Eve-0

AnjoOneElevenPress.com

First paperback edition May 2021

Cover design by Jerry Todd
Library of Congress Cataloging-in-Publication Data

Names: Gomes, Danielle, author
Title: EVE-0 [Book 1]
Description: ANJO One Eleven Press, [2021]
Identifiers: LCCN 2021905231

ISBN 978-1-7365992-1-1 (print)
ISBN 978-1-7365992-2-8 (ebook)
ISBN 978-1-7365992-3-5 (audio)

www.DanielleGomesWrites.com

To my husband Ben – Thanks for the adventures, laughs, and encouragement. I love you.

Eve-0

Danielle Gomes

Part 1

"To give us room to explore the varieties of mind and body into which our genome can evolve, one planet is not enough."

—Freeman Dyson
The Sun, The Genome, and The Internet:
Tools of Scientific Revolutions, 1999

CHAPTER 1

Pandemics

AS DR. GABRIELLE GALE reviewed the patient files from the night before, the shrill voice of the intake nurse, Martha, rose from the emergency room lobby. The lobby was typically quiet, as the public had learned to avoid emergency rooms. The University of Pennsylvania hospital had not had a single emergency walk-in for the past two months. On rare occasions, a new patient would be brought in by ambulance, but most new patients were transfers from other hospitals or medical centers.

Gabby set the small stack of files down, grabbed her mask, and made her way toward reception. Since the recent string of severe viral outbreaks, people had been avoiding crowded places, and hospitals had become an absolute last option. The business of virtual doctors had taken over a few years ago for regular medical needs. There were also infectious disease centers that handled most infections.

"Sir, you have to put a mask on and sit down. We have protocols to follow," barked Martha.

"I—can't—breathe, I . . . heart. Please—help me," pleaded a weak voice.

As Gabby pushed her way through the containment curtains into reception, she saw an elderly, unkempt, white-haired male. It was unusual to see someone's face not covered by a mask—Gabby could see the grip of pain across his tight, wrinkled expression. She guessed his age to be somewhere in his late seventies. He was gripping his shoulder. While his clothes looked like rags, he wore Cartier eyeglasses and clean New Balance sneakers.

"Martha, what's going on?" Gabby asked.

"I paged decon, but all three units are busy. He has to wait. He has to sit down and put a mask on," Martha said with panic rising.

Gabby secured her mask and eye shield; she already had her gown on, and added an extra pair of gloves. She grabbed a vitals cart, a dose of aspirin, and three doses of sublingual nitro and started toward the waiting room.

"Dr. Gale, you can't go out there. He hasn't been cleared yet. You can't treat him!"

"Martha, I have my gear on. Order an IV with morphine and heparin. Have it ready as soon as decon is able to clear him."

Gabby quickly made her way to the waiting room. The man was sweating profusely, even though the hospital's ambient temperature had been lowered in an attempt to slow the rapid rise in bacterial infections. Gabby gently guided him to the closest seat, where she took his blood pressure.

"Sir," Gabby said, while making sure that he was able to make and maintain eye contact, "what's your name?" She was momentarily struck by the clearness of his azure-hued eyes behind the turtle-rimmed glasses. His gaze was strong.

He cleared his throat. "Harold," he gritted in pain, "Mullen."

"I have a small dose of aspirin and a dose of nitroglycerine. Both will dissolve in your mouth. Are you able to take these?" Gabby asked, then glanced at the wall clock.

Though his jaw was clenched in pain, he was able to open his mouth and Gabby placed the tablets under his tongue.

She checked his pulse, which was erratic. His blood pressure was slightly elevated.

"Sir, have you ever had a heart attack?" Gabby asked.

He shook his head no. "I—" The man coughed and gritted his teeth. "I have high cholesterol and prediabetes," he said.

"Are you on any medications?" Gabby asked.

"I was, but since my wife died I . . . I haven't taken them like I should."

"Have you taken anything today or last night?"

Harold shook his head no.

"When we get you to a room, we will need a full list of your medications. Are you feeling any better?"

Harold shook his head 'no' again.

She checked the clock. "Mr. Mullen, it's been five minutes, so I'm going to give you another small dose of nitroglycerine, okay?"

Mr. Mullen opened his mouth, and Gabby placed another small tablet under his tongue. A minute later she asked, "How about now, are you feeling any better?"

"A little." The man rubbed his head.

The curtains to the waiting room swung open. Two individuals held the drapes aside while a third pushed in a cart filled with swabs and tinctures. All three figures wore white hazmat suits, goggles, and blue gloves, erasing any human characteristics.

"Sir, we are going to swab your nostrils, your throat, your ears, and your fingernails. Then take your temperature," a monotone voice stated from behind a masked face.

Mr. Mullen sat back as the three decontamination agents swabbed, doused, poked, and tested him.

"Sir, your tests were all negative for antibiotic-resistant bacterium as well as influenza and pandemic-related viral pathogens. You are cleared for intake. Oh, and doctor, please be advised that we will have to report your break in protocol."

With that, the decon team quickly vanished through the curtains, replaced by a team of nurses dressed in scrubs, covered in impermeable blue gowns, faces and eyes protected, wheeling a gurney.

"Get an EKG while you're getting his medical history and doing intake. I will be right in," Gabby instructed.

The nurse staff nodded and wheeled Mr. Mullen away.

Gabby followed them back, then headed to the sterility room. The small chamber glared with fluorescent light. Lifting the lid to the bio-hazard bin, she carefully removed her top layer of gloves from the wristband and dropped them into the bin. Next, she grabbed her face shield, careful to only touch the band that went behind her head, and dropped that in as well. Her protective gown was next, followed by her secondary face mask and gloves.

She pushed the foot pedal to close the bio-hazard bin. A pump of sanitizer and she rubbed her hands clean. She unzipped the plastic shield over the clean rack, labeled "A", pulled her thick, wavy brown hair into a tight ponytail, and began the process over again.

Although Gabby had only been the attending E.R. doctor at the hospital of the University of Pennsylvania for the past nine months, there was something about the containment protocols all hospitals had initiated three years ago that placed a seed of dread in the pit of her being. The world had been living in a state of panic following the first global pandemic of the 20th century, COVID-19, eight years ago, which ironically was actually very mild, with a mortality rate of around 3%. The new normal felt anything but.

For nearly a decade the world had been waiting to go back to normal, only things just kept getting worse. Much of her studies at Harvard Medical School and her dual-residency at Johns Hopkins in internal medicine with a focus on medical genetics and emergency medicine dealt with how to seamlessly institute these new and still-developing protocols.

In the past decade, the world had seen seven consecutive extreme influenza seasons that resulted in nearly three million deaths, an international spike in viral pandemics that accounted for close to another five million deaths, and localized outbreaks of fungal activity. Additionally, several outbreaks of antibiotic-resistant CRE bacteria across the country had resulted in the infection of nearly a million individuals with a mortality rate of 96.4%. With this, the practice of medicine had changed dramatically, particularly over the past five years.

The intercom in the sterility room buzzed. "Dr. Gale, this is Taylor. A patient in D-wing is coding, and you've been requested in level-C protection."

Gabby quickly unzipped the rack labeled "C". There were approximately a dozen white suits hanging there. She stepped on the sanitizing floor mat and started to slide the protective foot and leg covers on.

"Taylor," Gabby asked, "do you have a status on patient Mullen?"

"He had a heart attack, which was probably stopped with the nitro. We paged cardiology. They are prepping a room and admitting him."

"Thank you," Gabby said as she continued dressing.

Next came the full body suit with the connected hood that left only her large, almond-shaped, green eyes, her petite, slightly upturned nose, and her cupid's-bow mouth visible. Gabby was beautiful by any standard, though she had never paid much attention to her appearance. She placed the face mask on over her nose and mouth. Next came the external hood with a large plexi-face shield. Over that, the secondary apron, and finally the second pair of surgical gloves.

Gabby had this process down, and was able to safely dress in under forty-five seconds. D-wing was technically a quarantine unit—each room had individualized staff who had zero contact with any other patients. However, Gabby found that most of the patients in that unit were either indigent or had previously been in state-run facilities and now suffered from a variety of unusual ailments. Not a single case of the feared influenza strains, novel viral pathogens or antibiotic-resistant bacterial infections had been admitted to this unit.

Gabby had only been called into that unit two other times, both for cardiac arrest. As she approached the room, she saw that this time was different. Two nurses stood outside the door, leaning against the wall. Gabby could see the remnants of vomit clinging to the outside of their shielded hoods.

As she walked into the room, she saw that the patient was in the grip of a full-body, grand mal seizure. The patient, a morbidly obese, middle-aged man, shook uncontrollably, his eyes glazed. Gabby noticed small ruptures speckling the patient's skin as she joined the doctor and nurse working at his side.

"What's the status? Has he been administered Cerebyx yet?" Gabby asked.

"There's a dose on the tray. I've never seen anything like this," explained Dr. Chan, the attending doctor for the unit. "We have been trying to address the skin ruptures. The patient complained of severe abdominal pain, three times since yesterday afternoon. He was administered morphine. Then . . ." Dr. Chan's voice broke off.

Gabby quickly grabbed the dose as well as an alcohol swab. When she attempted to hold down the patient's leg, her finger broke through his tender flesh. Her brain struggled to accept what was going on. The patient's flesh quivered with the consistency of jelly. The slightest touch broke the surface. Each jerk of his seizure created another tear in his flesh. Gabby looked at Dr. Chan and his assisting nurse, whom Gabby didn't recognize; both were focused on delicately trying to tape flesh ruptures on the patient's arm and chest. They seemed to have shut down to the situation as a whole, focusing in on such a small effect.

Another jerk created a rupture in the patient's abdomen. Gabby stepped back, as did Dr. Chan and the assisting nurse. Her pounding pulse sent vibrations of terror ping-ponging through her core, wedging in her throat. Another jerk created a rupture that covered the patient's entire trunk and, with that, each jerk sent blood and flesh pouring out in tsunami-style waves of expulsion. The patient stopped moving, reduced to an almost shapeless, oozing, crimson mass. It was only then that Gabby noticed the blaring flat-line beep that brought her back to the present.

"Gabrielle," said a voice from the entrance to the room. Searching for anything to hold on to, Gabby stumbled back against the wall and turned toward the voice.

"Trent? What . . . what are you doing here?"

"My lab was called to test and seal this room and patient due to the unusual and severe circumstances. We have set up a special decontamination unit and holding room. I will meet you there."

"Wait, what—I mean, how—" Gabby struggled to get her words together. Nothing made sense. Her fiancé, Dr. Trent Martins, was a lead geneticist for

AmCorps Labs in DuPont, Delaware, and had only worked at the UPenn hospital one other time. Several years ago, Trent had created a virus that was able to cure a rare form of relapsing leukemia in a young girl.

"Gabrielle, some of my staff are right outside, they will take care of you," Trent said.

"Are we being quarantined?" Gabby asked.

"No, nothing like that. We're just taking every precaution. I will be there soon." With that, Trent pushed past Gabby, holding some sort of small machine in his hand. She managed to get her feet to carry her past the threshold.

All Gabby could see were yellow curtains. They must've been set in place in a matter of seconds.

"Dr. Gale," came a voice, "please stand still. We are going to spray you with a decontamination formula. It's completely harmless to you. It's basically a liquid copper spray that kills a wide variety of pathogens."

Within seconds, a gray mist filled the curtain tunnel. The mist cleared, and as an opening at the far end was unzipped, two agents pulled back the curtain for Gabby.

"Dr. Gale, we are going to spray you with a second solution. It's a sanitizer made from thymol." The two agents sprayed Gabby in unison.

She was then directed to the next tent. Her protective clothing was removed and she was guided to the doctors' lounge. Soft lighting, comfortable gray recliners, dark wood tables, floral-patterned chairs, and beige walls were a welcome departure from the harsh white fluorescence of the rest of the hospital. But it could not erase from her mind what she had just witnessed.

CHAPTER 2

Waiting Room

GABBY FOUND HER FAVORITE RECLINER and absently stared at the flat-screen TV mounted on the wall. CNN droned on in an endless stream of monotone voices. The two nurses Gabby had passed on her way into the room were in clean scrubs. They sat with their eyes open, though their stares were thousands of miles away and likely inspired by a dose of clonidine.

It was a look Gabby recognized from her childhood, growing up with a mother who suffered from severe PTSD. When she was just six years old, her parents had been at a fundraising meeting at the World Trade Center on September 11, 2001. Gabby's father didn't make it out, but her mother survived, although she was never the same and suffered from night terrors, anxiety, and depression for the next two decades until she passed away from lung cancer. Gabby had basically been raised by her grandparents.

Dr. Chan and his assistant were also directed to the lounge. Staff from AmCorp filed in and out. They took swabs of the inside of Gabby's cheeks. They took five different blood tests. Someone brought Gabby a cup of coffee. She wasn't sure how much time passed; Gabby's mind was not operating on seconds, minutes, or hours, but rather running circles around the event that had brought her here. Was she in danger? What novel disease could cause someone to quite literally dissolve? Was it contagious? *What the hell is going on?*

Eventually, Trent came into the room along with the hospital's C.E.O., Thomas Dooley, to address Gabby and the others.

"Nothing prepares us to deal with medical situations of this extreme nature, but I'm very proud of how you and our staff here responded," Mr. Dooley said.

"Our initial tests indicate," Trent began, "that the

patient had an extreme and fast onset of a rare genetic form of scurvy. He had absolutely no Vitamin C, D, A, or B in his system, and the connective tissue throughout his entire body failed simultaneously. We don't believe that this is contagious. In fact, we are virtually certain."

Watching Trent work in this capacity reminded Gabby of how they met. Trent had taught one of her genetics classes while she was in residency at Johns Hopkins. He was only three years older than Gabby, but had made some powerful discoveries very early. She still remembered the first time she saw him.

Gabby had been walking into her class, focused on finding a desk near the front but not in the first row. Trent was casually leaning against the teacher's podium, flipping through a notebook. She could see the chiseled lines of muscle where his shoulders met his biceps through his tee shirt. His sandy blond hair matched his golden-brown eyes perfectly.

As Gabby felt herself melting, she tripped on the leg of a desk. She didn't fall, but her faux pas made a loud enough noise that passersby in the hall made a point to look in. Her cheeks caught on fire and she crept to the nearest desk. Trent gave her a cool wink and slight smile.

"However," Mr. Dooley interrupted, bringing Gabby back to the present, "per our regulatory response to unknown conditions, any staff that came in contact with the patient during this medical event are required to be placed on paid leave for a minimum of three weeks. Think of this as a well-deserved vacation. We have to say that you are encouraged to remain at home and have as little contact with others as possible."

"But, keep in mind that at this point we are 95% sure that this is not contagious, and within the next twelve hours, we will know with 100% certainty," Trent said.

"But, we will still be placed on paid leave for twenty-one days, even if you know that this is not contagious?" Dr. Chan asked.

"That is a mandated protocol," Mr. Dooley responded, "but keep in mind that all staff are signing confidentiality agreements—no one will know about this. We have decided that in a time of such pandemic panic, the irresponsibility of the media could turn this into a situation that it's not."

"You will be cleared to go home shortly. In the meantime, do you have any questions?" Trent asked.

Gabby looked around the room. The entire D-wing staff was silent, not a single question. "I have several questions," she began. "What was this patient admitted for?"

"He was admitted from his state-run, adult-living facility for heart pain and spells of dizziness. He was being monitored for a leaky heart valve and aortic arrhythmia," Dr. Chan answered.

"How—" Gabby began.

"Gabrielle," Trent interrupted, "we can address these questions in your debriefing prior to your release. We realize that as the only care-provider during this event that was not part of the team, you will have more questions, and we will leave plenty of time to address all of your concerns in your individual meeting."

"Lunch will be delivered shortly, and then you should be cleared to go home," Mr. Dooley said.

The two men abruptly left the room.

A cart was dropped off with cellophane-wrapped sandwiches and a random selection of individual bags of chips, all of which remained untouched.

Just as promised, the five waiting were called one-by-one. Dr. Chan was first. An AmCorps Lab agent directed Chan into the conference room next door. Then it was his assistant, followed by the two nurses. Finally, Gabby sat alone in the room.

She had to wait longer than anyone else. All she wanted to do was to go home, soak in a warm bath, and forget about today. Eventually, the door creaked open. Gabby expected to see the same AmCorps agent, and was ready to let him know just how irritated she was that she had to wait so much longer than anyone else.

"Trent?"

"Come on, Gabrielle—there's a car waiting."

"I haven't had my meeting or been released yet."

"I know."

"What's going on?"

"Your meeting will be offsite. You've been cleared to leave; your tests were all normal."

"Why?"

"I'll explain everything at the meeting. Just come on, we need to leave."

"What's wrong? Why am I the only one that—"

"Nothing. Nothing is wrong," Trent interrupted.

"The hospital needs their space back and we need to have your meeting at the lab."

"But—"

"Gabrielle, just come on."

Begrudgingly, Gabby rose from her recliner and followed Trent through a back corridor and out through an emergency exit, surprised that no alarms sounded.

Outside, a black GMC Yukon waited, flanked by two armed military guards. The passenger-side guard opened the backseat door for Trent and Gabby.

"Trent, what . . ." Her voice trailed off.

"Don't worry, we have several government contracts. They provide security for our lab facility and sometimes, when needed, transportation."

After five years of dating, Gabby realized just how little she really knew about what Trent did. Sure, she knew that he studied the genetic and epigenetic processes of both humans and diseases. She'd heard about his breakthroughs in cancer treatments and virology. However, beyond that, she really knew nothing about what he did on a daily basis or what his life was like outside of their home.

"Can't we do this tomorrow? I'm tired. I want to go home," Gabby admitted.

"I know," Trent said and patted her knee, "but we need to do this now. We're almost there."

As soon as he said that, Gabby began to notice the long line of chain-link fence with periodic warning signs: *Warning—Do not cross—Military test site. Warning: photography prohibited. Warning: drones prohibited.*

Gabby checked the clock on the dashboard, which read 16:53. If she had worked her normal shift, she'd still have been at the hospital for at least two more hours. The car pulled up to a large steel cantilever gate. As the driver rolled all the windows down, two armed military guards stepped up to the car. The driver flashed his ID card, then the guards stepped toward the back windows.

"Dr. Martins, welcome back, and Dr. Gale—welcome to AmCorps."

The heavy metal gates slowly creaked open. The buzz-cut officer motioned for them to proceed. The windows rolled up and the car pulled through the gate.

Chapter 3

The Reader Gene

THE AMCORPS BUILDING was a simple, square, concrete structure. It looked like a leftover World War II bunker. There were only a few extremely small windows in the center, lower section of the building. The rest of the structure appeared like a series of stacked boxes. Gabby was surprised by how small the building appeared. It wasn't much bigger than a standard, middle-class, single-family, split-level home.

"This is your lab? How many people work here?" Gabby asked.

"Close to two hundred."

"In there?"

"Yes."

The car pulled to the front. An officer posted by

the building opened the car door for Gabby, and she followed Trent toward the building.

Trent had to scan a badge to get through the outside door. Inside, a secondary door granted him access following a retina scan.

Gabby immediately realized why the building was so small—the structure was built down, not up. The building was hollow inside, lit with a string of hanging, industrial, high-bay LED lights. The only furnishing was another security desk, with military guards who sat in front of a bay of exposed elevator shafts.

Trent handed his security badge to a guard at the desk, and the man scanned it.

"Ma'am, do you have your driver's license on you?" the second guard asked Gabby.

She nodded and passed it to the guard. He scanned her driver's license and handed it back.

"Sir, they are waiting for you in Crypto One," the guard told Trent. "I will send you there."

The center elevator pulled into its dock and the doors opened. Gabrielle followed Trent in and they began their descent.

"Trent, what the hell is going on?" Gabby asked

"Just be patient. You will understand very soon."

The elevator slowed and the doors parted to a small lobby, with another guard desk and two more guards. This lobby was entirely gray, with no hints of hospital lavender or whispers of laboratory sage, just a drab mix of black and white, a completely utilitarian scheme. It seemed that the walls, the desks, and even the guards in their powder-gray uniforms had been formed from concrete. A few small holes in the ceiling emitted an unnatural light.

"Hello, Dr. Martins. They're ready for you. You know the drill," a guard told Trent. Gabby swore every guard they had come in contact with looked the same—about six feet tall, stocky but fit, shaved head covered with a patrol cap, fatigues, and combat boots. Trent began to empty his pockets into a small bin on the desk.

"Dr. Gale, please empty your pockets and place all of your belongings in this bin. Once you're finished, I will scan you for bugs," the second guard directed.

"I've been decontaminated and swabbed at least five times today," Gabby responded.

"Not those sort of bugs, Ma'am. Listening devices. Then, I have a non-disclosure agreement for you to sign. This document will grant you top-secret security clearance. Consequently, if you leak any information that you receive in this meeting, you will be found guilty of treason."

The guard placed a single-page document on the desk. Gabby looked to Trent. In a single gesture, he nodded for her to sign it. She finished emptying her pockets. The guards placed the bins in a steel cabinet. Gabby started to read the document in front of her:

Dr. Gabrielle Gale, by signing this document you will be granted top-secret security clearance . . .

"Gabrielle, they're waiting," Trent urged.

She signed the document. The guards scanned them with black wands that looked identical to the TSA tools. Then one of them opened the only door in the lobby.

Inside the doors was a conference room where three gentlemen sat at a round, dark wood table. The room was a soft beige. An artful arrangement of DNA, bacteriophage, and mast cell watercolors decorated the walls. The effect should have been a relief after the too-stark interiors of the other areas. The heavy table was surrounded by five weathered navy leather chairs; the two closest to the only door in the room, which quickly shut behind Gabby and Trent, were empty and waiting. Instead of feeling relieved, Gabby felt her pulse quicken.

"Hello Trent, Dr. Gale. Thank you for meeting us." The man speaking wore a military uniform, and based on the number of stars, Gabby knew that he was high-ranking. He had a youthful appearance, his thick salt and pepper hair neatly coiffed and his olive skin smooth. It was only the gruffness in his voice that gave away his senior status.

"Trent knows us, but for your sake, Dr. Gale, I will quickly do the introductions. I'm General Robert Holton. Under the recent restructuring, I've taken leadership of the CDC. To my right is Dr. Lucien Sabara, Director of AmCorps and lead scientist on Project EVE-0. To my left is Dr. David Benjamin—I'm sure you know who he is," General Holton said.

"Yes, of course," Gabby replied. Of course she knew the Surgeon General of the United States. She kept her voice steady, yet every fiber in her quivered. The three most prominent men in the medical field in the nation, all of them already familiar with Trent, and now she was meeting with them? *What the hell is going on?*

"Great. So then, let's get started," General Holton finished.

"I'll start from the beginning," said Dr. Sabara. Gabby found the doctor to be striking, to the point it was almost difficult to focus on what he was saying. His pale skin appeared like porcelain, so thin and so fair. His eyes were a light shade of green, set against his strawberry hair. It wasn't that he was particularly attractive or unattractive; Gabby had just never seen another human being that shared even the slightest resemblance to this man. Taking a deep breath, she forced her focus, something she had become very good at in medical school.

"In 2003, I was one of the scientists who completed the human genome project. Though we had mapped the entire genome, we didn't fully understand the function of every gene. Following this project, I broke off, and initially through private funding, I began AmCorps, with the intention of discovering the interactions of groups of genes within the genome as well as epigenetic factors, which if you're unfamiliar, epigenetics is the—"

"The role of environmental factors on gene expression. I studied epigenetics with Trent," Gabby interrupted.

"Yes, of course. I'm so used to elucidating to our esteemed government that I forget how nice it is to speak to someone in the field," Dr. Sabara continued, with a sly smile. "AmCorps's focus was to understand the process of human evolution through genetic expression with the ultimate goal of identifying an evolution gene. We theorized that with this knowledge, we would be able to tweak our genes to make us resistant to disease—that's where many of Trent's breakthroughs on cancer treatments came from."

"Which, funny enough, weren't actually attempts to cure cancer," Trent revealed.

"What?" Gabby asked, confused, because for the entire length of their relationship, Trent had spent many hours telling her about his work curing cancer with genetics.

"I mean, we weren't trying to create a cure for cancer," Trent explained. "We've been trying to identify the genetic coding that sets cancer off. In other words, we wanted to stop cancer before it started.

The viruses we've created carry genetic information that has told the body how to fight cancer that is already present, and they have been valid and promising breakthroughs, just not our ultimate goal."

"You see, Dr. Gale," Dr. Sabara interrupted, "our goal has always been to stop diseases before they start, and we knew the key to achieving that would be to identify an evolution gene or sequence in the genome—from there, we would be able to understand how the human species evolves, and as a consequence, how various diseases are imprinted. Do you follow?"

"Yes, although it seems like a pretty big assumption to operate under. Isn't it a huge leap to assume that base evolution is tied to disease, when there are so many variants in what we define as disease?" Gabby replied.

"You're absolutely right in one sense," Dr. Sabara replied. "However, through this line of research, we theorized that we would not only be able to stop diseases before they started, but program the human body to be resistant to all forms of disease. But we're getting ahead of ourselves. Initially, like I said, we just wanted to know more about evolution. We were shocked when we were able to identify an evolution gene very quickly, which we named EVE-0."

"And even more shocked when we saw how closely it was linked to the immune system," Trent explained.

"With EVE-0, we learned that evolution is directly tied to the immune system. In fact, EVE-0 is more or less a reader gene that interprets messages from the environment and tells our bodies, our species, how to evolve," Dr. Sabara explained.

"What type of messages?" Gabby asked.

"Mainly viruses and bacteria, but what you have to understand is that the big breakthrough here is just how connected to and dependent we are on our environment," Trent said.

"Obviously, we all know that we're dependent on our environment," Dr. Sabara inserted, "but what this gene proves is that we're not only dependent, but directly linked. Our bodies communicate with the environment, including all other living creatures, through viruses and bacteria."

Chapter 4

The Messenger

GABBY RUBBED HER TEMPLES; this was a huge concept to grasp for a doctor who had more or less been fighting a war with germs. If this was true, they'd been approaching medicine all wrong. She'd known for years that there were good bacteria and bad bacteria, and the good bacteria were very important but the bad bacteria, well, weren't worth the risk.

Antibiotics had saved countless lives. Before the invention of antibiotics, life expectancy was forty-seven years. She also knew that only a small amount, roughly 10% of all bacteria, were harmful, and our bodies lived in harmony with many of these disease-causing bacteria on a daily basis.

The other 90% *showed potential* to help everything from mental health to digestive health to the health of our skin. But, bacteria could kill and they could kill fast, so wasn't it better to err on the side of caution? As far as viruses were concerned, they're still such a mystery. Virtually unstoppable, incredibly deadly, and yet a necessity to life.

"Do you follow?" asked Dr. Sabara.

"Yes, I think so. I mean, science has realized the importance of bacteria and viruses for a very long time, and its potential to kill. We've had to take some very drastic measures recently to combat outbreaks and drug resistance. But I'm not sure I understand what messages they carry or how," Gabby said.

"Drug resistance is part of this, too. Everything evolves. But we will get to that," Dr. Sabara said. "First, bacteria, both good and bad, carry messages that direct the evolution of humans on a multigenerational level. This isn't new; geneticists have observed how human beings evolve in the face of disease for years."

"In 2014, an immunologist in the Netherlands identified a mark the Black Plague left on the human genome. In the process of killing an estimated 25% of Europeans, the Black Plague tended to favor a cluster of toll-like receptor genes found on chromosome 4. Those that had this cluster of genes seemed to have survived the plague, and this genetic expression has been passed down to modern descendants."

"However, what we are realizing is that bacteria and viruses doesn't just transmit messages in extreme circumstances, like a plague, but in countless other less remarkable ways on a daily basis."

"Like Lucien said," Trent added, "we know that the immune system reacts and evolves on many levels. Take viruses, for example—the common cold, influenza, HIV, they all carry genetic material that interacts with our immune system and therefore our evolution. Viruses differ from bacteria in the sense that they are more like nerve impulses, quick messages that elicit a quick change. If you touch something hot, you move your hand."

"Viruses can be extremely powerful, too. Take the 1918 Influenza Epidemic—it killed close to one-fifth of the population. But, like bacteria, there are hundreds or even thousands of levels of viruses, some of which communicate genetic material across species lines."

He continued, "Throughout history, we can point out the dramatic evidence of this system in action. The plague cleaned up a population that was out of control. When a cluster of over-population of not only humans but bacteria and viruses as well created unbalanced conditions, nature responded and rebalanced the system, spurring the evolution of human beings."

"So, bacteria and viruses are the earth's immune system?" Gabby asked. "Responding to, what? Specific overcrowded areas?"

Trent shook his head. "No. It's more an implication of how dependent we are on the environment and its effect on a cellular level. Any imbalance throughout the entire system generates a reaction, and not always where you might expect. We have a tendency to look at things as individual systems rather than a whole body. For example, depression is a mental illness. However, it can be caused by an imbalance in the digestive system. These two systems are commonly viewed and treated totally separately."

"And, again, we discovered this very early on in

the project. We also discovered a problem," Dr. Sabara admitted.

"A problem?" Gabby asked.

"Yes," Dr. Sabara continued. "When we discovered the evolution gene, we also discovered that it has become dormant. Initially, we hypothesized that EVE-0 only activated during times of evolution. However, when we tested samples of DNA from different eras, we were able to conclude that EVE-0 had been fully active until around 1955, and by 1987, there were no longer any humans with an active EVE-0 gene. This change also corresponded with the hyper-evolution of bacteria and viruses." Dr. Sabara paused to take a drink from his water glass.

Gabby's mind was already making the connection. A shiver threatened her, but she waited patiently for the director's further explanation.

"Through the testing of a variety of species' DNA, we were able to conclude that all living animals carry this reader gene or evolution gene, EVE-0. With the deactivation of this gene, nature has taken us, humans, out of the evolutionary process. Or, in other words"— Dr. Sabara paused momentarily—"we have become disconnected from the collective system, essentially making us foreign bodies."

Gabby glanced at each of the men at the table, their faces somber. "And that's why we have faced so many unprecedented pandemics recently?"

Dr. Sabara nodded. "Yes. But what really turned us on to the urgency of this situation was the discovery that in every extinct species from which we were able to pull DNA and identify the evolution gene, this gene became dormant in the years leading up to their extinction. Granted, our testing has been somewhat limited. But through a combination of carbon dating and genetic testing, we have been able to conclude that EVE-0 was dormant in all naturally extinct species."

"We have even been able to pull enough genetic material from some prehistoric dinosaur material, and now have a completely new theory on their extinction. We have not come across a single anomaly in all of our research. Do you understand?" asked Dr. Sabara.

"We've stopped evolving. But why? Is it because of antibiotics or vaccines?" Gabby said. The time frame seemed right to her. Antibiotics were first used in the 1940s, and not widespread until the 1970s or so.

"Gabrielle, you're missing the point," Trent interrupted.

Dr. Benjamin interjected, "Dr. Gale may be partially correct, as we suspect that the deactivation of EVE-0 is due to a combination of several factors including antibiotics, vaccines, and the environment. And we will study this further. But, the much more pressing problem is that we are approaching mass-extinction much quicker than we thought it would happen."

Again, Dr. Sabara nodded. "Yes, much quicker. Events that we expected to take a century have happened in a matter of months. As you know, our antibiotics can no longer keep up with bacteria. The past seven seasonal influenza outbreaks have consecutively been the deadliest in history, even with vaccines. And there have been several novel and deadly viral pandemics. At this rate, the human race will be extinct in three to possibly five years."

"That brings us to today," Trent said looking directly at Gabby. "That patient was a willing participant in our twelfth human trial. We've attempted to reprogram a virus with chimpanzee DNA that included an activated EVE-0 gene in hopes of reactivating our evolution."

"Wait, your twelfth? Did they all end . . . like that?" Gabby's mind replayed the horrific scene, the man's tissues liquefying before her eyes, only hours ago.

"No," Trent answered quickly, his worried eyes watching her expression. Then he admitted, "But none have survived. We actually had high hopes for this patient. His EVE-0 gene reactivated two days ago. Then, unexpectedly, his connective tissue completely broke down. This is a very complex process."

Gabby nodded. She knew science currently had the ability to delete portions of DNA with gene-editing, through a process based on custom-made proteins called TALENs. However, they couldn't simply erase whole genes—not that they would necessarily want to if they could remedy the flaw within them.

Trent took a breath and continued, "Trying to reactivate the EVE-0 gene has been much more challenging, and we are having problems with cross-species effects. We have also attempted to reactivate the EVE-0 gene on developing embryos. We activate the gene very early, when the embryo is just a handful of cells, using the CRISPR system. However, regardless of what we do, the embryos develop mosaicism, which is a spotty effect of gene activation among different cells, and the embryos have always developed an unpredicted mutation."

From the liquified volunteer to mutated babies . . . Gabby was having difficulty holding her thoughts back. "Is this legal?" she asked. Or ethical? she wondered.

Dr. Sabara answered, "For any other lab, no, but we are working closely with the highest levels of our government and approaching this in the most delicate way. And considering the stakes—total extinction of the human race in just a handful of years—it's in everyone's best interest. I'm not exactly sure what labs around the world are doing, but I know they are experimenting with gene editing. We have taken some of our methods from labs in China."

"President Spiegel, along with the other nations' leaders, speaks bi-monthly, so if there had been a breakthrough, we would know about it. This is not just an American problem. In 2017, thirty people in Madagascar died of an antibiotic-resistant plague; it is now an epidemic and, luckily, their island has been quietly sanctioned off and completely quarantined from the rest of the world. We don't think there are any survivors left there."

"Diseases, of all kinds, are spreading at an unprecedented rate, and without an EVE-0 we have absolutely no chance of surviving this," Dr. Sabara finished.

"We've taken samples from across the world, including some very remote, underdeveloped areas and have not been able to find an active EVE-0," began General Holton. "Our last hope is to send a small team into the Amazon to locate an indigenous human that has never had contact with the modern world."

"Then what?" asked Gabby.

"Trent has the ability to program a virus with a small sample of blood or saliva. The equipment, the virus, everything is ready—we just need to isolate an active EVE-0 in another human," General Holton explained.

"What if your team can't find someone with an active EVE-0? What if the virus doesn't work? Who else knows about this?" Gabby blurted out.

"There are a lot of what-ifs, but based on science

this is the only treatment, and it's our last chance," Dr. Benjamin said.

General Holton leaned toward her. "Every country is trying to stop the pandemic onslaughts. As you can imagine, we want to be the first to find a fix; otherwise, there may no longer be an America to speak of."

"We are going to send a small team of three, including Trent, into the Amazon under the auspices of a biochemistry team searching for a new broad-spectrum antibiotic," explained Dr. Benjamin. "We have to keep this top-secret because, as you can imagine, if this hits the media it could result in any-thing from panic to international conflicts. Of course, we will share our work with the rest of the world once this has proven out, and then we can begin rehabilitating our country and the whole world. You're here because we would like you to be the team's doctor."

"Me? Why?" asked Gabby.

"For a number of reasons. We need a doctor with frontline emergency medical experience on the team. You also have a strong background in genetics. And, your absence for a few weeks would neither impact nor be questioned by a family situation," explained Dr. Sabara.

The last part was definitely true—no one would look for Gabby or be inclined to ask many questions. Her only surviving relatives were her grandparents who were both in assisted living, battling late-stage Alzheimer's disease.

Trent looked directly at Gabby, "I know what a great doctor you are and I advocated for you. I don't need to tell you how important this mission is. I want the best with me. That's why you're here."

Gabby smiled ever so slightly.

"The team is set to leave tomorrow at 0600. Everything has been arranged—documentation, visas, we've even packed the equipment including clothes and personal items. We have an operative in Brazil who will get you into the Amazon. You are to have no contact with anyone outside of this mission from here on out. As far as everyone is concerned, you've been quarantined at home pending the results of today's event," General Holton said.

How could she say no? The only person she really had in her life was going. And, if their facts were accurate, she and Trent could only have a few short years to live their lives together if they didn't succeed. "Okay, but I want to see my grandparents tonight," Gabby replied.

"That can be arranged, but you do understand that once you are outside the confines of this room, you can't speak about this mission, even to Trent, even when you are at home. The risk of bugs is too high," General Holton warned.

Gabby nodded in agreement.

"Gabrielle, I have a series of vaccinations for you," Trent said as Dr. Benjamin passed a plastic medical supply case to him.

Gabby had spent her career accepting vaccinations and prescribing antibiotics, and now everything she had known seemed to be in question. "We're so reliant on vaccines. If that's part of the problem, what's the future look like if we are able to survive a mass extinction?"

"It looks very different, I can assure you of that. But what you have to understand is that what we thought would take fifty to a hundred or more years to fully actualize is happening in a matter of months.

We need to survive the present situation, but rest assured, we are looking toward the future," Dr. Sabara assured her.

Gabby looked at the director of AmCorps. "It just seems like we need an immediate plan if we are able to reactivate EVE-0, right?"

"It's not as straightforward as you might think. It goes beyond vaccines and antibiotics. A lab at Rockefeller University identified a genetic mutation that stops your body from producing interferons, which makes it nearly impossible for the body to fight off a simple influenza infection," Trent said as he handed Gabby an alcohol swab.

"When this mutation was first discovered, it was considered very rare—about 1 in 10,000 were thought to carry this gene. However, it's now estimated to be carried by 35% to 65% of the population, and without the vaccines that we have, we'd be completely unable to fight off any infection," explained Trent as Gabby prepped her arm for the series of vaccinations.

"That mutation's related to EVE-0?" she asked as he handed her the first shot, and she administered her first vaccination.

"Yes, which means that EVE-0 has not only stopped us from evolving, but it is changing our DNA so that we're not able to fight common infections," Trent said, as Gabby administered a second and much more painful shot.

Dr. Sabara said, "Dr. Gale, this is our last hope. We know, point blank, that in order to survive we need to reactivate EVE-0. But, we also know that it is capable of being active in the presence of vaccinations and antibiotics. We've tested several domesticated pets and they all had active EVE-0 genes. Which is very promising, but no less urgent for us."

"Three days from now, on March 23, the president, along with the leaders of every country, are going to announce a full ban on all travel, even within our own country. Airlines and airports will be fully shut down," Dr. Benjamin said.

"Can they do that?" Gabby asked.

"In a state of emergency, such as pandemic events, yes—although, as you know, in the past, and albeit on much smaller scales, partial travel bans have not been effective in preventing the spread of disease," replied Dr. Benjamin.

He continued, "With travel down 85% across the

board, it shouldn't come as a surprise, but we still need to get you out tomorrow morning. There will be very limited travel following this announcement."

"Will we be able to get back?"

"There will be limited military travel, it won't be a problem. We just need to get you in quietly," General Holton responded.

"In the weeks following the travel ban, strict quarantine protocols will also begin to roll out in stages, so we want to get you out while there are still some people out in the streets. Like General Holton said, we need to keep this operation quiet," Dr. Benjamin explained.

Trent gave her a handful of pills to swallow and a book on rainforest fauna.

"The third member of the team is set to meet you in the morning. He will be your security detail. Lt. Christopher Silver is a PJ." Spurred by Gabby's confused expression, Dr. Benjamin continued, "An Air Force Special Warfare Pararescue Specialist. He also holds a master's degree in epidemiology and has served on several high-risk missions that include bioterrorism, combat rescue, and outbreak control."

"That will be it," General Holton declared. "Thank you for agreeing to serve your country on this mission. Godspeed."

The men quickly rose and ushered Gabby and Trent out.

CHAPTER 5

The Apple

THE SAME MACHINE-ESQUE MILITARY escorts drove Gabby and Trent to Seven Oaks, where Gabby's grandparents had been living for the past three years. The Dutch Colonial building set in the serene hills just outside of Philadelphia was always a welcoming sight for her.

Despite the inevitable pain of her visit, just being around her grandparents was enough to wrap Gabby in the warm arms of nostalgia and calm any emotions that threatened to bubble over.

Trent waited in the car while Gabby went in. Like always, she signed in at the front desk and offered a thermal reading of her temperature. Gabby was always a cool 97.9. She took the empty elevator to the third floor.

Visitors were not allowed into the facility. Family members could only see their loved ones through video chats. People had become terrified of any sort of medical facility, and outbreaks were particularly devastating to nursing homes. Gabby was only allowed in because she was a doctor.

"Hi Gabby. When I saw the elevator light up, I knew it was you. How ya doin', sweetheart?" asked Libby, the nighttime attending nurse. Libby's curly blonde hair was speckled gray.

"I'm good, how are you?"

"Oh, I'm fine." Libby paused a moment. "I just want to warn you, today hasn't been a good day for your grandparents. They haven't said a single word all day, you know—they've just been zoned out."

"Okay, thanks," Gabby said as she pushed open the door to their room.

Her grandparents' room was large, a hybrid of a living room and a hospital room. Family pictures and paintings from their old lives hung on the pale sage walls. There was a small sitting area with two recliners that faced a television. Just past that,

Gabby's grandparents lay in their hospital beds. They stared at the blank, wall-mounted TV.

Gabby froze; she wasn't sure she could continue. There had been many visits with forgotten names, but there was always a sense of warmth and a deep recognition. Now, her grandparents just seemed empty. She wasn't sure she could face them.

Suddenly, Gabby's grandfather turned his head and locked eyes with her. "Hi sweetheart, how was your day?"

"Hi Pop, how are you doing?" Gabby replied as a tear broke free.

"Oh, I'm fine, just enjoying the excitement of this place," he said, and coughed out a chuckle.

"Gabby, angel, I'm so glad you're here," Gabby's grandmother suddenly proclaimed.

"Hi Nana, how are you feeling?"

"I thought we told you to stop asking us that, three years ago when we moved in here," Nana said.

"You did," Gabby said, "but I worry about you."

Pop said, "Sweetheart, we're in here safe and just waiting; you're the one we worry about. The way that you have to practice medicine now is wrong. We sure made a mess of things. When I was practicing, I was never comfortable with the way things started going. You know, I banned those drug reps from my office, do you remember why?"

"Yes, we talked about that—remember, that's why I studied genetics. You taught me there was a better way to help the body heal itself," Gabby replied.

Pop had been revolutionary for his time. He was a Harvard-trained internist and family medicine practitioner. However, he'd gained particular notoriety for being one of the first doctors to approach medicine holistically, and in doing so received an equal amount of praise and scorn from the larger medical community. He really blazed the way, for future doctors would enjoy media popularity for their naturopathic methods.

"Enough work talk," Nana interrupted. "How are you and Trent?"

"We're good, just both busy with work."

"That's alright for now, but when you're ready to get married, you find someone who puts you first and who you will put first. Work is important, but love should always come first," Nana said.

"Okay, Nan," Gabby said with a very slight and inadvertent roll of her eyes.

"Gabrielle, your grandmother is right. Love should always come first," Pop said, "and don't let her bite the apple."

"What?" Gabby asked.

Pop looked at Gabby, frowning now at the realization that what he'd said didn't make sense. She could see the fog rolling back into his gaze.

"Oh, nothing, just be careful. Don't prescribe all those drugs they push on you."

"I won't. I'm going to head out and let you guys get your rest. I just wanted to tell you how much I love you and how much I appreciate everything you've done for me," Gabby said, letting deep breaths out so that she could fight back her tears.

"Oh, sweetheart, we love you too. So much. You're our world," Nana said as Gabby hugged her.

"We love you, Gabrielle," Pop said as she hugged him as well, then pulled her even closer. "You be careful, do you understand me?" He held her tight. "Only do what you know is right. Don't trust them."

"Who?" Gabby asked, but there was no reply.

Just like that, their momentary clarity had been

replaced with emptiness. Pop and Nana went back to staring. It was like they weren't even there. Their care team had warned Gabby of fleeting episodes like this, but it was still difficult for her. Wiping her tears, she made her way out.

The car drove Gabby and Trent to the apartment they had shared for the past year. It was a small but luxurious one-bedroom flat that overlooked Boathouse Row. She immediately drew a warm bath laced with lavender essential oil, and forced her mind to go blank. When she got out, Trent had made a pot of soup, and they sat down in the living room with the TV on and a bottle of Malbec.

Before Trent spoke, he put his finger over his mouth in a hush gesture to remind Gabby that they could not speak freely. "Gabrielle, I realize how hard work is, but you're doing the right thing."

She took a deep breath and nodded, opting to remain silent for fear that she might say something she shouldn't. She had wanted to tell her grandparents that she would be likely unable to visit for a few weeks, but feared even that could not be shared out loud. She wondered if they would know how much time had passed anyway, and tried to set aside the thoughts of their condition.

Instead, she gazed at the talking heads on CNN, showing color-coded maps of the most recent outbreak numbers and causes. The U.S. was starting to look like an overlapping mosaic built on color-coded, disease-labeled tiles.

"You should know," Trent began, "I fought for this. I—I can't imagine a life without you. I love you."

Startled, Gabby looked at Trent. She knew they loved each other, but she had never considered herself the romantic type of person. She didn't need to hear the words "I love you" to make them real. Both her parents and her grandparents had said "I love you" to each other virtually every time they spoke on the phone or left the house.

Trent believed that actions were more meaningful than the silliness of words and had taught Gabby to not "need" their empty reassurance. With Trent, she had found a sort of independence. But never-the-less, sometimes it felt good to hear.

"I love you too," she replied.

Chapter 6

Child of Light

DR. SABARA WAITED TILL HE HEARD the elevator ring and knew Gabby and Trent had left.

"Thoughts?" he asked the others.

"Dr. Gale was a poor choice," General Holton said. "She could become a problem once she becomes aware of the complete situation."

Dr. Sabara agreed, but felt she was not much of a threat. "She's there because Trent is comfortable with her capabilities as an emergency doctor should a situation arise. He just didn't want to overload her all at once. Beside, she's one rather small girl—what could she possibly do when the full team is sent in?" he replied.

"Personally, I think we should have been more upfront to begin with," Dr. Benjamin inserted.

"Trent knows her well. It was his decision, and he felt more comfortable with her learning the situation in stages," Sabara said.

General Holton shrugged. "Either way, it's done now. Where do we stand on Operation Blockhouse?"

"Each safe house is up and running. Our tech and service crews have gone through the quarantine and decontamination process. We are cleared to roll out Phase One," Sabara reported.

"That's great news," replied Dr. Benjamin.

"Yes, great news," added the general. "I love when things are ahead of schedule. Let's push everything up and begin Phase One tomorrow. I will let the president know." He abruptly stood up. Following his cue, Dr. Benjamin stood up as well, and the two swiftly left.

Dr. Sabara sat back in his chair. While the others might have been terrified of the situation at hand, this was precisely what Lucien was born for.

For Lucien Sabara, life had not been easy, at least not in the typical sense. He was born with a genetic mutation that made him highly sensitive to natural sunlight, xeroderma pigmentosum. He was lucky, or so he was told, that his case was considered mild and his parents had been so protective that a single ray of sun had never touched his skin. His vitamin levels were strictly monitored and maintained. By every standard test, Lucien was considered extremely healthy.

He was also lucky from another standpoint: Lucien's parents were tremendously wealthy. His father, Edward Sabara, was a successful real estate developer and owned several high-rise buildings in Manhattan. His mother, Beatrix Candergie-Sabara, came from one of the wealthiest families in the world. In fact, before leaving the hospital following Lucien's birth, Edward and Beatrix had every window on the penthouse floor of his Upper West Side building bricked up and even installed special fire escape slides to be within code.

Lucien had never seen the light of day. There was protective gear that he could wear, if he had to go out during daylight hours. But his mother couldn't handle the stares and whispers this "spacesuit" drew, so they simply did everything at night. He only wore it in rare instances when he traveled to or from the private jet or other brief yet unavoidable situations. He'd seen Paris, London, Tokyo, and even the Parthenon gloriously lit up at night. He'd swum in the crystal-clear waters of the Aegean under the light of the moon, but he'd never know what the sun felt like.

Lucien never felt bad for himself; in fact, he thought this whole situation was a bit comical. Beatrix always said, "Sweetheart, we chose your name because it means 'light.' We picked it before your diagnosis. You are destined to be a light to the world. You are meant for great things, my bright boy."

Beatrix had not been particularly religious until Lucien was born. But as the years went by and the prayers became more desperate, Lucien's mother made his father convert from his Judaic roots to Catholicism, and then they began taking pilgrimages to all the great churches of the world, collecting relics along the way and leaving large donations in their wake.

However, they were also deeply committed to the family's long-held tradition of supporting the science of eugenics. Beatrix and Edward knew that Lucien's condition was the result of a poor breeding choice that his maternal great-grandmother, Althea, had made. At sixteen, Althea had become pregnant by the property caretaker's son. He was seventeen, and came from very poor stock, helping take care of the manor's sprawling landscape.

Following this scandal, the young father was forced to enlist in the army, shipped off to the trenches on the Western Front, and never heard from again. Althea eventually married a more suitable gentleman who agreed to adopt her son along with a hefty dowry.

Luckily, Lucien's grandfather, William Candergie, took after his mother's line. He was handsome and intelligent, and proved extremely deft at financial investments. Under his guidance, the family became one of the wealthiest in the country. His only daughter, Beatrix, continued to add to the family's fortunes when she married the up-and-coming real estate mogul, Edward Sabara.

In order to make amends for Althea's poor choices, the family donated very large sums to the American Eugenics Society. AES was dedicated to "improving the genetic composition of humans through controlled reproduction of different races and classes of people." They built onto the work of the Station for Experimental Evolution at the Cold Spring Harbor Laboratory in New York, as well as the Race Betterment Foundation in Michigan. Through this work, the Candergie family funded thousands of forced sterilizations at mental institutions and prisons.

Their work with the AES became extremely controversial following World War II, specifically after Hitler praised the United States' work in eugenics. Regardless, the family continued to quietly support the AES, funding early genetic studies in breeding and forced sterilizations. By the time Lucien was born in 1966, only a handful of states still allowed them. In 1972, Beatrix and Edward served on the Board of Directors for AES when they voted to change the name of AES to the Society of Biological Demographics. The SBD continued to support genetic studies, through which Beatrix hoped to find a cure for Lucien's condition.

From a very young age, Edward and Beatrix had taught Lucien about the roots of his condition and what they had learned through their genetic research. He proved to be quite the student. At just fifteen, Lucien completed his high school education, taking every AP class offered and graduating with a weighted GPA of 5.0. He was accepted to Columbia University at sixteen.

They even made special arrangements—accompanied by a large donation to the school—so that he was able to attend all night classes. They built a special wing of classrooms in the biological sciences center that included lighting more conducive to Lucien's condition.

Lucien completed his undergraduate studies in two years, a period of great growth for him. He found his purpose; he found his independence. His focused shifted completely to his studies, and he quickly became a young star in his field of genetics—after all, this was what he was clearly born for. Following graduation from Columbia, Lucien attended medical school at the University of Michigan, where he met his mentor, the famed "gene-hunter" Francis Collins. Under Collins's leadership, Lucien and his team began uncovering the genetic markers for several diseases.

In 1993, Collins was appointed Director of the National Center for Human Genome Research. Lucien, now officially Dr. Lucien Sabara, joined

Collins and led a team working on the Human Genome Project. In this position, Lucien was able to open his own independent lab while continuing to work on the genome project. Through private funding, AmCorps Lab was created.

AmCorps was built on the foundation that eugenics was the human species' obligation. As the only free-thinking species on the planet, it was our duty to create the best version possible. Granted, in the early 1900s, science wasn't where it was today. Now, eugenics was not only scientifically possible, but it was rapidly becoming a necessity. With the increasing rate of cancers and auto-immune conditions, no one disagreed with genetically altering the species so that we did not suffer such a demise.

That opened the floodgates for Lucien to work toward a genetically superior human race.

CHAPTER 7

Green Hell

AT 3 A.M., THE BLACK YUKON ARRIVED. As Gabby
got into the SUV, she noticed the full moon and clear
sky. It made her remember the hours she spent with
her dad, as a little girl, staring into the night sky, the
wonder she felt when he tried to explain how space
goes on forever and has no end that we are aware of.
He pointed out the constellations, and they waited
for falling stars.

Tonight, she easily picked out the Big Dipper and
Little Dipper and felt like it was a sort of wink or
nod from her dad.

The two officers from the night before handed
Gabby and Trent their travel packs. These folders
included the necessary visas and credentials, including

a brand-new passport for her that mysteriously had stamps from previous travels to Peru, the DRC, Italy, Great Britain and Australia (all places Gabby had been), as well as credit cards and cash. They headed to the Philadelphia airport, with one quick stop on the way.

They needed to pick up the third member of their party.

Lt. Christopher Silver was staying at a small Sheraton in Philadelphia. He was waiting outside when the car pulled up. With a floppy mop of messy, thick brown hair, khakis, and a lived-in Endless Summer sweatshirt, this was not the Airforce Special Forces lieutenant that Gabby was expecting. He was big and bulky—he might have been muscular, but it was hard to tell with his baggy clothes. Chris had naturally tanned skin and looked like he spent his days on the beach.

"What's up?" Chris said as he nudged Gabby over and jumped in the side seat. "Hey Trent, and you must be Dr. Gabrielle Gale. I'm Chris. Nice to meet you."

"Nice to meet you too," Gabby replied.

Chris had big brown eyes, a strong jaw, and a

hearty smile, which made him look kind, more like a teddy bear than a military machine. Gabby found it hard to believe that he could be capable of hurting anything larger than a gnat.

"This car has been scanned and is safe, so this will be our last time to talk," Trent began. "Is everyone clear on their roles?"

Gabby nodded; she had studied her field notes the night before. She knew her cover was as a botanical chemist, so she'd brushed up on the fauna she would be studying. She'd also read about the FUNAI, a Brazilian governmental protection agency for native interests and their culture, and their rules for protecting the indigenous peoples of their country.

"We have a field agent picking us up, who's currently an anthropologist at the Federal University of Amazonas. He has prepared our expedition and will get us into the jungle," Chris said.

"Gabrielle, do you have any questions? Do you know your role? It's essential that we make it in as quietly and unnoticed as possible," Trent said.

"I'm a botanical chemist, and I'm looking for microbes in the soil of the jungle that resemble Teixobactin. I will also be looking for other microbes that show antimicrobial promise and testing ways to reproduce and isolate those microbes," Gabby answered.

"And, Chris, are you familiar with Teixobactin and your role?" Trent asked.

"It's an antibiotic that was discovered in soil. It treats many bacterial infections that have become resistant to common antibiotics that treat tuberculosis, staph, septicemia and C. diff. It was grown in soil and isolated through the use of a specialized computer chip, called the iChip, and that's where I come in. I'm a microbiologist who studied under the iChip's inventor, mmm—" Chris paused for a moment. "Dr. Slava Epstein. I'm going to help grow and isolate any of Dr. Gale's new discoveries in our lab," he said as he playfully nudged Gabby with an elbow.

Trent nodded. "Just for cohesiveness, I'm the lead scientist for this mission. I'm a medicinal chemist and molecular engineer. I will be assisting with all functions as well as preparing and securing any samples for transfer. As you know, we are all employed as scientists with AmCorps, which has paid the Brazilian government a hefty 'legal' fee to get in."

"We have a private transport, but we have to leave out of the Philadelphia airport and arrive at the Eduardo Gomes International Airport in Manaus, so that we can go through customs," he explained.

"Got it," said Chris, "and while we're speaking freely, are you both prepared for this mission from an operational stance?"

"Of course," replied Trent.

"I've set up a quick weapons training session before we head into the jungle," Chris said.

"What?" Gabby asked.

"With only three of us, you're going to need to know how to carry and fire a gun, and be comfortable doing it. There are some animals that can pose a threat, but for a large portion of our way in, we will go through an area that's a known passage for drug traffickers and illegal loggers. Multiple expeditions have been attacked in this area before, so we need to be prepared. Granted logging has slowed down, drug trafficking has been more active than ever," said Chris.

Gabby felt sick to her stomach. It wasn't that she was afraid, it was that her whole world had changed so drastically and so quickly.

"Have either of you been in the jungle before?" continued Chris.

"No, but I'm sure I'll be fine," said Trent.

"I was in the outskirts of both the Amazon and the Congo for a Doctors without Borders mission," Gabby said.

"Do you know what the Amazon's nickname is?" Chris asked.

"Green Hell," Trent responded with a slight roll of his eyes.

"Yeah, and it fits well. It's hot, humid, infested with biting insects, and miserable. I mean swarms—no, clouds of mosquitos will attack you ridden with some of the most horrific diseases imaginable. It's . . . it's hell," Chris stated matter-of-factly.

"Oh, insects!" Trent said. "Gabrielle, you still need your second dose of the anti-malarial."

On cue, the front-seat guard passed Gabby a bottle of water, a small cup with a single pill, and a banana. While she typically tried to avoid medicines at all cost—she didn't even like to take the occasional acetaminophen or ibuprofen and was one of the only doctors in the United States that didn't trust the seasonal flu shot—she took this without hesitation.

"Your blisters will get infected almost immediately," Chris continued. "Let's hope no one gets sick from a bug bite—forget malaria, there's also Dengue Fever and Chagas. Leprosy is endemic in the Amazon too. Then you have the venomous snakes and spiders, jaguars . . ."

"You forgot frogs and piranhas," joked Gabby. "I glanced through the contents listing of my medical kit and it's well-stocked with antivenom and antibiotics." She laughed.

None of this was funny, but at this point, all she could do was laugh. She was so exhausted. Gabby briefly considered the fact that all of this could be a nightmare. When she was little and would wake up in the grips of a nightmare, Nana used to hug her. The old woman would always say, "Oh my little angel, you're so perfect, I must be dreaming, and I should pinch us both to wake up." Nana would start pinching and tickling Gabby until they were both rolling in laughter. The night terrors would vanish, and Gabby would easily fall back to sleep and wake up happy, usually still snuggled in Nana's arms.

Now, Gabby gave it a shot. She pinched her leg, knowing she'd still be squished between Trent and

Chris but hoping that little pinch might bring back a little nostalgic comfort. The pinch just made Gabby long for simpler, warmer times.

They pulled up to a private airline terminal, Pacific Aviation, which operated out of Philadelphia International Airport. A second black Tahoe pulled up behind theirs with two more Marines, and everyone, except Gabby, began unloading duffle bags, equipment, crates, and supplies. Trent handed Gabby a large duffle bag backpack that weighed at least eighty pounds.

"This is your bag. Follow me," Trent said.

Gabby struggled to get it on her back. Chris gave her just enough help to settle it comfortably in place.

Trent, Gabby, Chris, and the four marines with all the cargo made their way into the empty terminal. Light blue industrial carpet gave way to white tables and tan chairs. The private terminal resembled any other airport terminal in function, but the similarities ended there. Rather than crowded walkways, angry travelers, and unapologetic airline employees, this terminal was empty except for a few calm employees who sat lazily with slight grins, waiting.

Tom (Gabby read his gold-plated name badge)

stood to acknowledge them. "You must be the AmCorps Lab group. Customs is ready for you. You received special clearance to have your military escort load your cargo. I just need to scan your military IDs, then I will take you"—the agent looked directly at the marines—"and the cargo to the plane. The three passengers can continue on through customs, which is straight ahead."

Tom had the air of a five-star concierge sprinkled with the sagacity of a federal agent. His thinning blond hair was neat, and he was dressed smartly under his florescent orange vest.

Gabrielle, Trent, and Chris continued on through a small lobby to a security check-point, staffed with only one TSA agent and one customs official.

"Tail number please," the TSA agent requested.

"N2AMC," replied Trent.

"Thank you. Can you place your bags on the x-ray machine, and then we will get your passports checked," the TSA agent said, then moved to the operator's seat of the extra-large baggage x-ray machine and turned it on.

Trent placed his suitcase on first, took out his passport, then put his backpack on and stepped over to the customs officer. Gabby took her travel documents out of her small bag and tossed it on the belt. Before she had the chance to attempt to get the large duffle off her back and onto the belt, Chris grabbed the heavy bag for her.

"Thanks."

"No worries." He smiled.

The team went through security and customs without a single question or problem. They were on AmCorps's private 747 in less than five minutes. Gabby had never been on a private plane, let alone a super jet. The front section had a conference table that could seat ten, flanked by soft leather couches on each side. Then came the fully stocked galley. Soda, water, wine, and beer set in perfectly straight lines were visible through the glass door of the refrigerator. Baskets of chips, protein bars, and cereal sat neatly on the counters.

Behind that were four semi-private sleeping stalls with an area to secure their bags. Each stall had a twin-size cot with a seatbelt and a cubby underneath for a suitcase, along with a flat-screen TV, a set of headphones, and a privacy curtain.

Trent went up to the cockpit to talk to the pilots, and returned five minutes later.

"We've been cleared for takeoff. Make sure your bags are secured, then buckle the seatbelts on your beds. The next seven hours may be your best chance for sleep in the coming weeks," Trent said.

Gabby heard the engines power up. She kicked off her shoes, got under the blankets, loosely buckled the seatbelt, grabbed the headphones, and turned the TV on. Skimming through the film selection, she settled on an old movie, *Avatar*, but was asleep before the opening credits were over.

After sleeping a solid five hours, Gabby woke to the smell of freshly brewed coffee. Trent and Chris were already up.

"Coffee?" Chris asked.

"Yes, please."

He poured her a large cup. Gabby sat down on the couch and looked out the window toward the setting sun. Trent passed her a notebook with the first day's itinerary.

Day 1:
Quick briefing in safe house.
Weapons training.

Dinner.

Midnight departure.

Gabby nodded, then handed him back the notebook. Trent sprayed a solution on the page and the ink vanished. The plane had been scanned and was considered safe, but due to the sensitivity of this mission, they had agreed that it was best not to risk any information breach. In the high-profile private lab world, pilots were notorious for flipping to the highest bidder; several patents had been lost in that manner.

Gabby, Chris, and Trent remained quiet for the rest of the flight. She savored another two cups of coffee while she reread *Jurassic Park*; it had been her dad's favorite book. Gabby had read it at least five times. Then they were landing at Manaus, much too quickly for her liking.

PART 2

"I suspect that some people also dislike the idea that natural selection has no foresight. The process itself, in effect, does not know where to go. It is the "environment" that provides the direction, and over the long run its effects are largely unpredictable in detail."

—FRANCIS CRICK
What Mad Pursuit, 1988

Chapter 8

The Marlow

WHEN THE JET DOOR OPENED, a small force of machine-gun-clad officers was waiting. They all had black N99 face masks on, leaving only their eyes visible. Gabby's mouth immediately turned to cotton, and she wasn't sure that she could do this.

"Dr. Trent Martins?" the highest-ranking officer yelled over the sound of the jet engines. His jet-black eyes scanned them as they walked off the plane.

"Yes, are you Officer Figuero?" replied Trent.

"I am. My men will help you unload your equipment and take it to your transport," Figuero said.

"Thank you," Trent replied as he reached into his bag, grabbed a thick envelope, and passed it to Figuero.

"This is Lazarro—he's our customs agent. He will stamp your passports, check your bags, and get you cleared through customs," Figuero said.

They passed Lazarro their passports, and he stamped them and handed them back with a grinning wink. At that, Chris passed him another envelope; Gabby could see an American bill peeking through the open flap.

The crew quickly unloaded their cargo, wheeled it through a guarded gate, and loaded it into three waiting army-green Land Rover Defenders.

Gabby suddenly felt extremely nauseous. It was a combination of too much coffee and the heat. Not to mention machine-gun-wielding soldiers. Her body wasn't ready for this. She had to bite her tongue hard to fight back the urge to vomit. This was happening so fast. She jumped into the back seat of the third Defender, next to Chris. Trent took the front seat.

The driver turned to the back, and Chris leaned forward. They embraced in a strong handshake and hug. "Chris, man, it's been a while. It's good to see you, and nice to see someone that still hugs."

"You too, buddy. Tomas, this is Trent and

Gabrielle. Tomas is our guy. In his other life, he's an anthropologist who has worked his way through a series of posts here in Brazil. Tomas's parents are Brazilian, but he's American. We actually went to school together."

"Nice to meet you," Gabby said. Tomas gave her a warm smile. His curly brown hair had specks of blond, clearly from years spent in the tropical sun.

"Everything is set. Your crew is waiting. My partner, Mari, has connections with FUNAI, so they've already been out and approved the expedition. You're set to leave," Tomas said.

"Partner? Was she cleared?" Trent asked.

"Yes, Trent," Chris said, "she has all the same security clearance that Tomas does. I told you that his team would handle getting us out."

"You've had a long trip. Relax. We have a twenty-minute drive," Tomas said.

Gabby stared out the window at a gritty metropolis carved out of jungle. Ghosts of a once-busy city hung heavy. As they easily moved fast, the quiet buildings became a blur of concrete, fading colors, and stunning graffiti. An occasional dirt bike or small car periodically darted around their entourage, but there was not much life to the city, at least not out on the street.

"With so many sick, not many people leave their homes anymore. It began with Zika and just got worse," Tomas explained.

Soon they were pulling up to a small dock and old warehouse. There was a single wooden boat floating there; it looked like an old steamboat without the paddlewheel. Gabby hoped that this was not the vessel that would take them into the jungle. White and blue paint had chipped from the wood. The shallow draft and tall cabin made the boat seem as if it would tip over at the slightest ripple. *Marlow*, the name of the boat, was painted in large, light blue block letters on the front third. As Gabby peered into the black water, she thought she saw a large fin break the surface.

The warehouse was constructed from a mishmash of various shades of red and yellow corrugated iron panels. As the sun went down, a fog began to settle over the water. A deep sense of foreboding washed over Gabby, that sort of anxiety you feel in the pit of your stomach that seems to drain all the blood from your extremities. She had dealt with flushes of dread like this for as long as she could remember. Usually they were the result of a memory rather than impending doom. With a deep breath, she pushed the growing knot of angst back down to a manageable size.

Tomas led them into the warehouse. Gabby was relieved to see that the inside appeared much sturdier, with solid steel beams and a clean concrete floor. Supplies were neatly packed in various sections. Tomas suddenly let out an ear-shattering whistle. Gabby jumped.

"Sorry, it's just such a large building," he said.

Gabby smiled while trying to hide her embarrassment. Then a back door opened. A stunning woman walked through. She had glossy black hair that was twisted behind her head. Her tan skin glowed. Her perfect plump lips parted into a warm smile. She was fit, with hints of toned muscle that gave way to soft curves.

"This is Mari. Mari, this is Trent, Chris, and Gabrielle," Tomas said.

"Chris, I've heard so much about you," Mari said.

"It's all true, but don't hold it against me," Chris said with a confident wink and joking grin.

"Trent and Gabrielle, everything is set up for your weapons training. I thought we could do that while Tomas introduces Chris to the crew and they finish loading," Mari said.

"You're going to teach us to shoot?" Trent said.

"Yes," the woman said with a smile.

"You're qualified?" he pressed.

"Oh, very," Mari replied, and motioned for Gabby and Trent to follow her.

A makeshift target range was set up inside the next room. Silhouette targets were set against the far wall with a thick backing. Three long tables displayed a variety of guns.

"Gabrielle, what's your experience with guns?" Mari asked.

"I've never fired a gun before. I . . . I don't even think I've ever actually seen a gun in person."

"That's alright—I have some firearms that are really easy to work with. Trent, what about you?"

"I'm pretty comfortable shooting. I've been to the range several times and shot a variety of guns."

"Great, do you have a preference?"

"I guess a handgun, if I'm going to have it on me all the time," Trent replied.

"Okay, so a Glock, M9, something else? I think I even have an old-school Chief's Special 45," Mari said.

"Ah, whatever," Trent replied.

"Okay. Personally, I think you should have a handgun on you at all times, then something bigger close by," Mari said.

For some strange reason, Gabby began to feel a tickle of excitement at the base of her spine. She'd grown up with a strong disdain for guns, but now found herself both fearing their finality and welcoming their protection. In her college years, she was protesting gun violence. She petitioned for stricter gun laws, and whole-heartedly believed that guns had no place in modern American culture. Then again, modern American culture had taken such a sudden departure from any future she had pictured. And besides, she stood now far from it, in a secluded warehouse in Brazil only hours from the dangers of the jungle.

"Gabby, I'm going to give you two handguns. The Chief's Special, for backup, is light and easy to carry. And the Glock 17 is a really good gun and pretty easy to work with. Trent, you seem like a Beretta guy to me."

Mari handed them each their guns, barrels down. She demonstrated where the barrel should always be pointed, and how to drop the magazine and check the ammunition. Then she showed them how to rack the slide and make sure there were no rogue bullets.

The woman had Gabby and Trent practice with unloaded weapons over and over, to get the feel of them. Gabby was surprised by the lightness of some guns, while others were quite heavy. Each felt a little different. As much as Gabby despised guns, there was something empowering about holding this cold metal in her hand.

Then, they loaded the weapons.

"So now we shoot," Mari announced. "First, place your dominant hand around the grip with your index finger resting on the trigger guard. Next, use your other hand to provide support. Once you feel comfortable, close one eye—"

"I'm shooting," Trent interrupted.

"Please," Mari replied.

With one arm outstretched, Trent fired five shots in quick succession. They formed a tight circle around the heart on the silhouette target.

"Excellent. You should've told me you're such a pro," Mari said.

"My dad made me learn to shoot a gun when I was a kid," Trent said. "It's been awhile, but I guess it's like riding a bike."

That was the most Gabby had ever heard him say about his father. She knew the man was not part of Trent's life anymore, but that was all he would say.

"Gabrielle, focus on the far sight. Center it on the target and give it a go," Mari instructed.

Gabby took a deep breath, bit her bottom lip, and pulled the trigger. The gun kicked back, but not as hard as she'd expected.

"Not perfect, but still fatal. Nice job, Gabrielle. Next time, make sure that your wrist is straight. Think of the gun as a natural projection of your arm, not something you are trying to hold," Mari said.

Gabby aimed. Trent stepped closer. He gently put both his hands on her elbows and brushed down to her wrists, where he softly corrected her alignment.

"You're doing amazing—just relax and try it again," Trent whispered.

He stepped back. Gabby took a deep breath and

let it out, then pulled the trigger. It was perfect. She pulled the trigger three more times. All on target.

"You two are naturals, and such a good team," Mari said, clearly beaming.

Gabby felt good. The power was intoxicating. She liked shooting a gun; actually, she liked shooting them all. The M4 was big, but she liked feeling the kickback on her shoulder. The handguns were sleek. She liked staring down the sight at her target. Her arms were tired, but she felt strong. She felt powerful.

After their weapons training, Mari helped Gabby and Trent pack up the weapons. She fitted them with holsters and they took their handguns, and she gave Gabby an extra pistol to conceal as well.

Chris came in as they were finishing up, accompanied by their guides.

"This is Paulo, our captain. He has extensive experience on the Amazon," Chris said.

"It's nice to meet you," Paulo said in English so perfect that Gabby would've thought that he was American. "Just as Chris said, I have a lot of experience on the river, from my time with the military and as a luxury Amazon cruise captain, until tourism dried up a few years ago." Paulo had black hair that had begun to gray around his temples. His skin was tanned and creased, but still showed strong, chiseled features. He had large, muscular forearms covered in faded tattoos.

Also in tow were four men from the Sapanahua Tribe who had been hired to get them as deep as they could into the Amazon.

"And this is Kukulcan—did I say that right?" Chris said.

"Sim, but can call to me as Kukua. More easy," Kukua said.

"Kukua, was the chief of his tribe," Chris said. "He was the one that sought contact with the outside world."

Gabby smiled at them. The men were all small, about the same 5'5" as Gabby's slight frame. They wore modern clothes but maintained some of their tribe's traditions. They had no body hair or facial hair, including eyebrows. The hair on their heads shaped into a bowl with the crown shaved; it reminded Gabby of a monk's hair from the middle ages.

"The Sapanahua Tribe have only recently come out of isolation," Mari said. "Many of them have died from diseases that drug traffickers and loggers spread to their villages, and those who survived were forced to make a difficult decision."

"Hard for my people," Kukua said, "many get sick. Us no have choice."

"If you should run low on food," Tomas said, "the Sapanahua are one of a very few groups that are still allowed to legally hunt in the rainforest. More importantly, they actually know *how* to hunt in the rainforest. Which, trust me, is nearly impossible for even the most experienced hunters or survivalists."

Gabby ran a few basic health analyses on the captain and crew; everyone checked out.

CHAPTER 9

Check In

THE TEAM SET SAIL in the darkest hours of night. Chris agreed to take watch, so Gabby and Trent retired to the main cabin that they would all be sharing. Its pine walls were lined with two stacked cots on each side. There was a small bathroom that doubled as the shower, though due to the limited amount of fresh water, they were only allowed to shower every three days. There was also a single desk.

Gabby was exhausted and lay down on a bottom cot in her clothes.

Trent said, "I have to contact the lab to let them know that we made it past check one, but you should get some rest. I'll try to be as quiet as I can."

Trent had a spot beam satellite communication system that went through multiple levels of encryption to avoid any information or location leaks. It took nearly thirty minutes for him to set everything up. Gabby wondered how it all worked, and found her gaze wandering his way as she lay still, hoping for sleep. When he turned around to check on Gabby, she quickly closed her eyes. She didn't know why, other than she felt a little like she was spying. Nevertheless, though she felt silly pretending to be asleep, she continued to watch what Trent was doing.

From where Gabby was, she could clearly read the computer screen. The way the system worked was that each message was typed, encrypted, transferred, then erased. There were only two computers that could understand this communication: Trent's and the home base computer.

This is Tsep, checking in. We made it through checkpoint number one, Trent typed.

Good news. Any issues? The message flashed on the screen then vanished.

No, all went exactly as planned, Trent typed.

Very good. Phase One at home base began today.

Phase Two will begin in three weeks. All went better than expected. No issues.

Great. Why the push?

Situation outside progressing faster. Much worse than predicted. We have decided to push all phases 3—5 months ahead of schedule. We are making arrangements for C1 to go in as soon as possible. More info to come at next check in. The screen flashed then went black.

Trent closed his computer and Gabby quickly closed her eyes. Feeling slightly guilty for spying, she sat up in bed, startling him.

"You're still awake," Trent said.

Gabby nodded. "Is everything alright? At home?"

"Yeah, it's fine."

"What did you mean by phases one, two, and three?"

"Oh." Trent paused. "We didn't have time to brief you on this before we left, but there are a series of plans in place to initiate a sort of shelter-in-place in safe houses that we have constructed to be resistant to any pathogen spread. You know, we need to do more than just go virtual."

Gabby sat there silent for a moment. "Safe houses for who?"

"Our president and other high officials will be the first group in. We need to preserve as much of our society as possible, till we're able to find a solution."

Trent closed the computer, quickly packed up his system, then lay in the cot across from Gabby.

She tried to fall to sleep but couldn't. As a doctor, she had seen the signs for years, but now watching it actually happen was so much more terrifying. It was hard for her to imagine a good outcome.

After a few minutes, Trent got up and slid into Gabby's tiny cot.

"This is scary for all of us," he said as he brushed her hair behind her shoulder. "There are a lot of difficult decisions that are crucial in order for us to save the best fraction of humanity possible."

Gabby swallowed and let out a slow breath. "Yeah, but who is making these decisions? There is so much more going on than the pandemic risks we are dealing with. Shouldn't people be more informed?"

"It's a very complex, sensitive situation. There is so much still unknown. The president and the most intelligent people in our country are doing everything they can." Trent paused. "In the morning, I'd like you to help me test the captain's and our guides' DNA. You'll feel better once you start working toward a solution."

"Yeah," Gabby replied.

"Try to get some rest," he said as he made his way back to his cot.

She closed her eyes, listening to the soft splash of water against the hull as thoughts still tumbled through her mind.

CHAPTER 10

Mole

AS LUCIEN SAT IN FRONT OF HIS computer waiting for the video conference to begin, he scanned through the latest headlines. More of the same. More infections. More deaths. The numbers had slowed slightly following the mass quarantine and complete shutdown of all public gathering places including essential operations. Lucien knew that this was just temporary and the infections would rebound.

Lucien's living quarters took an entire floor at AmCorps' subterranean complex. The entire apartment was disinfected daily with a state-of-the-art UVC light system. Every day, when he left his apartment, the UVC system disinfected every surface in his living space. The system was built-in to deliver strong ninety-second bursts of intense UVC light.

The irony in this was that this system, while deadly to pathogens, was perfectly safe for most humans—except Lucien. He'd installed tight controls, and ensured he was the only person that had access to them. There were also thermoregulated safeguards that prevented the system from activating when a heat source—like a human body—was present.

As a specially created, secured Virtual Meet notification chimed, Lucien answered, "Hello Mr. President, David, Robert. How are you doing?"

"So far, so good. It's been much better than I expected," President Spiegel said.

"Great," replied Lucien. "I trust that you're finding the level of service suitable and your living quarters are comfortable and well appointed."

"Yes. The public will not even notice that I'm not quarantined at the White House," laughed President Spiegel.

"Our quarters are perfect, too," Dr. David Benjamin said.

"The system was very well thought out," General Holton added.

"I'm glad to hear that. As the phases continue to roll out, nothing will change for you. Your decontamination quarters and then living quarters are much like your current quarantine area. In your individual pods, you are completely separated from others. Anything that is brought in goes through three levels of decontamination. Once you're in there, you can remain pathogen-free indefinitely," Lucien said.

President Spiegel's image leaned into the screen. "Let's just hope they bring the treatment back soon and we can put this behind us."

"The team got in, completely unnoticed," Lucien reported.

General Holton countered, "Good, but not completely unnoticed. There has been some intel that another agency is tracking them. IFP, Interfaith for Peace, has been nothing but a fucking pain in the ass. We suspect there may be a mole imbedded with your team or staff with ties to those broke bastards."

"A mole?" Lucien asked. "Where did this group even come from?"

"When the first bid went out for the safe house construction, they found out," Holton replied.

"They're not happy with how we are allowing individuals into our safe houses."

President Spiegel nodded. "They think we should have taken a selection of religious leaders, artists, and intellectuals in for free. They also think that 50% of the people that we bring into the safe houses should be from a public lottery," he added with a roll of his eyes.

General Holton scoffed. "We already have leaders from every religion, artists, and many of the smartest minds in the world that have paid their way in. Right now, we don't have the luxury of charitable services."

"Pastor Hughes and Rabbi Shmuley both have said, many times," said President Spiegel, "that if the wealthy and powerful are able to get their hearts right with God, they will dispense their blessings to those that look up to them. That's what this year's National Prayer Service was all about."

"Pastor Hughes, Rabbi Shmuley, Baba Ramlev, and Edin Mecada have all made it through Phase One quarantine. And thanks to Edin, we were able to get our team into Brazil unnoticed," General Holton said.

Lucien sat back, his arms folded. "Nature has given us this incredible opportunity to fix many of the problems that plague the human race. Everyone will want what we have. Until we have identified the treatment and have it back here, we are in a precarious situation. Don't screw this up—security is your responsibility."

"We have a large team of special-forces soldiers in a temporary decontamination unit. They are protected from pathogens, healthy, and ready to deploy as soon as they get the call for extraction," General Holton assured him.

"Great, but how big of a problem is this IFP group going to be for my team that's there now?" Lucien asked.

"We've received some intel that they're aware of your team in Brazil and that they may be sending a unit to intercept them. But, I wouldn't worry. For one, they don't have the money to fund any sort of real operation. Secondly, I don't see how they could even get into the country. If they are actually able to do anything, we will be two steps ahead of them. They're a nuisance, nothing more," General Holton said.

Chapter 11

Static

WHEN GABBY'S EYES FLUTTERED opened, she felt even more exhausted than before she'd laid down. Fleeting dreams kept her mind racing and her body tossing through the night. She thought she had been awake all night—though she must've slept, because the sun was up and she was alone in the cabin. She quickly got up, changed her clothes, brushed her teeth, and made her way up on deck.

The scenery was wildly different. The vast Amazon river, earlier banked by city buildings, was now strangled by thick jungle. The air had become oppressive without Gabby noticing until such a heaviness hit her that just taking a breath seemed an effort. It was so humid, the air itself felt wet. Beads of moisture clung to Gabby's skin and immediately dampened her clothes.

"Gabrielle," Trent yelled from the aft deck, "Chris just made some coffee. Grab a quick breakfast and then we'll start collecting samples."

Gabby took a deep breath. She could already feel her lungs adjusting to this heavy atmosphere.

After breakfast, she found Trent in the makeshift lab. She was shocked by how completely he had transformed the small third cabin into a fully functioning laboratory. Solar panels had been fixed to the upper deck and a tight bundle of wires carried enough energy into this small room to power this high-tech workspace. The room seemed to buzz with the hum of machinery and the click of Trent at the keyboard. He had set up three ultra-fast, high-performance thermal cyclers, a micro tube plate cooler, two computer stations, five digital microscopes, and two DNA sequencer machines.

While each machine was deceptively small, Gabby could feel the surge of power in the room. Every apparatus was top-of-the-line. At least half-a-million dollars filled this eight-by-twelve-foot space.

"Wow." Gabby cleared her throat. "When did you set all of this up?"

"Chris helped me this morning." Trent looked up from his computer. "Ready to get started?"

She nodded.

"The collection kits are in a box marked *AmCorps Precision Phred-Score—L3 Solution*. They're in a container under the table with the gloves. We'll start with standard saliva collection and see what we get."

"Okay."

"Ask Chris to help you; you're going to have to come up with a reason that will make our crew feel comfortable enough to offer up their spit. Just make up something. Don't even mention genetics."

"I don't want to lie to them."

"It's not lying—they just can't comprehend this, and they have so many crazy superstitions."

"They should know what we are doing."

"Please, just make this as easy as possible. I'll send Chris down, they seem to like him."

Gabby didn't like lying—it went against what she believed patients deserved in terms of honesty. And she tried to ignore Trent's implication that the others didn't like her. She pushed back her discomfort and started looking for the supplies.

"Don't screw this up," Trent said, and vanished.

Now she *was* irritated. She most certainly knew how to process specimens! Gabby found the box. Inside were dozens of small clear plastic tubes, pre-filled with solution, marked with the logo *APP-L3* and sealed in protective plastic sleeves. She gathered up five kits.

"Hey . . ." Chris loomed right behind her and Gabby jumped, dropping the test kits. "Sorry, I didn't mean to scare you. People usually hear me coming," he joked.

Gabby could feel the fire in her cheeks. "I'm not usually jumpy." She smiled, realizing the circumstances truly had made her more distracted and irritable. Chris gathered up the sealed kits that Gabby had dropped.

"Thanks," Gabby said, "I'm trying to figure out how to get our guides to fill these tubes up with spit."

"Just ask them," Chris replied.

They found the crew sitting on the back deck, joking around. Everyone appeared happy and relaxed.

"Hi Kukua, I hope I'm not interrupting," Gabby began.

"Interrupting?" Kukua questioned with a smile.

"Mmm, bothering you," Gabby said.

Kukua shook his head. "No, no, you no bother. Sorry English is no so good. What it is, you want?" he asked.

"Your English is great, it's really amazing."

"Friend teach so can watch Spongee Bob, you know?"

Gabby laughed, "I do."

"Is favorite."

"Well"—she glanced up and down the deck, but Trent was nowhere to be seen—"so, we are looking for a very specific medical treatment that will react to everyone differently based on their genetics. Because you are indigenous to this part of the world, we would like to get a sample from you to test in our lab. All we need is for you to fill these tubes up with your spit." Gabby paused, unsure what to say next. "Do you understand?"

Kukua looked at her with his head tilted. "Want DNA in spit?" Kukua asked.

Stunned, Gabby hesitantly replied, "Yes, you know about DNA?"

Kukua smiled. "No do school, but learn DNA from Spongee Bob, it so funny. Plankton took Pa-treek's DNA. He make Bikini Bottom so dumb. You no do something like that?"

"No, no . . ."

"Kukua make joke." he laughed "that no possible."

"Oh." Gabby laughed as well.

"Sim, do for you. Gabby have good soul. Trust you. Chris good too."

Chris laughed. "I'm glad you think so. What gave us away?"

"Listen to wind. Make noise. By Chris and Gabby, wind calm, soft. You good. Wind by Trent sound like," Kukua said, then made a *schuushcuuuuush-cooo* sound, "like TV not work."

"Static?" Gabby asked.

"Sim," Kakua nodded.

"He's a good guy," Chris smiled, "you just haven't spent enough time with him."

"Maybe Trent scared in jungle," he relented. "Kukua give spit first."

The boat captain didn't want to know why Gabby

and Chris wanted his saliva. Paulo, busy navigating and keeping to the strict schedule, quickly offered it but declined wasting time on an explanation.

Gabby had the samples complete and in the lab within an hour. Trent took over from there and told her to rest up for her night watch.

She spent most of the day reading on a deck hammock. There wasn't much else for her to do and it was far too hot to be in her cabin. The river was so wide that it left little for Gabby to look at. All she could see was lines of green where the river met the bank. She dozed sporadically, but deep rest was nearly impossible in this oppressive climate. Surprisingly, sporadic swarms of flies and mosquitos began to find their way to the *Marlow*, driving Gabby farther from the rest she craved.

Eventually, exhausted from chasing sleep, Gabby made her way to the galley.

"Hey Gab, want to help me make dinner?" Chis asked with a big smile.

"I'm not really that good in the kitchen, I burn everything, but I'll try."

"Awesome." Chris paused. "We only have a few more days of this easy sailing, so this is my way of winning over our crew." A brief serious note flitted across his usually relaxed manner, but it faded quickly. "How are you at chopping?"

Gabby smiled. "I'm a skilled surgeon; I could probably chop you into a corner."

"Oh, it's on," Chris replied, and flicked a knife to her so that its point stuck into the worn wooden cutting board perfectly.

Gabby gave him a sly nod, then picked up the knife and got to work.

Finally, time seemed to start moving again. Two hours passed in what felt like five minutes. Chris and Gabby joked and didn't mention current affairs once. She learned that Chris was from San Diego, and had grown up in Solana Beach. His dad was a chemist who had invented a series of antibiotics, following the first phase of antibiotic resistance. Chris wasn't sure why, but his dad suddenly retired, opening a surf shop and spending his days surfing or talking about surfing.

Chris's mom still worked as a journalist. She was Afro-Portuguese, and had grown up in Hawaii before moving to California for college. Chris had a younger sister who was a professional surfer and healthy-lifestyle blogger in Hawaii. Chris's family traveled a lot—it sounded like they had fun, and like Chris had enjoyed an amazing childhood.

"It wasn't all great," he finished. "At the time, I didn't appreciate what I had. I was one of those spoiled, obnoxious jocks. I partied too much, abused everything around me, and got into some trouble. I guess that's what led me to the military. But enough about me, what about you?"

"I was a boring book worm, that's it."

Gabby was not one to open up easily, she never had been. The conversation quickly turned lighter again, as Chris explained that they were making his self-proclaimed, world-famous fajitas and salsa. This was how he had started every mission for the past five years. Mari and Tomas had had to go to three different markets just to get the ingredients.

As Gabby was putting everything out on the large, rear-deck table, Chris brought the captain his plate and went to gather the crew and Trent.

Trent was the first to the table.

"The first sample, Kakui's—"

"Kukua," Gabby corrected.

"Kukua, *sorry*, is extracted, quantified, and

processing. We will have the results in a couple hours," Trent said.

"That's great!"

"Yes!" He gave her a big hug. "Dinner looks amazing!"

While it was hot and humid, covers over the food were needed to keep the bugs away, and space was cramped, an air of relaxation had settled over Gabby and Trent. At home, seeing face after face covered with surgical masks was a constant reminder of what they were facing. The steady stream of spreading epidemics on the news created an unending state of anxiety. Without those daily aides-mémoires, Gabby couldn't help but think that maybe there was a place on this earth that was still safe. It was incredible just how quickly those fears had faded.

The crew and Chris filed in next.

"Sit down, let's eat," Chris said.

"What us eat?" Kukua asked.

"These are called fajitas." Chris took a tortilla, then passed them around the table as he showed Kukua and the crew how to build the perfect fajita.

They all laughed watching each other try to eat the fajitas. With each bite that made it to their mouths, three bites fell out of the tortilla and back onto the plate. Chris, Gabby, and even Trent were in tears of mirth. Finally, Chris showed them a trick to folding the tortilla to keep the meat inside the shell.

"Us like. Make," Kukua pointed to his mouth, "hot, but it good."

"These are really great," Trent agreed.

"Thanks, Gab helped."

"Wow, Gabrielle," Trent said, "I'm impressed. You may have to start cooking when we get back home."

She smiled. "Don't get too excited, all I did was chop and stir."

The dinner went well. Everyone was relaxed, and it felt comfortable. The two 'crews' bonded. Gabby thought it was the perfect start to their mission.

Chapter 12

The Joker

AFTER DINNER, TRENT WENT BACK to the lab. The crew retired to their hammocks on the back deck. Gabby helped Chris clean up. When they were finished cleaning, Chris showed her where the supply of Red Bull, coffee, and caffeine pills were. Then he took her to the deck to give her the breakdown on what she would spend the night doing on her watch.

Gabby was to watch for any lights. She had to keep a lookout for other boats as well as any activity on shore. It was not likely, as they were in what Chris had determined was a safe zone. It was undeveloped but still close to populated areas, so it was not trafficked by drug smugglers or illegal loggers.

"It'll be good practice," Chris said. "You can even

bring a book; just do a quick scan every couple minutes or so. You'll be fine."

He finished and went to bed, having been up for nearly forty-eight hours. Gabby grabbed a Coke and her book, and went to her spot on the bow.

A soft breeze had pacified the unbearable heat. It was so calm and peaceful, and Gabby was enjoying herself. She had not been this serene in years.

"Gabrielle . . ." Gabby quickly sat up and her Coke clattered to the floor. "Shush," Trent cautioned. Though the wood floors on the deck of the boat were old, they were strong and did not creak under footsteps.

"Sorry," she whispered.

"Listen." He sat very close to Gabby and spoke in a barely audible whisper. "I have Kukua's results. It's not what I expected. It's . . . it's the first sample that we've come across like this."

"What is it?"

"The EVE-0 gene mutation involves a specific deletion of a single base pair of genes. Genes we need to function in our environment. We have attempted to replace those missing genes using the CRISPR method, and isolating genes from chimps and preserved genetic material. Kukua does not have the active EVE-0, but the base pairs are there, they are just in a different order."

"What's this mean?"

"To be honest, I have no idea. I'm going to classify it as a VUS." Trent paused.

Gabby knew that a VUS, or variable of unknown significance, meant he really didn't know anything about this missense mutation. "Have you considered a possible frameshift mutation?" Gabby knew mutations did not happen in one step, but sometimes in several stages. Maybe Kukua was in mid-change.

"I have, and that's a possibility. I think we've caught Kukua in the process of an actively mutating evolution of that gene. There must be some specific, potent component that every single civilized human being is exposed to, one that abruptly begins to cause this mutation."

"So now what?"

"I'm not willing to risk any human experimentation at this stage. I'm going to play around with it in the lab."

"This is great news, though, right?"

"You have no idea. Everything is going better than

we even hoped in our initial assessment of this mission." With that, Trent kissed her and disappeared into the cabin.

Gabby picked up her book and started reading. She'd borrowed Chris's copy of *On the Road*; the allure of *Jurassic Park* had faded ever so slightly while she was in the jungle wrapped in a strange genetic world. She was careful to scan from bank to bank every eight pages. It was astoundingly peaceful. Gabby's body had adjusted to the heavy, humid atmosphere. The soft hum of the engine was the bass to the contralto buzz of jungle insects and distant soprano chirp of wildlife awake in the night. The soft breeze, just enough to keep the insects mostly at bay.

Gabby checked her watch—it was 0220. Scanning the banks, she saw that all was calm. She had to admit that she was enjoying this peacefulness. After almost a decade of constant anxiety, it was nice to be separated from it all. Gabby hadn't had this much time to herself since she had been in school. A slight pang of guilt came over her at this bit of calm enjoyment, and then she heard the unmistakable click of a gun cock and felt the hard metal barrel jab the back of her head.

"Put your hands behind your head, Cadela, and turn around slow."

Gabby recognized the voice immediately as the officer who had checked their passports and so jovially welcomed them to Brazil the day before.

As Gabby turned, she saw that another shadowed man had a gun to the captain's head, while at least three other shadows moved around the boat. The man on Gabby was dressed in black, his face covered with a bandana that had a wicked Joker's grinning mouth. His black eyes glared callously at her.

"What do you want?" Gabby asked.

"Don't be stupid. Nobody has been allowed into Brazil like you were in years. How much did you have to pay for that?"

"I don't know." Gabby's eyes started to burn. She had never had a gun pointed at her. She was mad. Even worse, she felt like she had let her team down. "We are here to find medicine."

"Enough with your lies." The man jabbed the butt of the gun into the side of her cheek, and she felt a sharp pain radiate through her teeth.

"Look," Gabby snapped, "I know who you are.

Your stupid mask isn't doing anything but making you look like an idiot."

He pulled his arm back. Gabby reflexively jumped and he laughed.

"It's not for you, galinha—you'll be dead soon anyway."

"You can't do this. You stupid piece of . . . we're here to save your life and the lives of everyone you love."

"Gabrielle," Trent yelled as he was being marched up on deck with his hands zip-tied, "don't waste your time. Don't say any more to them."

At the same time, Kukua, the crew, and Captain Paulo were marched onto the deck. Gabby counted at least four more masked men. Each carried a large assault rival, and each of their masks bore a different, twisted, vile grin.

"Where is it?" the joker asked.

"What?" Trent replied.

"You can make this easy, or you can make this hard," he said.

"I don't know what you're talking about. But you have to listen—we brought several samples of dangerous bacteria. If you break the wrong sample in my lab, you will be infected and there is nothing that can cure you. You will die slowly and painfully," Trent spat.

"Enough." The joker grabbed Gabby by the hair and pressed his gun against her temple. She heard a shot fire. Her world froze. She looked to Trent and mouthed, "Chris." The joker yelled something in Portuguese and dropped her.

This was all her fault—she should've been more vigilant. Tears soaked her cheeks.

The joker yelled again, then sent two of his guys into the cabin, pushing one as he walked by. Gabby quickly crawled close to Trent. As she did, she felt the bulge in her sock and remembered the small handgun she had stashed there this morning.

"Tell me where the fuck the gold is," the joker said as he aimed his gun at Kukua and pulled the trigger. Kukua's body flew back, then collapsed on the deck. His head made a hollow thump on the hard wood floor and a stream of blood spread from under the limp body.

The joker laughed. He aimed his gun at Trent. Gabby pulled out her Chief's Special, aimed, and pulled the trigger. The joker jumped and the bullet grazed his arm. The shot serrated his bicep and left a splash of blood in its wake, causing him to drop his gun. Gabby tried to cock it to shoot again, but the weapon jammed.

"Sua puta," the joker cursed, stepping forward and backhanding Gabby with his good arm. The man's fist jammed right between her temple and jaw, twisting her neck and sending her head into the boat's deck. He picked up his Glock with his left hand and awkwardly aimed it at Gabby.

As she lay on the floor, fighting to hold on to consciousness, she noticed a red laser spot on the joker's chest. He noticed at the same time and froze. There was no sound, just a red mist rising up behind him. The man's eyes were wide open and gazing up, but the rising crimson haze made him look as if he were slowly falling. His painted smile didn't move.

Seconds later, the joker collapsed on the floor in a pool of blood. At the same time, a barrage of gunfire seemed to explode from somewhere far away. Then everything went silent. Gabby's vision blurred and she went out.

When she came to, Trent was holding an ice pack to the side of her face and gently rubbing her head.

"That was really brave—I had no idea you had it in you," Trent said.

In a panic, Gabby sat up and looked around.

Kukua was sitting up. Mari was cleaning and bandaging his wound.

"It's just superficial. He's fine," Mari said, and Kukua smiled.

"What happened?" Gabby asked Mari. "How . . . how did you get here?"

"We got some intelligence and knew what they were planning. We tried to intercept them, but they got here before we could," Mari said.

Still foggy, Gabby rubbed her head. "Wait. So, you knew this was going to happen?"

"Yes—in order to get you into the Amazon unnoticed, we had to bait them so they would not record your entry," Mari replied.

"You let them kill Chris?" Gabby cried.

"What? No," Mari replied, "Chris is fine. He knew about this too."

"What?" Gabby repeated.

Chris walked out from the cabin.

"Hey Gabs, you're awake. How are you feeling?" he asked.

"You set me up. Kukua could've been killed. I—*I* could've been killed," Gabby said.

"Look, I know this is a hard pill to swallow. But, if we hadn't done it like this, they would've kept coming until they actually killed us. Or, even worse, the government could've gotten involved."

"Why didn't you warn me?" Gabby yelled.

"It's not like that," Chris replied. "We had to get them all together, and our only chance was to have an element of surprise."

"You still should've warned me," Gabby said.

"I couldn't. I'm sorry."

"If it makes you feel any better," Trent added, "I didn't know the specifics either."

Gabby took a deep breath and rubbed her throbbing head. "So, what's going to happen now?"

"You need to help us clean up and get rid of the bodies. We need to do it before morning, and Mari and Tomas need to leave." Chris paused to look at his watch. "Now."

Gabby stood up and immediately became light-headed. Chris grabbed her elbow. "You okay?"

She pulled her arm away. "I'm fine."

"Good. For the record," Chris added, "everyone is really impressed with how you handled yourself."

Gabby rolled her eyes. "What needs to be done?"

"If you don't want to help dispose of the bodies, I understand. We could use your help cleaning."

"I can handle bodies and I can help clean up."

"Good. We only have about two hours till sunrise, and this mess has to be gone before that."

"Gabrielle," Mari interjected, and grabbed Gabby's hands, "nice job. It's been a pleasure working with you. Take care. Godspeed." She held her hands an extra moment, then gave Gabby a hug. People had stopped hugging so long ago, it felt strange but good to hug again. Mari hopped over the side of the *Marlow* and into a small speedboat where Tomas was waiting. They quickly vanished into the winding blackness of the Amazon.

The joker's crew had used a small raft to sneak onto the *Marlow*. Tomas was able to easily locate their actual boat, which they had anchored less than 1,500 meters upriver. While Mari was helping clean up the mess, he towed the boat upriver and tied it to the *Marlow*.

The joker's craft was clearly a military vessel. It

was a matte-army-green, twenty-two-foot speedboat. The exterior had been built up so that the deck and much of the boat was protected. This worked in the AmCorps team's favor. They could easily trap all of the bodies inside the cabin and sink the whole thing.

Chris had already found the tracking and radar identification systems that the Joker's men—as security guards—had snuck into their gear at the airport. He sent the device with Mari and Tomas so that they could send out a few false pings before they sank the device far from where the boat and bodies were.

Gabby was helping Trent carry the bodies up from the cabin. They were heavy and awkward, but what surprised her most was how little emotion she felt. To her, it felt akin to gross anatomy—it wasn't nice or pleasant or fun, but it had been a necessary part of her education in medical school. And it seemed a necessary part of this new and tangled world of intrigue and jungle where she found herself.

"What did they mean by gold?" Gabby asked Trent while they were dragging the second body up on deck.

"Gabrielle, we don't have much time, and he's heavy. What are you talking about?"

"He said he wanted the gold. What gold?"

"It's a common practice for expeditions to bring gold. We do have a small amount; I guess that's what they were after. Now please, I'm tired and I want to get this over with."

When they carried the body up the wooden step, its balled fists made a knocking noise on each rung, sending a chill down Gabby's spine. They finally managed to drag the body to the pile on the rear deck. A tarp was down so the bloody drips would make less of a mess.

Gabby could feel the burn in her biceps and an ache in her lower back. She took a deep breath and a step back. Her focus froze on the pile of bodies. It was a mass of black peppered with gray-tinged hands, dead eyes, and wicked grins. A wave of nausea crashed over Gabby and she threw up over the side of the boat.

"Are you okay?" Trent asked. "Maybe your concussion is worse than we thought."

"I'm fine," Gabby replied, "I just need an Advil."

"We have a few minutes until Chris finishes preparing their boat. Let's take a break," Trent said, and led Gabby back into the galley.

She sat at the table while he grabbed a couple bottles of water. Then he sat down with her.

"I got a bad report from home. Concerning your grandparents," Trent began.

"Are they okay? What happened?" Gabby panicked.

"They're fine, but institutions like the one they are in are going to be forced to close. With the latest quarantine protocols, they can't find enough people to work in them."

"What do you mean?"

"The updated quarantine would include a 'stay-in-place' protocol requiring workers within a live-in institution to be there full-time. There are not enough medical workers or workers in general that are willing to work and essentially live at these institutions."

"What's happening to the people in those care facilities?"

"It's only been a couple days since the updated quarantine was initiated," Trent replied, "but an overwhelming number of places have already declared an emergency. For now, all medical facilities are being condensed."

"Where are my grandparents?" Gabby's eyes filled with tears.

"I assumed that you would want them taken care

of despite their request to stay where they are, so AmCorps has moved them to a small home with a husband -and-wife care team. They will be able to follow the recommended quarantine protocol there."

"Oh, thank God," Gabby said, and gave Trent a hug. "Thank you."

"Trent, Gabs, are you down there? We have to get the bodies on the boat fast so I can sink it within the hour," Chris yelled from the deck.

The three of them and the crew helped heave the bodies onto the military boat, then hastily shoved them into the cabin. Paulo sealed a small section of the cabin, then welded the exterior door shut, creating a secure, underwater mausoleum. They couldn't afford any floaters to give away what had happened.

Gabby could see the first rays of morning working their way to the eastern horizon. The black sky had taken on an eerie navy hue. This meant that the team had less than an hour to get the boat completely submerged.

Paulo finished, then quickly jumped back on their boat and began taking his clothes off. He worked his way into a form-fitting black capped body suit—a wet suit.

"Paulo," Gabby asked, "why are you getting in the water?"

"Not just Paulo," interrupted Chris. "I'm going in, and either you or Trent need to go in, too."

"Not me," Trent said. "I need to check the lab and make sure they didn't do anything in there."

"What?" Gabby asked. She had a world of thoughts swirling through her mind, stoked by the winds of adrenaline, but the only word she could get to her mouth was another, dull-sounding, "Whaaat?"

"Have you ever been scuba diving?" Gabby shook her head. "That's alright. You're not going deep," Chris said, "just breathe normal and don't panic."

She just stood there looking at him.

"What are you doing? Put your wetsuit on—we're really short on time," Chris ordered.

Paulo was pulling the tight hood over his thick hair. Gabby took a deep breath, stripped down to her underwear, and began to wiggle her way into the tight suit.

"Paulo and I are going to cut holes in the hull. That will make the boat sink quickly and quietly. We need you to be our signaler. Paulo and I will each be underwater on opposite sides of the vessel, so out of view of each other. We are going to signal you when we are in position, and once you get both of our signals, you are going to signal us to start. Got it?" Chris asked.

"How am I going to signal you?" Gabby asked.

"Paulo and I are both going to have hyperbaric cutting rods. When we're in position and ready, we are going to give you a long pull on the rod, which will just look like a bright light. Once you see both of our signals, all you have to do is light an underwater flare. Then you can head back to the boat," Chris said.

"How will I know when I'm in position?" Gabby asked.

"We will swim out toward the boat together. You can stop about thirty feet short of the ship," Chris said as he strapped on his rebreather and handed Gabby hers.

"Wait," she said, "how will I know when I'm thirty feet out?"

"I'll tell you, don't worry. All you have to do is go underwater ten feet and point due west and follow me," Chris said.

"But—" Gabby began.

"Here." He handed her a wristwatch. "This tells you your depth and your direction. It even has a built-in, back-lit screen. It's easy. The rebreather will do everything for you."

Gabby strapped her rebreather on. It looked like a small, black backpack with two tubes coming out of it that formed a mouthpiece.

"We are currently at a depth of close to three hundred feet, which is very good for our current need, but obviously this is very deep water. So just be careful," Paulo said.

"What do you mean? Careful of what?" Gabby asked. She didn't want to appear scared, but she had never been scuba diving.

"Just be mindful of your position. In three hundred feet of dark water, it will feel very big. That's all," Paulo said.

"You might need to adjust your pressure. If your ears start to hurt, just look up and yawn," Chris said. "When we get to your position, I will tap your arm like this." He grabbed Gabby's arm and tapped it twice. "Alright, let's go."

Gabby was surprised by how focused the man had

become. It was almost like he was a completely different person.

"Wait, why can't you just blow a hole in their boat or something like that?" she asked.

"This is still a populated area of the jungle, especially around the river. We have to do this quietly so no one sees what's going on," Chris said.

Paulo jumped in the water, followed by Chris.

"Gabs, you're with me. Are you ready?" he asked.

She nodded, unable to get words to form.

"You can do this. Just stay calm and focused. You'll be back on the boat in no more than twenty minutes. Don't. Let. Yourself. Panic," Chris said.

Gabby nodded, swallowed the lump in her throat, and jumped in.

She was not prepared for how dark the water was, despite the warning. Almost immediately she was completely engulfed in a complete blackness like she had never experienced. Gabby could feel herself start to panic. She couldn't see anyone or anything. Forcing herself to breathe in steady respirations, she swam down, already able to feel the pressure of the dark water.

Gabby checked her depth gauge, which glowed a

soft blue. She was facing south and only at a depth of six feet. She thought for sure she had gone at least fifteen feet down and could feel her heart start to race even more. Turning to face west, she tried to adjust the pressure in her ears. Her ears were throbbing, and no matter what she did, she could not regulate them.

The pain was radiating into her jaw—Gabby thought her eardrums might burst at any moment. She tried to swim farther down to find Chris, but the pain was debilitating. In agony, Gabby arched her back and pulled her neck back, opening her mouth as if she were going to scream. Her eardrums cleared and the pain vanished. When she got down to ten feet, she started to head west, but bumped into Chris.

They swam directly west for about ten minutes. Then Chris stopped, grabbed Gabby's arm, and tapped it before continuing on. It took absolutely everything Gabby had to stay calm. She felt like she was floating in space, completely alone. Then, she felt something big brush up against her. She froze, too afraid to turn around. She had heard of bull sharks swimming far up the Amazon. Then she felt it again, this time harder.

Gabby had gone into this knowing that there was a chance she might not make it through, but death by shark had never even been a blip in the wild realm of possibility. She could barely make out a large flurry of movement in front of her before she felt another bump against her back. Something was circling her.

Gabby clapped her hands—she'd heard a story as a kid of sharks being scared away from attacking a family when the people clapped their hands under water. A dark shape moved in front of her, but it was too dim to make out anything other than movement.

Then she clearly saw a long flash of bright light. In the glow, she thought she the shadow of a long, pointed snout a few feet away. Then a second bright light. She took out her flare, pulled the cap off, and it lit up. She clearly saw the outline of something very large swimming away from her, toward Chris and Paulo.

Gabby swam to the surface to get her bearings. Subtle streaks of orange had already begun to light the horizon. The sun would be up soon. She was happy to see the boat only about a hundred feet away, and she started to swim as fast as she could. Gabby quickly realized that she was swimming against the current, which tired her quickly. She managed to only make it halfway before she exhausted herself.

As she struggled to keep afloat, Gabby felt something grab her arm from the side. Too tired to fight, she turned, expecting to see a wide mouth full of teeth, but instead saw Chris with his scuba mask up. He wrapped his arm around her and helped her the rest of the way.

"Gabs, we did it. See, nothing to it," Chris said.

Gabby ripped her mask off of her face. "We have to get out of the water—there's something down there. Something big. I think it's a shark."

"Stay calm. Don't panic. We will be out soon," Chris calmly replied. "We're almost there. Swim at a steady pace."

They made it to the boat, where Chris helped Gabby up. Then he caught her as she tripped over her flippers.

"You know, it probably was a shark. Bull sharks are actually pretty common here."

"Is Paulo still in the water?" Gabby asked.

"Sharks usually don't bother divers. He's an experienced waterman. If the shark was hungry, he would've gotten you when you were swimming at the surface. That's what bulls like to do."

"Look, there's the fin," Gabby pointed.

"That could definitely be a big bull," Chris said. "Hopefully Paulo comes up near the boat."

They took off their equipment, leaving just their black wetsuits on.

"What if something happened to him while he was sinking the boat?" Gabby asked.

"No. It went down perfectly. Exactly how Paulo said it would. Just scan the surface," Chris instructed, "look for any water movement or bubbles. You take the port side and I'll take the starboard. We will start back here and work our way up."

Trent walked up on deck as they started scanning from the aft deck. "What's going on?" he asked.

"Paulo hasn't made it back to the boat yet," Chris said.

"What? Without Paulo, we're done. We can't possibly navigate our way in without him."

"He's fine," Chris assured.

After three slow scans up and back, there was still no Paulo.

"There's the fin again," Gabby said.

"Fin?" Trent asked.

"There might be a bull shark near the boat," Chris said.

"What the fuck?" Trent said.

"Be ready—when Paulo surfaces, we need to pull him out of the water as quickly as possible," Chris said.

"The shark got him. I know it."

"He's fine. The shark is just curious," Chris said.

"The shark bumped me, hard. It's not curious, it's hungry."

"If it was hungry, it would've eaten you, not bumped you. Just keep scanning."

They continued their watch. Finally, Gabby saw a flurry of movement about fifty feet away from the boat.

"I think I see him," she called.

"Where?" Trent asked.

Gabby directed their attention out from the back of the boat, but the momentary movement vanished. It was completely flat. Then a pointed fin clearly cut through the water. Gabby's heart turned to stone, then sank. Like a wrecking ball, it seemed to collapse her very core from the inside out. The mission was over before it even started. With that, their hope for any return to normalcy was gone.

"Don't panic. Stay alert," Chris said.

Gabby stood there, still frozen. Then, out of the corner of her eye, she saw a rush of bubbles off the back of the boat.

"Look." Gabby pointed toward them.

The shark's fin circled toward the boat and went under.

"Gabby," Chris calmly ordered, "light a flare and throw it toward the shark." He and Trent readied to pull Paulo out as quickly as possible.

Gabby took a deep breath, then flung the flare. It sailed through the air, then sank below the surface. The shark was underwater, so whether or not it would work was a complete guess.

Suddenly, Paulo shot up out of the water. Chris and Trent grabbed his arms and heaved him onto the boat. The shark's fin surfaced moments later, then sank back below the surface. Paulo ripped off his mask and took a deep breath of fresh air.

"What took you so long?" Trent asked.

"I was playing with a few sharks," Paulo said.

"Playing?" Trent yelled.

"Glad you're back. Ready to head out?" Chris asked.

"Yes, pull up the anchors."

"Awesome." Chris immediately began cranking the chain to pull up the anchor. Over the noise, he yelled, "Gabs, you get today and tonight off. Trent, do you want day or night watch?"

"What?" Trent yelled.

Chris finished pulling up the anchor, then yelled to Paulo, and the purr of the engine kicked on.

"I said, Gabs gets today and tonight off. And I asked if you prefer the day or night watch?" Chris repeated.

"I guess day. I just need a couple hours to work. Does this mean that we are safely in now?" Trent asked.

"Yes, the bait worked. They never recorded our expedition; they wanted to attack us without record of our ever being here. Which means Brazil does not know we're here," Chris said.

"I know we have to limit showers, but I'm making today my shower day," Gabby interrupted.

"We have very limited means, Gabrielle. We're not

supposed to take showers for two more—" Trent began.

"It's fine," Chris interrupted, "we'll all take showers today instead. Gabs, go enjoy yours."

She didn't wait for anyone to change their minds, heading right to their cabin where she jumped in the shower. It was harder than she'd thought it would be to get her wetsuit off. Her adrenaline high abruptly wore off, and it took every ounce of strength to strip the damp neoprene from her skin.

The water only came out in one temperature. It was tepid at best, but still felt amazing. Gabby tried to be as quick as possible, but her fingers stumbled over the knot on her cheek bone and brought images from the past night flooding back. She saw the joker's wicked grin and dead, black eyes; she felt the bump in the resounding blackness and felt a predator circling. Gabby started crying and wrapped herself in a tight ball in the corner of the shower.

"Gabs," Chris called from inside the cabin, "I'm in the cabin. Trent is going to take the watch today, and I'm going to be on tonight. So, I'm going to catch some sleep."

Gabby couldn't get words to form—she couldn't

move. She was stuck in the corner of the shower, crying and shaking.

"Gabs? Can you hear me?" Chris knocked on the door. "Are you okay?"

She couldn't move.

"Gabs, I'm coming in."

Chris opened the door. "Oh Gabs, you're fine," he said with an air of relief. Turned off the shower, he grabbed her towel, wrapped her up, and helped her into the cabin.

"Listen, take a few deep breaths. You're crashing from the most intense adrenaline rush that you've probably ever had. It's causing an anxiety-like attack. It happened to me, after the first combat situation I was in. It won't happen again. Next time, your body will know how to handle this chemical flood," he said as he rubbed Gabby's arms.

She slowed her breathing down. She didn't want anyone to see her like this. Nothing like this had never happened to her.

Chris wrapped his arms around her to try to control her shaking. He had used deep pressure therapy throughout his career as a way to help anxiety or PTSD. But really, Chris's parents had always valued hugs over handshakes and, military training aside, Chris was a hugger. The power of human touch was ingrained in his being.

However, person-to-person contact had become taboo over the last five or so years. Social distancing had taken over, and mental illness had shot up. Over 80% of the population was currently on some sort of prescription med for anxiety. Chris's hug worked, though—at this moment, Gabby felt safe, and her body slowly stopped shaking.

"Deep breaths. You're going to sleep really well, and when you wake up you will feel like yourself again. You're feeling the effects of your body's defense hormones—you know, fight or flight—regulating back to normal levels. This is a completely standard reaction," Chris said.

His voice was soothing and, more importantly, he was reengaging Gabby's intellect, which was what she needed to pull out of this spiral. Everything he had said she had known, and even explained to several patients of her own as they faced the demons of death and disease. But experiencing such gut-wrenching trauma herself gave those words a new dimension. After a few minutes, Gabby had calmed down and stopped crying.

"See, I told you, you're okay," Chris said with a smile.

"Yeah, I'm fine," she acknowledged, and even managed a smile, then bit the corner of her lip. "Please don't tell anyone about this."

"Of course not, but it's really not a big deal. You need sleep. I'm hopping in the shower."

Gabby smiled and nodded. Chris jumped up and got in the shower. She wrapped her hair in the towel and grabbed whatever was on the top of her suitcase to put on, a loose pair of light khaki shorts and a white tank top. Then she lay down and instantly fell to sleep.

CHAPTER 13

Smooth Sailing

GABBY SLEPT THROUGH THE DAY and most of the night. With a sudden gasp, she rejoined the conscious world. It was just before 5 a.m. She had slept so deeply she didn't dream; she didn't even remember falling asleep. It took her a moment to remember where she was. Everything seemed so far away. Trent's deep, rhythmic breathing brought reality crashing back. He was sound asleep and appeared as exhausted as Gabby had been.

She found Chris on the deck, scanning the shores with night-vision binoculars.

"Hey Gabs," Chris said while still scanning.

"Hey, I brought you up a cup of coffee," Gabby answered.

"Thanks. Feeling better?"

"Like a new person."

"What did I tell you?"

"You were right. Thank you for—ah, well, I'm sorry I lost it like that."

Chris stopped scanning and put the binoculars down.

"Gabs, stop. Do you know how many times I've helped the toughest guys you'll ever meet the same way? Believe me, it's normal."

Gabby smiled. "Is Paulo still up there driving?"

"No, yesterday he trained Kukua to navigate the boat, so he's sleeping in a hammock up there. We have another couple days in easy water, so Kukua should be able to give Paulo some relief."

"Did I miss anything else?"

"Not really. Trent's been doing whatever it is he does in the lab and on his computer. And we do have some bad weather coming in that we're trying to get ahead of, but that's it."

"What kind of bad weather?"

"Just rain, but really heavy rain."

"Will it affect us?"

"If we don't get ahead of it, it could hold us up for a few days, even a week or so."

"In that case, do you want me to take over for a bit and you can catch up on some rest?" Gabby asked.

"Only if you feel up to it."

"The sun will be up soon—I'll be fine."

"Alright. I'm going to take a quick power nap, then I'll make a big breakfast," Chris said, his face looking more relaxed already.

"Perfect."

Chris left her the night-vision binoculars. He also left the book he had been reading, *Lost Horizon*. Gabby dog-eared his page then scanned the shores. The detail she was able to see through the binoculars was amazing. Gabby could see the rustle of palm leaves. She even thought she saw a jaguar or some kind of big animal dip down for a drink of water. The banks of the river had tightened dramatically from where they were twenty-four hours ago.

Watching the moving shoreline was mesmerizing. Except for the purr of the motor, the boat was nearly silent as it cut through the glass of the river. Every sound from the shore carried across on the warm breeze. Although the sun wasn't quite up, the birds began their days early, feasting on the insects that swarmed the night.

With the binoculars, Gabby could see the flurry of activity on the banks of the river. Nature continued in nearly the same exact way it had for eons, despite the drastic changes humans consistently inflicted on their environment. This was the first time in her life that Gabby saw the true irony in all of this. Nature had flipped the self-destruct button on human beings.

"Gabrielle . . ." Trent came up slowly behind her. "How do you feel?"

Gabby pulled her gaze from the riverbank. "I feel good, but this doesn't make sense. What caused the evolution gene to turn off?"

"We aren't sure. It could be antibiotics, vaccines, maybe a virus?"

"A virus? You didn't tell me that before."

"Lucien, uh, Dr. Sabara, did," Trent replied.

"No, he didn't." Gabby shook her head in confusion.

Trent shrugged. "The fact is, we don't know. Those are all just theories anyway."

"If it is a virus, aren't we carriers, and couldn't we infect and deactivate EVE-0 in any indigenous groups we come in contact with?"

"No. We've all taken a strong antiviral that renders any viruses that we carry unable to spread."

"What? That doesn't make sense. Why wouldn't we just give this treatment to the public and the problem would be solved?" Gabby had heard such serums were being researched but not that any had been approved.

"They don't work in the long term. It's like putting a bandage on a cut, where coagulation is the problem." Trent replied.

"When did I take it?"

"With the vaccines that you took to come here."

Gabby reflected how willingly she had accepted the scant knowledge and the unknown meds before this mission. She shook her head, determined to be more alert in the future. "How do you know that will work?"

"I took it and measured my own viral expression and activity. It won't cure a virus, but it will block old ones from spreading."

"What is it? An HIV antiretroviral?"

"Yeah, basically. It's a form of that."

Basically. A form of that. Too many things loomed uncertain and, in Gabby's estimation at this moment, unknowable. Even at this late stage in the game of survival, humans were again mucking around with more unknowns. Maybe nature did have an end goal, and humanity's destruction had caused the imbalance.

"Something about this whole situation seems wrong. Have humans done so much damage that nature has just decided to get rid of us? I mean, if we are looking at the world as one body, in this situation—" Gabby paused. "Humans have become the equivalent of cancer. Maybe we should just let nature run its course."

"It's not like that. You're not thinking clearly."

"Maybe," she acknowledged.

"We are on the precipice of our growth into our next era. The only difference is that we are educated enough now to realize what is happening and to control it."

"Then why have we stopped evolving? Why does our world want us eradicated?"

"You can't take words so literally. You're getting

lost in the rhetoric. We've simply defined a term as evolution. However, when we are able to specifically control how and when we grow as a species, that's truly evolution. The highest form of evolution."

Gabby had to admit that Trent had a point. How could she say how, when, or why humanity should evolve? How could she pretend to know what image God—or Allah, or nature, or whatever you believed in—had in mind, when the human race came into existence? How could she say that science didn't have the right to edit nature?

She cleared her throat.

"Life without disease would be incredible. But, are you setting any boundaries?" Gabby asked.

"Boundaries? Do you think Phidias saw boundaries in the stone he used to create the Parthenon? Do you think Galileo saw boundaries, or Michelangelo, or Columbus, or Alexander Fleming, or Louis Pasteur, the Wright brothers—I could go on and on. The greatest strength of the human race is our ability to see past boundaries."

Gabby nodded her head in agreement. It was a solid point; maybe she just needed to move past her need of these "boundaries" she lived within. She realized that she innately viewed the world through an "us versus them" lens: nature versus nurture, medicine versus disease. Although, it was hard to shake the feeling that the human race's inability to see lines was what had created this entire situation. Ultimately, she decided that she had to force herself to not dwell in doubt. Only one thing was certain: humanity was dying from pandemics. And saving it had to be their primary goal.

"So, did I miss anything yesterday?" Gabby asked, hoping to change subjects.

"Actually, I couldn't wait to tell you this. Yes, I finished the decoding of the rest of the crew's DNA. They all had the EVE-0 gene, but it varied from the genetic coding that we are looking for. After talking to Kukua, I've been able to conclude that they are in the process of deactivating. In fact, they all joined modern civilization at different times, so they are at different stages of this genetic mutation."

"That sounds promising."

"It's more than promising. It supports our theory. Now we just need to find a group that has not had any contact with modernity at all. I can take over; it's my turn anyway. Will you make us some coffee?"

Gabby made her way to the galley and found a fresh pot already brewing.

"Hey Gabs, is Trent up?" Chris called out.

"Yep," she said as she poured two cups of coffee.

"Good. I got some bad news, and we need to decide what to do. Meet me on the foredeck in five—I need to run something by Paulo," Chris said, and vanished.

Gabby made her way back out, with two cups of very strong coffee. Chris was not far behind.

"It looks like the storm that we've been trying to get ahead of has intensified and picked up speed. We have to make a decision. We can either try to outrun it, or we can look for a safe spot to wait it out," Chris said.

"We need to outrun it," Trent snapped.

"That's extremely risky. If the storm continues to intensify, there's a good chance that it could sink the boat. It will take out trees with its heavy rain and high winds. I mean, we are talking about a very dangerous situation. If we opt to wait it out, we will need to find a sheltered spot—shallow water and no trees. Either way, it's risky."

"So then why wouldn't we take our chances with outrunning it?" Trent scoffed.

"If we get caught, unprepared, we could lose everything," Chris replied.

"What are the chances of outrunning this storm?" Gabby asked.

"Right now, the storm is heading towards us at twenty miles per hour, but it is rapidly intensifying and picking up speed. It's expected to ramp up to fifty miles per hour by tonight. We can't outrun that," Chris answered.

"You said 'expected,'" Trent retorted. "Weather prediction is woefully inaccurate. For that matter, the storm could completely change directions or die down. Why would we base our plans on what's expected and not what is currently actually happening?"

"It's about calculated risks. If we get stuck in the storm, it would leave us at the bottom of this river. Is that a risk we should be willing to take in order to save a few days? I say we don't risk it, and instead find a safe spot till it passes," Gabby said.

"I agree," Chris replied.

"I don't. We can't afford to waste any time. This is my mission, and I want to continue on," Trent said.

"You're out-voted," Chris replied.

"Technically, if you read your mission mandate, then you know it states that as mission leader, my vote counts as two, and when the decision is tied, I am able to set the ruling," Trent stated.

"Oh, I read that. However, our captain is given a vote as well. He wants to stop. So, it's three to your two. We are stopping," Chris replied.

"Gabrielle, change your vote," Trent snapped.

"I think we should stop," she replied.

"Fine," Trent said with a slight roll of his eyes, "but you'd better be right."

"So, what's the plan? You do have a plan, right?" Gabby asked Chris.

"Paulo knows a potentially safe tributary; he's just not sure if we can get in there. It all depends on the water levels. It's close, and if we can get in, it will be the safest place to be."

"What if we can't?" Gabby asked.

"If the storm gets as bad as it's projected to, then we're in trouble. We can't go into the forest because falling trees and flying debris are dangerous, and we can't stay on the open water . . ."

"Because the boat will sink," Gabby finished.

"I'm going to give Paulo the go-ahead. Do you

mind staying on watch? Watch for drug smugglers and loggers. Just keep an eye out for any movement on the shore. Anyone with a brain will be looking for shelter, so we should be okay." Chris paused as he saw Gabby's expression. "It's just extra precaution, so we don't get blindsided," he said, instantly regretting his choice of words.

"Just go talk to Paulo."

As Gabby watched the shore, she began to notice the subtle movements of nature. The banks were about forty feet away on each side, but felt much closer because of how lush the greenery was. It was almost like the jungle was trying to darken the open sky left by the river.

Suddenly, Gabby was struck by a movement that didn't seem natural. While the jungle seemed to move in graceful strokes, this motion near the shore had been jerky and erratic. She figured it was probably an animal that she hadn't seen. Then heard a loud pop, and a bullet ricocheted off the boat's heavy wood railing.

"Gun! Gun, someone's shooting at us!" Gabby yelled up to Chris and Paulo.

"Gabs, get down!" Chris yelled from the top deck.

She had already planted herself on her stomach. From the top deck, Chris and Paulo unleashed a couple rounds of automatic gunfire on the jungle shore.

"Port side!" Gabby yelled.

Another round of gunfire went off, then silence.

"Gabs," Chris said.

Uncovering her head, she saw Chris standing above her.

"Stay down just a little longer, but I'm pretty sure we got them all. It looked like a small crew of poachers or smugglers that were left behind. They probably thought they could steal our boat and get out of here before the storm hits," Chris finished.

Gabby rolled to her back but stayed on the floor.

"Are you alright?"

"I'm fine." Strangely enough, Gabby mused, she really was okay. Her racing heart had already started to slow. She wasn't shaking. Maybe after one near-death experience, they really did become easier to handle.

"We're about forty-five minutes away from the opening to the tributary. I'll finish out the watch," Chris said, setting his AR-15 down next to him.

"Sounds good," Gabby said as she hopped to her feet.

"Can you ask Kukua to start inflating the kayaks? We'll need four, maybe five."

Gabby found the man and his crew trolling off the back of the *Marlow*.

"How can you fish with all this commotion?" she asked.

"Us get down and wait. Mad if they shoot fish," Kukua answered.

"What are you fishing for?"

"Dinner," he answered, then grinned. "Tambaqui, best place to get. Us catch two."

Kukua then said something to his crewmate in their language. With a huge smile, the kid held up a huge, silvery fish.

"Tonight, us eat this . . . how you say?" Kukua touched his side.

"Chest?" she offered. He shook his head no. "Intestines?"

"No, no. Bone, here." Kukua poked his sides up and down.

"Ribs?"

"Sim, eat tambaqui ribs. Favorite food."

"I can't wait." Gabby gave the kid a thumbs up.

As he put the fish away, she noticed just how young he looked. He was the smallest of the group, not even five feet tall. Then she looked at Kukua, his sun-baked skin contrasting the youthful sparkle to his eyes.

"Kukua, how old are you?"

"Old man, twenty-six."

"That's young."

"Not in jungle."

"How old are they? Can you introduce me?"

"That Bob, he fifteen." Kukua pointed to the smallest as he put the huge fish back in the basket.

"Bob?"

"Yeah, take new names when leave jungle. Me chief so keep name."

"Bob, it's nice to meet you," Gabby said, and held out her hand to shake his. Bob wasn't sure what to do, so Gabby grabbed his hand. Bob laughed and his childish innocence beamed through. Gabby hadn't shaken someone's hand in nearly ten years, but in this moment it felt natural.

"This Jim, he seventeen." Gabby shook his hand with big smiles all around.

"And this Patrick, he twenty." Gabby smiled and shook Patrick's hand as well. The man smiled, but looked down. He wouldn't make eye contact with Gabby. He had a long, jagged scar that crossed his face.

Suddenly, the wooden pole jerked and Kukua and the crew started pulling the line in together. Patrick dipped a net in and pulled out a gigantic fish.

"Big Tambaqui, it biggest us get," Kukua said. "Us have good dinner."

"Okay, I just hope it tastes better than it looks." Gabby laughed, pointing at the massive blob of bloody scales, but the crew just looked at her. "Anyway, can you help me inflate the kayaks?"

CHAPTER 14

Calm before the Storm

CHRIS, GABBY, KUKUA, PATRICK, AND JIM each readied a kayak. They had to check the depth of the tributary and the lagoon where they would take shelter. The depth needed to be no more than six feet and no less than four. Ideally, they were looking for a spot away from the trees, where the lagoon was just slightly over four feet deep and the *Marlow* could rest in shallow water.

"Gab, try not to flip your kayak. In these shallow, stagnant areas, the water is full of some nasty parasites and bacteria," Chris cautioned as they prepared to put-in.

"What?"

"You'll be fine, just try to be a little careful. I

know a couple of guys that got sick from swimming in water like this, and they've got some lasting stomach issues."

"Forget it, I'm not going."

"You'll be fine, just try to stay in your kayak, which is easy. If you do fall in, just keep your head out of the water."

"I'm joking. I'm a doctor, remember? I'm pretty well-versed in the dangers of dirty water."

"Just making sure." Chris smiled.

"But, maybe you should tell Kukua." Gabby pointed over to Kukua, Patrick and Jim who were happily splashing and swimming in the water.

"Kukua!" Chris yelled.

"Chris, I was joking again. They're fine. Their bodies grew up on this water. Our hyper-sanitized systems just can't handle it."

Chris held the kayak as she climbed in. The other three were now in their kayaks and heading to the inlet.

As Gabby paddled toward the cove, every ripple sent a shiver vibrating down the steps of her spine. She wasn't afraid of the water, but there was something else at work here. The earthy jungle seemed as if it were trying to strangle the life out of the water, while the water was trying to slice through an emerald artery of the jungle's blood. Nature existed in a delicate balance that often gave way to silent wars, leaving scars that wouldn't be seen for thousands of years.

She noticed a splash along the shore as something slithered into the water, but didn't see what it was.

"Is it just me," Chris asked as he quietly paddled up next to Gabby, "or does this place give you a strange feeling?"

"It's creepy, really creepy."

"Good, the jungle isn't driving me crazy . . . yet." Chris laughed. "You take the right side of the inlet, I'll take the left. We need a depth of at least five feet."

Gabby nodded. She was so tense, her muscles were starting to hurt. She did not want to go close to the shoreline.

Kukua circled back to them. "Where us to check?"

"Can you guys check the lagoon? Look for the safest area to secure the boat."

"Okay, us do. Ah"—Kukua paused, his brow furrowed slightly—"don't whistle. Tunchi here."

"What?" Chris asked.

"Tunchi bad spirit. Tunchi guard forest. But him not too strong. Tunchi find you when you whistle, like bird, or you hurt forest. Then he get in." Kukua pointed to his head. "Make you do bad things. Us see Tunchi take people."

Normally, Gabrielle wouldn't believe in something like this, but the Amazon world didn't play by the rules she knew. This was the first time she could ever remember getting goosebumps in oppressive heat.

"Our Father," Chris whispered, "who art in Heaven."

Gabby joined, "Hallowed be thy name." They continued to pray in the slightest whisper.

She couldn't remember the last time that she'd prayed. She was surprised that she even remembered the "Our Father" prayer. Although she'd been half-heartedly raised Catholic, she had completely given up religion when she started learning about science. If nothing else, praying at this moment distracted her. More importantly, it quelled the urge she had to whistle.

When Gabby lifted the weighted line to measure

the depth, her kayak wobbled. First she over-corrected her weight, nearly flipping her vessel. Then she heard a loud splash behind her, and saw a large shadow move beneath her kayak. She paddled in the opposite direction of the dark shadow.

"Gabs," Chris yelled as quietly as he could, "where are you going?"

"There's something in the water," she answered, still heading toward land.

"There's lots of things in the water."

"It was as big as my kayak." Gabby froze, realizing that she was too close to the land.

"How deep is your side? Mine's over six feet deep," Chris said.

Gabby dropped her weighted rope. On the boat, they had quickly marked four feet and six feet.

"Wow. It's deeper than six here too," Gabby replied.

"Move up thirty feet and check again. I hope there's not too much water here."

Gabby paddled forward and dropped her rope. She was getting used to the tips and dips of her kayak, and trying to ignore anything under the water.

"Still deeper than six," she said.

Chris and Gabby got back to the boat first.

"So?" asked Trent.

"The entire canal is deeper than six feet, so we can definitely get into the lagoon," Chris answered. "Kukua is checking the lagoon for the best place to anchor."

"The decision that we make based on this information is crucial, and you're trusting Kukua with that job?" Trent snapped.

"I'm comfortable with Kukua handling it," Chris abruptly replied.

The deck went silent. Trent sulked back down to his lab and Chris made his way to Paulo.

Gabby momentarily lingered on the deck, but the quiet was too eerie. She found her way to the kitchen. It was hot and stuffy, but at least she felt slightly protected. She grabbed a Coke and waited for what felt like hours.

Finally, she heard Kukua on the deck. She made her way back out as Chris and Paulo remained deep in conversation. Eventually, Trent came back up.

"Kukua found a large sandbar in the center of the lagoon where we need to be," Chris said.

"Can't we pull up next to it?" Trent asked.

"The problem is, it cuts right across the middle of the lagoon. There is not enough space to anchor on the safe side. And if we anchor on the other side, there's a chance the storm will drag us to the sandbar and capsize the boat," Chris answered.

"Just get to the point. What are our options?" Trent snapped.

"No options. We are going to anchor with our bow toward the sandbar. You just need to know the danger we face when storm comes in," Paulo added.

"Fine," Trent said, and started to walk away.

"Wait," Chris said. "Trent, you need to be on watch while we move the boat into position. Gabs was on watch and needs to sleep."

"I'm fine, I can—" Gabby started.

"We should stick to our schedule," he interrupted.

"She's fine to stand watch," Trent inserted. "I'm working." He walked away without another word.

Paulo pulled Chris's attention away from Trent's retreating back. "I'm going to move into the lagoon. Then Kukua can take a kayak to the sandbar so I can see where we need to be positioned."

It was easy to get the boat through the tributary, but inside of the lagoon the water was murky, which made it difficult to avoid any underwater hazards. Slowly, they eased the *Marlow* farther into the lagoon. Kukua took a kayak to the sandbar and Paulo pulled the bow as close to the sandbar as possible. They set anchors from the bow and the stern.

Gabby needed to secure the ship's interior. Everything fragile had to be wrapped and packaged. Anything loose had to be put into secure storage.

When Gabby finished, Trent was still in the lab with the door closed. Chris and Paulo were still securing the decks. Kukua and his guys were cleaning their catch. The sun had just begun its descent, and Gabby sat on the deck, watching Chris and Paulo. After a minute, she decided to see if Trent needed help securing the lab.

She stopped short of the door when she heard Trent talking.

"We are losing a few days because of weather," Trent said. After a brief pause, he continued, "I tried, but there's really nothing I can do. . . . Has intel picked up anything? . . . What? Here? Are you sure? . . . That's impossible. We're the only group that knows this. Why would any other team even leave their lab? . . . Fuck. . . . Alright."

Gabby heard something slam. Then she knocked

and opened the door. The lab was completely packed up and secured. It was so impeccably neat, it looked as if a lab had never existed at all in that small space.

"Is everything okay?" Gabby asked.

"What did you hear?"

"Nothing really ... just that you cursed and seemed upset. Why? What's going on?"

"I didn't want to scare you yet, but there are other groups that are trying to profit off of this situation."

"What do you mean? How?"

"There are groups that are trying to steal our work to sell to private investors."

"That's insane. Can't the government stop them?"

"It's not that easy. It's a complex situation, and there are many political layers."

"That's very cryptic. What do you mean? Are other countries trying to steal your treatment?"

"Yes, and we received intel that there is another group tracking us. We purposefully came with a small team so that we would have a very small chance of getting noticed. If Brazil actually knew that we were here, they would've never even let us in."

"But their customs checked us in, right?"

"No, those customs officials were not operating

above board. Brazil doesn't know the US has a team here. We didn't force them to try to rob us, but we certainly laid the groundwork to motivate them into attacking us, knowing that if they were dead, we'd be in a much better position."

"I thought you didn't know about that."

"I didn't, but I knew that they were baited."

"That's wrong," Gabby admonished.

"No, it's not. They were really bad people." Trent shrugged.

"So why is someone after us now?"

"For the power they will own with this knowledge and the ability to save the human race."

"Who would do that?"

"More people than you could imagine. All we can do is try to stay ahead of them."

Chris yelled down, "Gabs. Trent. Can you come up here?"

When they got up on deck, he and Paulo were talking.

"The storm is still about five hours out, but water has started washing in ahead of it, which indicates that it will be bad," Chris said.

The boat lurched forward, then bounced back.

Gabby stumbled, cracking her chin on the deck. Her skin split open and blood poured out. It happened so fast that no one noticed.

"Paulo," Chris shouted, "what the fuck was that?"

"A big log. It's okay, it didn't damage the boat," Paulo yelled from the stern.

Gabby was holding her chin.

"Gabrielle, you're bleeding. A lot," Trent said.

"I realize that."

"Gabs," Chris said, "you're gonna need a couple stitches. Come with me, unless—Trent, you want to stich her up?"

"I'm not that kind of doctor. You better do it."

"Come on," Chris said, helping her up. "Actually, you're dripping blood everywhere. Stay here."

Gabs sat back down, holding her chin.

"You need anything?" Kukua asked. Gabby shook her head. "Us make dinner."

Gabby nodded and tried to smile, but her bruised and bloodied chin hurt too bad.

"I'm going to check on the lab and specimens. Are you alright if I leave?" Trent asked.

Gabby nodded. Chris came back with the first aid kit as Trent was leaving.

"Are you sure you know what you're doing? You're not a doctor," Gabby said.

"Yeah, but I've probably given more stitches than most emergency room docs."

"You better be neat. I don't want a jagged scar across my face."

"Scars add character. Now hold still."

"Seriously, please be careful."

"Gabs, even with the ugliest scar, you'd still be beautiful."

Gabby blushed but couldn't hide her slight smile.

"Oh please, you're just trying to flatter me so I don't get mad at your handiwork."

"No, I mean it. Now hold still, you're bleeding everywhere."

Gabby felt flutters in her stomach. Trent hadn't told her that she was beautiful in a very long time. He told her she was brilliant, and of course that was what mattered to her. They connected on a pragmatic, intellectual level, and she knew it's those sorts of connections that last long after youth fades. But there was something carnal that stirred in Gabby when Chris called her beautiful. Maybe once you see someone as beautiful, you always see that beauty through the lines of time, she thought.

Gabby quickly gulped those musings down, buried them deep in the pit of her stomach where anything difficult, silly, or sad, or that otherwise clouded her judgement, was laid to rest.

"All done, and it's my best work yet," Chris announced.

"That was quick."

"You should get some ice on your chin. It's starting to swell."

"Thanks," Gabby said, getting a little dizzy when she stood. Chris went to steady her, but she knocked his hand away.

"I'm fine."

"I know."

"Us eat now," Kukua beckoned, peeking his head through the cabin door.

Gabby and Chris were the last to join the table.

Piled on the table were platters of grilled ribs, rubbed with spices and slightly charcoaled.

"Ribs? Where in the world did you find ribs?" Chris asked as he quickly grabbed for a platter.

"No, wait," Kukua instructed. "Us need give thanks for fish river give."

"Sorry," Chris replied, and whispered to Gabby, "Where do you see fish?"

"Shush," Gabby chided in a whisper. "The ribs are fish ribs."

Kukua began to chant while Patrick, Jim, and Bob hummed in the background. It was beautiful. It sounded so foreign to Gabby, more like a song than a prayer.

Kukua finished and they bowed their heads.

"Us thank river for food and ask winds to send protection," Kukua said.

Gabby quietly said "amen" and made the sign of the cross; it had become a compulsion lately.

"That's beautiful, Kukua," Trent said. "Sometimes I wish I could believe in a god."

"It no easy. For you, us hope one day you can," Kukua replied.

"No, unfortunately or fortunately, I chose science," Trent said.

"Okay, while you guys talk about philosophy and theology, or science or whatever, I'm starving." Chris grabbed a platter of ribs.

Kukua smiled and handed Trent a platter as well.

"You may be surprise," Kukua said.

"This is the most delicious thing I've ever eaten," Chris said. "I can't believe it's fish."

"It's really good," Gabby added. "I wish my chin didn't hurt so bad when I chew."

The tambaqui tasted more like a combination of pork and veal, it was tender but hearty and savory. The conversation fizzled as they ate. It was so quiet, the normal sounds of the jungle seemed to have disappeared.

After dinner, Gabby went up to the top deck to catch the remaining rays of the day. She could see a black wall of clouds in the distance.

"It's time. We must take shelter inside," Paulo called to her.

CHAPTER 15

Intel

"MARTIAL LAW WILL GO into effect tonight. Then, it will be much easier to move the bulk of Phases Two and Three in," General Holton said.

Lucien's computer screen glitched momentarily, which always frustrated him. He was dumbfounded by the fact that after nearly ten years of an intense economic reliance on the internet, it still could get overloaded.

For Lucien, quarantine was the norm. Most of his meetings had always been via virtual applications. He'd grown up completely isolated. The rest of the world had sporadically dealt with this lifestyle for the past several years, but this was the first time martial law would be fully instituted. Lucien suspected that it would not be received well. The panic incited by an unseen pathogen was very different from the terror found on the receiving end of military force. However, at this point it wouldn't matter.

"We're ready on our end," Lucien replied.

"The president said the process and the living situation is well thought out and relatively easy," General Holton replied.

"Of course it is—what did he expect?" Lucien replied.

"We trust your judgement, but what you need to understand is that we are not as familiar with this world as you are. These are extreme measures," General Holton said.

"Soon, you'll see for yourself. It's not as bad as you think," Lucien said.

"We're ready. My family and the team going in with me have had absolutely no contact with anyone for the past three weeks. We start full decon tomorrow, but I'll still have full access to communications while I'm in, right?" General Holton asked.

"Yes, your process will be exactly like the president's. Your decon area is fully equipped. Your current devices will be destroyed, and you will only be out of comm abilities for approximately an hour, just while you are completing the intake process," Lucien said.

"An hour is manageable, but the main reason for our call is a situation that's come up. We've received intel that another unit is close behind your team."

"How is that possible?"

"It shouldn't be. Most of the people that even know your team is there are dead. As you know, we've suspected a mole for a while, but we've narrowed it down to being in your unit in the jungle."

"That's impossible," Lucien snapped.

"I agree. It should be, but all intel indicates that there is a double agent on your team."

"Absolutely not. Everyone has been thoroughly checked and vetted."

"What about Dr. Gale? What do you actually know about her?" General Holton asked.

"Trent knows her very well, and your team did a background check on her," Lucien snapped.

"Yes, in a week. This mission was not supposed to leave for another month, so we didn't have as much time as we normally would take," Holton retorted. "But what matters now is figuring out how this outside team is tracking your unit."

"Do you have any idea who the other team works for?"

"You're not going to believe it, but we still suspect Interfaith for Peace," General Holton said.

"You're fucking kidding me. How did they get into Brazil? We barely got our own team in."

"Actually, they have an idiot, billionaire backer. He was easy to identify as he was the only one rejected from this program. He's a Jewish billionaire—his father founded a comm company that he now controls," General Holton said.

"Thomas Williams?" Lucien asked.

"Yes. He apparently grew some sort of conscience and wants to see everyone saved."

"What an asshole. He was a fragile x gene and cystic fibrosis carrier. Does he really think we plan to carry a genetic predisposition for mental retardation into the future of the human race?"

General Holton shrugged on Lucian's screen. "I don't know what he thinks. All we know is that he has been funneling tens of millions to Interfaith for Peace."

"Does he have a history of supporting them?"

"No."

"Is there any other connection to suggest this organization is behind this other mission?" Lucien asked.

"A few months ago, they began a pseudo-grass-roots movement resisting the current uptick in quarantine protocols. They claim that America has been classist in their handling of these pandemic situations and are perpetuating an even greater socio-economic divide," General Holton said.

"First it's sexism, then it's racism . . . now it's classism. Just when I think people can't possibly become more stupid. I can't believe how many people buy into their hypocrisy, and then the media praises it. The world is over-populated with complete imbeciles. When will people come to terms with the fact that everyone is not created equal? Some are smart while some are stupid," Lucien said.

"Yeah, well, I think we can all agree on that. The problem right now, however, is that they have the capability to track your team."

"I realize what the fucking problem is. What are you doing about it, General?"

"Our intel so far has been able to follow them, so you will be able to keep your team ahead of them. The problem is that we can't send a unit in to intercept them without being noticed and risking breaking quarantine before extraction."

"We can't risk that. We can't send anyone else in, not until we go in to retrieve the target," Lucien said.

"I realize that. So, our best option is for you to keep Trent and only Trent informed. He will have to keep the team moving and try to uncover the mole," General Holton said.

CHAPTER 16

The Storm

IT WAS HARD FOR GABBY to take her eyes off the dark curtain as it roared closer. In the distance, she heard booms. Bright flashes of electric fury illuminated the utter darkness headed toward them.

"Gabrielle, come now," Paulo shouted.

There was something beautiful in the chaos of nature's wrath.

"Come," he called again.

Everyone wore lifejackets. They crowded in the galley, away from windows. Within minutes, the first winds of the storm began lashing the boat. The old wood of the boat creaked and moaned. Waves pounded in relentless succession. Soon, everything was shaking in violent tremors. *This could be it,*

Gabby thought. She became numb, thoughts distancing themselves, and she felt almost as if she were watching a movie. Everyone around her sat in silence, their heads bowed.

Gabby looked at Trent, who was motionless except for the rapid tapping of his foot. He was looking at his hands. Bob began to cry, and Chris put his hand on his shoulder. With tears in his eyes, Bob looked like a child, like the fifteen-year-old that he was.

The boat suddenly listed, and the team were thrown on the galley table. A large beam of wood broke off of the door jamb and tumbled toward them. Jim shoved Bob out of the way and took the brunt of the beam's force. The beam slammed into his chest with brutal force. His ribs were crushed. He gasped for air between shrieks of pain, barely audible over the howl of wind.

"Lay him flat on his back," Gabby yelled over the storm's rage.

Chris and Trent moved the debris and cleared a spot for Jim. The blood drained from the man's face with every shallow gasp.

"He has a pneumothorax," Gabby said.

"What?" Chris yelled.

"—ah, a punctured lung," Gabby said.

Jim's skin began to take on a bluish tint.

"It's severe," Gabby yelled. "He's going to go into shock. I need to clear the air out of his chest cavity, so that his lung function can return." She got up.

"Stop," Trent yelled, "you have to stay here."

"I need my medical kit in our cabin," Gabby replied as lightning exploded nearby.

"You're not going. It's too dangerous maneuvering to get back there," Trent demanded.

"Jim will die if I don't restore his lung function," Gabby pleaded.

"Jim we can risk; not you," Trent said.

"Gab, Patrick go," Kukua interjected. "You tell Patrick where."

A strobe of light set off by the constant lightning lit the cabin and sent pulses of electricity through every fiber of Gabby's being, as she yelled directions to Patrick. Her senses were on fire, and she could feel Jim's heartbeat fading.

"Roll him on his side," Gabby instructed.

Trent sat there as if frozen.

"Roll him on his side!" Gabby yelled to him.

Trent finally pulled Jim onto his side. Now she couldn't hear any air going into the man's left lung.

"Now roll him onto his other side."

"I can't do this," Trent said.

"What?"

"I can't do this," Trent said quietly, and pulled away, his voice lost to the chaos of the storm.

Flashes of fire lit the cabin. In this chaos, time seemed to freeze. It was the first time that Gabby had a moment to think, and she realized that there was a good possibility that they were all going to die.

The world around them was ablaze in a violence like nothing she had ever experienced. Gabby had seen first-hand the worst of man's violent temper, but mother nature's fury felt far more severe. There was no anger or hatred behind it. It was simply, plainly, and utterly destructive. A cool bead of sweat dripped down Gabby's spine, sending shards of icy chills through her veins.

Patrick appeared with her medical trunk. "Find." He handed it to her.

"Stay calm. It'll be alright. You got this," Chris said as if reading her mind.

Those simple words were all that it took to reset her mind. She could focus on the task at hand.

"Roll Jim onto his left side and hold him very still. I'm going to give him a shot of Novocain, but it's still going to hurt. I have to release the air from his chest so that his lung has a chance to inflate," Gabby said.

Chris and Patrick held Jim as still as they could with the waves bouncing the boat. Jim was unconscious and limp, and the boat felt as if it might break apart under the force of the wind and violent shaking.

Gabby made a quick incision in his side. Jim's body stiffened and he let out a moan so full of pain, Gabby felt it like a splinter in the pit of her stomach. As a doctor, you don't want to see your patients in pain, let alone be the cause of their pain. She quickly shoved a thin plastic tube into the cut she'd made. An audible rush of air made its way through the tube as Gabby taped it in place.

"Okay, gently lay him on his side. Grab a pillow and make him as comfortable as possible," Gabby instructed. The boat was tilted so dramatically they had to prop Jim up against the wall.

As if in a schizophrenic rage, the storm continued to beat the *Marlow* with punch after punch. There was nothing rational about the fury with which nature attacked. A part of Gabby couldn't help but feel the storm was trying to get to them. She told herself it was just her imagination, but in the jungle, everything seemed different, alive, almost human.

Then, as suddenly as it began, the wind died down to non-existent. It gave up. The world around them became completely still.

The boat had been pounded into the sandbar. It listed nearly 60 degrees to its left side and had sustained a significant amount of damage. They would have to wait until the water level rose high enough to lift the boat upright. Only then would they be able to push it off of the sandbar. According to Paulo, this could happen in a couple days or a couple months—the water levels were very unpredictable.

For Trent, this was tantamount to death, or certain failure. Anything longer than a day, and they might as well give up. Word from home base allowed him only a three-day grace period.

Jim had been stabilized, but after two days of waiting, his condition began to deteriorate, along with the stability of the crew. Trent had only left the lab twice: once to get a saliva sample from Jim, and the second time to get blood, or rather to have Gabby draw it.

Just before sunrise on the fourth day of their watery imprisonment, Trent started acting erratic. Gabby was woken by his incessant pacing between the lab and their cabin. Just as the first rays of sun began creeping up the horizon, Trent woke everyone up.

"We have to get out of here, now," Trent told the crew. "I just received intel that another group is tailing us, two days back at most."

"The only way we leave today is without a boat. We can take rafts and then hike," Paulo suggested.

"We can't. Jim wouldn't make it," Gabby said.

"How far behind would that put us?" Trent asked.

"Not far. We have to leave the boat in a couple weeks anyway. We move faster on the rafts than on the *Marlow*, but it will be much, *much,* more difficult," Paulo said.

"Okay. Start packing. We leave in an hour. We will have to torch the boat," Trent decided.

"No, Jim won't make it," Gabby said.

"He's not going to make it anyway," Trent scolded.

Chris stepped into the conversation. "Gab, we can't stay. We're sitting ducks here."

"Talk to Jim," Kukua said. "Us decide."

"While you're talking, everyone else needs to start packing," Trent said as he walked out, followed by Paulo. Gabby hesitated only a moment, and then followed Kukua.

CHAPTER 17

Tepi

JIM'S CONDITION HAD DETERIORATED while waiting on his makeshift hospital bed onboard the *Marlow*. For the past two days, the man had drifted in and out of consciousness. His wakeful moments had become few. Kukua pulled out something that looked like three small bones joined with carved wooden beads to form a slowly tapered curve. He held it over his friend, and Gabby recognized this as some type of ceremony.

"Tepi for rapé," Kukua said.

"Should I leave?" Gabby asked.

"No, stay. This very important for my people," Kukua explained as he poured a tan powder into the wide end of the instrument.

Kukua closed his eyes and chanted. He placed the narrow end of the Tepi into Jim's nostril and blew. Jim's eyes opened immediately, and he took a deep breath in. Kukua placed his forehead on Jim's. They spoke a few words in an unrecognizable tongue. Then they chanted together. Kukua reloaded the Tepi and blew one more time into the other nostril. Jim laid his head back and closed his eyes.

"When us go, Jim go in water. Jim say him ready. Jim spirit start journey already. Jim say guides here," Kukua said, motioning in the air. Gabby's eyes took in the close quarters of the cabin, wishing she could sense those guides herself. So much inhabited this indigenous world and primitive jungle that she didn't understand, and today counted as proof one more time of that fact. Then Kukua stood and left the room. A moment later, Gabby crossed herself and followed.

The team had three soft-hull, black military Zodiac boats with shallow water thruster engines. Their supplies for this part of the journey had been prepacked, so they were ready to leave the boat in less than an hour.

Trent and Paulo were in the first Zodiac with the

communication and lab equipment. Gabby and Chris were in the second with the medical and shelter supplies. Kukua, Patrick, and Bob were in the third with the food and hunting supplies. They also brought Jim with them. Once everyone was off of the *Marlow*, Chris and Paulo poured gasoline throughout the cabin. The three boats pulled away.

It was still early, and while it was hot out, the full, suffocating swelter of midday had not yet set in. Once they were a safe distance away, Chris shot a flare onto the deck of the *Marlow*. Within moments, their ship was awash in an orange and blue firestorm. It was beautiful and destructive. The ship was disintegrating into a dangerous beacon.

"We have to move fast these next couple days," Chris said, but it was hard for Gabby to pay attention. She was focused on Kukua, Patrick, Bob, and Jim. They had paused and were gently lowering Jim into the water. Jim was awake, his face painted with the most gentle smile. He caught Gabby's stare and his smile deepened, then his gaze softened back to his crew. Kukua led a chant as they placed Jim in the water. He floated at the surface as they pulled away and back in line with the other Zodiacs. They did not watch as Jim's body floated, caught in the slow current.

"Gab, don't watch," Chris said.

"He's all alone—we can't let this happen. Go get him," Gabby pleaded.

"This is on his terms; this is what he wants. There is honor in this choice for him," Chris said.

"That's bullshit. We can save him," Gabby said.

"Who are you to question their beliefs? You're in their world. You think prolonging his suffering is better?"

"No, but he could at least have the chance to get better."

Chris shook his head. "He wouldn't make it in this environment. This is the rite of his culture. The Shoshone tribe abandoned their elderly when they needed to move on for food, in order to do what was best for the tribe. This was his choice."

"Hitler also killed the old, sick and imperfect."

"This is survival, not racial cleansing. This was their choice. Why would you presume to know what others want? You'd rather have him suffer for your own conscience as a doctor than allow him to go in peace?"

"You just didn't want to risk your own life to save him."

"He was probably going to die anyway," said Chris. "If we tried to bring him, he would've died and been in pain the whole time. And, if we tried to stay, we would all have been killed. If we broke up our team, the entire mission would have failed. Jim chose this on his own. If you refuse to see that or believe that, well, that's your choice. But your refusal to step outside of your privileged existence is taking a bit of Jim with it. Let him go in peace. Respect his decision and honor his culture."

For the rest of the day, Gabby remained quiet as they weaved through streams and rivers. At times, the water was less than a foot deep. They did not break for food or rest. There was a bucket in the boat that served as a bathroom, and they took turns driving. The plan was to move as quickly as possible for as long as possible.

Gabby had never felt heat as oppressive as this. There was a weight in the broiling vapor that held her captive. When she realized that there was no way to cool off, her initial reaction was to panic. Once she was able to relax into the heavy hotness, the panic faded to nausea, then lassitude.

They only stopped once the night had strangled every ounce of light from the sky. They were still too close to the team that was tracking them, so they couldn't set up a proper camp. That meant no fire, so it was MREs in the dark. Paulo and Chris sat off to the side of the group, going over the latest intel that Trent had received, under the softest glow of a small lamp. Finally, they rejoined the rest of the group.

"We are not making up the time we need. Today we moved too slow. This part of the forest is difficult," Paulo said to the gathered crew.

"That's not going to work," Trent said.

"No, but our only other option is to go through the firestorm section, and it's very dangerous," Paulo said.

"Too dangerous," Kukua said.

Ten years ago, fires had swept through the Amazon and left certain portions barren, except for small, fast-growing, dry brush and eucalyptus trees. This highly combustible flora fueled more fires, so the problems continued to grow. A new phenomenon had also developed in this area of the Amazon: flash fires. Blazes that tore through the remains of the jungle, killing everything in their path then burning out. There was no warning, no prediction. Science had not been able to say exactly how or why this was happening, although deforestation and farming had both contributed.

Large portions of the rainforest had been cleared for many types of farming, including eucalyptus tree farms. Though not native to the Amazon, these trees grew quickly. They had a type of seed pod that was released in forest fires, and when the first fires started, they spread eucalyptus outside of the farm confines. This strangled essentially all other plant and animal life out of this section of the Amazon.

"There is a river off-shoot we can take. It will give us some protection," Paulo said.

Chris nodded. "After going through the intel with Paulo, this is really our only option. The satellite images show another group moving toward us quickly. We are not sure how they're tracking us, but this route will give us a chance to lose them."

"Then we're doing it," Trent said.

"Too dangerous. Us not fight fire," Kukua said.

Chris reasoned, "We either take a very calculated

risk with the fires, or we will face some sort of fight with whatever group is tracking us."

"What's the calculated risk?" Gabby asked.

"There was a recent surge in fires, and then that storm that came through this area dampened the forest. According to our data, we should have a short window to cut through, one that the group tracking us will not have," Chris said.

"When are we leaving?" Trent asked.

"We should go now; there will be no stops for maybe thirty or so hours," Paulo said.

"No us sleep? How see in dark?" Kukua asked.

"Take shifts sleeping and driving. We have night-vision goggles. Same boats as before. Make sure your gas, food, and water are easy to access. Let's roll out," Chris said.

Gabby's legs froze. In her residency, she'd treated a vet who had tried to commit suicide by lighting himself on fire. There weren't enough pain medicines in the world to quell his constant suffering. He couldn't move without his scarred skin screaming. He suffered for months until eventually, his heart gave out.

"Gab, come on," Chris said. Everyone else had already pulled their boats out.

"Burns are a terrible way to go," Gabby said.

"We have guns, just in case," Chris said.

It took a moment for the meaning behind his statement to sink in, but strangely enough, it made her feel a bit better.

CHAPTER 18

Fire Forest

WHILE THE AMAZON HAD MORE plant species than anywhere else in the world, this section of forest was different. The eucalyptus gave off an eerie blue haze that carried a faint medicinal scent. It was quiet—there were no animals, no insects, no life.

"Do you want me to drive?" Gabby offered after a few hours of silence.

"Yeah, I've gotta piss," Chris said.

"Humans have really messed things up," she said.

"I guess we're learning as we go."

"No, things are really fucked up. We are on the brink of extinction and we've literally created pockets of Hell on Earth," Gabby said while keeping her focus on driving the raft.

"You can't think like that. We made mistakes, but we will fix them."

"Maybe this is the planet's way of fixing the problem."

"Gabs, everything is relative. You can look at things from a perspective of failure or a perspective of resolution," Chris said.

"But, just look at this place." Gabby gestured toward the wasteland that had once overflowed with life.

"We're going to fix it. We're human, we learn."

"I'd like to think you're right. I just feel so stupid for not realizing how big of a problem all of this was until now." Gabby's voice trailed off.

"You know what they say, hindsight and all. Here." Chris handed her a cup. "I made a coffee protein shake with an extra dose of caffeine."

"If we get caught in a fire, you have to kill me. I won't be able to do it," Gabby said.

"Gab," Chris said.

"Just promise," Gabby said without taking her focus from driving.

"I promise."

This part of the Amazon felt completely different.

She kept thinking that she saw sparks flicker, so it was easier to drive the boat. While she certainly didn't want to die, if she did, at least she wouldn't have to worry about the future.

"Are you worried about your family?" Gabby asked.

"They're heading into a safe house," Chris said.

"Safe house? What do you mean?"

He looked at her. "Wait, you don't know about the safe houses?"

"No, what are you talking about?"

"The government and AmCorps have been building sterile safe houses designed to withstand any sort of outbreak."

"Since when? Where?"

"Only a handful are ready, but there are a bunch under construction, with plans for more. The president and our highest-ranking officials have been moved in, along with some doctors. I'm pretty sure that they also included some artists, writers, and educators along with some private investors in the first phase."

"Phase One, which was moved up . . ." Echoes of Trent's conversation sent chills down her arms even though she sweated in the oppressive heat.

"Right. So, you do know?"

"No. Who's paying for this? Why doesn't the public know?"

Chris shrugged. "For the most part, I think it's been privately funded. It's been kept quiet because there just aren't enough places for everyone yet. This has all happened much quicker than anyone expected."

"How did your family get in?"

"It was part of my deal for taking this mission."

"Where are the safe houses?"

"Mostly in the Midwest. There's one in California and two in the Northeast as well."

"Are they all in the U.S.?"

"Yes."

"What does the public think?"

Chris was quiet a moment too long. "The safe houses have remained classified. As far as the public knows, disease transmission has slowed. For the most part, people have been staying home, so they don't know anything but what they've been told. There have been some gangs that have raided and terrorized some neighborhoods, but that has been put under control with the martial law order." He turned to her with a puzzled look. "Trent hasn't given you the updates?"

"No."

A tree nearby sparked, and flames began licking its branches. Gabby's stomach turned to stone, leaving her frozen.

"It's still too damp to fully ignite," Chris assured her.

"You hope."

"Yeah. What the fuck, yeah, I hope," he snapped.

"Sorry," Gabby said.

"Being in places like this messes with your head. You have to force yourself to think in the moment. Right now, we are here to survive, and to survive we have to be present and focused. Things are fucked, I know, but right now, we have to focus on getting to our goal, which at this moment is to make it out of here as quickly and efficiently as possible," Chris said.

Gabby took a deep breath. The air smelled medicinal, with smoky undertones. If there's a hell, she thought, this is it. Things can't get any worse. There was absolutely no other living creature in this part of the Amazon. The only sign of life was a splattering of ashen remains littering the bases of these sparking trees. The black-scorched earth streaked with the remnants of red clay soil gave way to the monstrous fire trees that had taken over.

These trees looked similar to eucalyptus trees in structure. However, this version's bark was a mottled black, which fed into a greenery unlike any Gabby had ever seen. The leaves were shaped like any other eucalyptus leaf, but instead of the soft, silvery green of the normal tree, these leaves were a sickly, disgusting, dark, vapid shadow of green. If evil had a color, Gabby thought this was it.

"Have you talked to your family? Do you know what the safe house is like? Are they all together?"

"I haven't talked to them, but I know they're safe and healthy. And they're all together."

"You never got married? No girlfriend?"

"Nope, no girlfriend, no fiancé, no wife. I came close, but my job pretty much put an end to it. I wasn't home nine months out of the year; she got tired of being alone."

"Did you love her?"

"Yeah, a lot. I still do, we're good friends. I went to her wedding. She married a really nice tech guy at Berkley."

"Did she work?"

"Yeah, she's one of the top veterinarians in the world. She's an expert on endangered species preservation. She helped a lot of zoos and animal sanctuaries around the world develop their species preservation plans."

"Wow."

"Now they have two kids, a picket fence, all of that."

"Is she safe?"

Chris nodded. "As far as I know. She has a completely self-contained compound in Alaska where they would spend summers, and she used it as her set-off point to research arctic animals, which was her latest project. They went there with enough food to last years, and she knows how to hunt and live off the land."

"I used to think"—Gabby paused— "well, not think, just feel sad that I didn't have any family, except my grandparents, who don't recognize me most of the time. But now, it makes this so much easier."

"My college buddies are always posting pictures of their babies and coaching tee-ball, and I thought I wanted that or I was starting to regret my career choice. But now, I don't know what I'd do if, you know, things ever straightened out."

"Yeah."

"What about you and Trent?"

"It's no secret that we were in a relationship."

"Were?" He cocked his head with a silly smile on his face.

"Are. You know what I mean."

"I know. I'm just joking. I was a little surprised that they put you on a mission together, but I guess he's got some pull."

"They needed a female, and I fit the bill."

"I know. I didn't mean it like that. I was really impressed when I read your brief. You and Trent are quite the power couple. Are you guys planning on marriage?"

"We decided that it would be career first for both of us, then once we were satisfied with where we were, we'd probably get married."

"Be careful. Or maybe not careful, but mindful. There are a lot of career-minded people who will never be satisfied. They always need that next accomplishment. Trent strikes me as that sort of guy," Chris let out a breath, "take it from me. I didn't realize what I was missing till it was gone."

"He's driven, but I don't know that that's a bad thing. It just somehow works for us—we're comfortable together."

"Comfortable?"

"It's," Gabby stammered, "it's not—"

"I'm not trying to upset you or criticize your relationship. But, I learned the hard way, and you're different than Trent."

"What do you mean?" Gabby snapped.

"Don't get mad. Trent is just one of those people only focused on career. He has no interests outside of his work, and he's molded his life to fit or to serve that. I don't think he has any feelings—he's purely intellect. You have feelings. You have formed your life through all of your experiences. You love your grandparents, you're sad about your childhood and the loss of your parents, you cared about Jim and worry over the environment and the world. You're human."

Gabby shook her head. "Trent has made some incredible discoveries that have saved lives. His work has meant life or death for some. He's had to learn to compartmentalize emotion. To be successful, he has to operate purely on intellect, but he has emotions."

"I know you understand what I'm saying. Do you really want to give up so much living for career accomplishments?"

"You say that like it's a bad thing and you've known us for, what? A whole two weeks."

"Time doesn't bring people together, situations do."

"Did you read that in a fortune cookie?"

"Actually, yeah," Chris laughed, "but it's a good one."

"I do appreciate your input, but I can't think about the future while we're in here, while we might . . . I mean, the whole human race might not even—I—"

"I know, it's pretty ironic. I didn't mean for our conversation to go so deep." Chris winked at her.

"Seriously though, what updates has Trent given you?"

"Not many. There have been no breaches, no infections in the safe houses. That's actually going better than expected. Only forty-three of those going in were stopped for infections. They were quickly turned away and pushed back to the next phases, dependent on their recovery. The quarantine protocols are working."

"That's good, I guess. Do you know what's happening outside of the safe houses?"

"With martial law, there's been strict curfew restrictions. The military has begun patrolling with robotics, mainly drones, which have been very effective."

"What do you mean, effective?"

"Healthy people stay home. The only people that go out are either sick, or criminals."

"What do the drones do?"

"They stop them before they can infect or harm anyone else."

"How?"

"Gab, don't make me spell it out. It's not pretty, it's not nice, but it's necessary if we want the human race to have any chance of survival."

A shudder hit Gabby and it took all she could do not to visualize the carnage. "How is that legal? And what do you think those rotting bodies are doing in the streets? Spreading disease. Haven't these geniuses studied disease transmission and plagues? Diseases aren't just spread through human-to-human contact."

"Gab, I'm not sure what the exact protocols are. I had and have nothing to do with what is going on back at home, I'm just telling you what I know. But, they are warned to return home if they refuse they are disposed of, and there are incineration vehicles that are dispatched immediately following any altercations."

"This level of control must be costing billions, and it's going to be impossible to maintain. Is it everywhere, every small town? When did they create all of this? This is crazy."

"Those are questions for Trent."

"Now I'm definitely glad that I don't have any family and probably never will."

"Don't say that," Chris admonished.

Gabby just shrugged. "Can you take over for a few?" she asked.

Chris moved up and took the wheel. "How about some food while you're back there?" he asked.

"Asian beef strips or southwest chicken and black beans?"

"Southwest."

The following twelve hours went by much like the first. They took turns napping and driving. Once the initial panic wore off and her adrenaline crashed, it was difficult to keep her eyes open. She got some of the best rest she'd had since coming to the Amazon, even as their raft passed sparking trees and smoldering remains.

CHAPTER 19

The Crossing

"GAB . . . GAB, WAKE UP."

Gabby pulled herself out of her deep, almost drugged, sleep. The boat was idling.

"What's going on?" she asked as she forced her eyes open.

They were still just inside the fire forest. Ahead of them was a long section of desert. There was not a tree, bush or even shrub in sight for miles. It was completely barren and exposed. It had been cleared as a way to prevent the fire forest from spreading. Just beyond this stretch, the Amazon jungle returned as thick as ever.

"We are just about out of the fire zone. We have a stretch of river that's completely exposed, which leaves us vulnerable."

Chris pulled the boat up alongside Trent's. Kukua was just on the other side. They had lightly beached their rafts on the scorched bank. Trent had his computer open with the satellite connection up.

"We have a problem," Trent said. "Intel can't locate the unit that was tracking us."

"Did they follow us into the fire zone?" Chris asked.

"They don't think so."

"How do you know?" he pressed.

"We've had an ISR aircraft that has been doing remote surveillance. They saw us go into the fire forest and have gotten sporadic pings from us while we've been traveling through. They saw the team tracking us up to the forest, but then they disappeared. The ISTAR team has limited capabilities when we are in the thick of it, but on most waterways they are able to track us, and so they were able to basically follow us through. That's why everyone is very confused as to why they can't see the others," Trent said.

"Were they possibly picked up by a heli?" Chris asked.

"They don't think so," Trent replied.

Chris snapped, "Don't think so? Who's providing this intel? Why am I always getting it second-hand from you? How reliable is it?"

"Blackwater. I couldn't tell you, because they are not officially part of this mission. AmCorps privately subcontracted a surveillance detail to provide intel directly to me. Just as"—Trent paused—"a sort of safety net."

"Blackwater? Who paid for that?"

"That's not important. What matters is that if they had not been providing intel, we'd all be dead, floating in that lagoon with our guide. Dammit, this comm keeps failing." Trent rapped his hand on his computer.

"Enough," Paulo interrupted. "You figure this out later. We need to decide our plan. Fast. We cannot stay here."

"Like I was saying. We need to move, but we will be completely exposed, which puts us at risk of discovery and attack," Trent said.

"If it's a trap, I would think that they want to take us, or at least Trent, alive. We should cross in teams," Chris suggested.

"Yes, I think so too," Paulo agreed. "I'll go first

and send a signal if it's safe. Patrick, you come with me. Trent, you go with Chris and Gabby. Kukua and Bob, you come last."

Trent began moving his cases onto Chris's boat. Patrick climbed onto Paulo and Trent's vessel and began helping Trent move his protected cases.

"We will have to use the radios," Chris said. "Do not talk over the air. One beep means trap. Two beeps means proceed. Is that clear?" Chris handed a radio to Paulo. "They are already on and set."

"We go," Paulo snapped. "Patrick, merda, pressa."

Patrick quickly finished helping Trent, then pulled away with Paulo. This was the first time that Gabby had noticed Paulo appearing nervous. He was always so stoic.

"Something doesn't feel right," she turned to tell Chris, but he'd left. Gabby saw him with Kukua and Bob. They were unloading and deflating the third boat.

"What's going on?" Gabby asked Trent, but he didn't answer. He was arranging his cases on Chris and Gabby's raft.

The burnt sand cracked under Gabby's boot as she stepped off her raft.

"What are you doing?" she asked Chris.

He handed Bob his hat, then undressed down to his boxers and gave his clothes to the boy as well.

"Gab, can you help Kukua load those boxes onto our raft?" Chris asked.

"Yeah, but tell me what's going on."

"We'll fill you in as soon as we're ready. Now please help Kukua."

Gabby did as requested, but her anger began boiling.

"What's going on?" she asked as Trent and Chris were breaking down Kukua's raft.

The team just continued working, loading the raft onto Trent's. Chris and Kukua changed into head-to-toe camouflage wetsuits.

"Isn't this too much weight for the raft?" Trent asked.

"No. It's not ideal, but it will be fine," Chris replied.

"What the fuck is going on?" Gabby snapped.

"Intel suspects a mole on our team. I just got comm that we are heading directly to the team that has been tracking us. This is a trap, and the only person that could've set it is Paulo," Trent said.

"Kukua and I are going to hitch a ride underwater. Bob is filling in for me. If this is a trap, we will counterattack."

Chris looked at his watch. "It's been nine minutes. We should get our signal soon." Chris put on his scuba gear. "Kukua, just breathe normally. I rigged a towboard. So just hang on and stay relaxed. Before we come out of the water, I will turn off your air intake—"

"What do you mean, turn off air?" Kukua asked.

"Your breath is in this tank. You will just breathe normally in this mask and hang on—"

Chris was interrupted again, this time by a beeping sound.

"Wait, Kukua. When the boat stops, I will guide you to the river bank, but don't go up. When I tap your shoulder, hold your breath. I will turn off your tank and take it off of you. Then we have to come out of the water very slowly. Don't make a sound. Do you understand?"

"We have to go," Trent said.

"Wait. Do you understand?"

"Sim, yes," Kukua nodded.

Chris pulled Kukua's mask on. "How does it feel?

Good?" Chris showed Kukua a thumbs-up gesture. "Or bad?" He flashed thumbs-down.

Kukua gave a thumbs up in return. Chris pulled his mask down and they disappeared beneath the dark, murky surface.

"Bob, let's go. Keep your head down," Trent said.

Bob pulled Chris's hat a little lower over his eyes and kicked the engine on.

As they pulled into the barren section of land, the glare of the sun made it difficult for Gabby to keep her eyes open. By this point, she had become used to being hot, but now she felt like an unlucky ant caught in the glare of a kid's magnifying glass.

"How could those assholes let a mole lead our team?" Trent said, more to himself than Gabby.

"What?" she asked.

"If they're powerful enough to get someone on our team, we're fucked."

Gabby recalled Chris's words. "At least you know you're safe. They need you for your expertise."

"I'm not doing all of this to give away my work. I will kill them before they—"

"Stop," Gabby interrupted. "Stay calm so that you can stay focused. Do you have your gun?" She couldn't believe the words that were coming out; it was almost as if she could hear herself talking, but was somewhere else entirely.

"Yes. You?"

"Yes."

As the jungle came into view, it loomed larger than ever. Its sharp claws seemed to pull at the earth, making just enough room for the river to cut in.

When they crossed in, it became much darker. There was no sign of Paulo, so they kept going.

A loud whistle seared through the jungle sounds. Paulo was up on the right bank and was waving them over.

"Bob, don't pull over to him. I will stand in front of you to talk to him. Just get a little closer. Even if everything seems okay, stay quiet," Trent said as he stood and moved up toward the front of the raft and stood in front of Bob.

"Why are you stopped?" Trent yelled to Paulo.

"Pull over. We radio for Kukua here," the other man said.

"No, we need to be ready to move. Get back into your raft," Trent instructed

"Okay, do what you like," Paulo said. "I radio

them now." He began walking towards his boat.

Gabby looked down and noticed the third radio on the floor toward the back of the raft. It was still on. She jumped up.

"I need some coffee," she announced, much louder than she should've. She knew she sounded ridiculous.

She got to the back of the boat, bent down, and reached the radio dial just as the first beep was coming through, then quickly turned it off.

Gabby looked around—Paulo was watching her.

"Pull over," Paulo yelled, "you're drifting. We need to regroup."

"No, I don't feel comfortable stopping here. Get back in the raft and get ready to go," Trent directed.

A gunshot pierced the air. Gabby looked around, but didn't see anyone. Bob slumped over and fell onto the floor.

"Pull over or Gabrielle gets shot next," Paulo yelled. "It does not need to be like this. You need to do what is right."

Trent shoved Bob out of the way and jumped behind the wheel. Gabby heard another burst of pops, then felt a sharp pain in her shoulder blade. Reaching back, she felt a warm trickle of blood. She watched Trent collapse. Then she looked at her crimson-stained fingertips as the world around her began to tunnel. It was like she was on a ride, moving backward. The tunnel got smaller and smaller, faster and faster, until a swirling black darkness overtook her.

Chapter 20

Wake Up

"GABRIELLE. GABRIELLE. Listen to my voice. Gabs, open your eyes."

Somewhere in the darkness, Gabby heard her name, but it seemed so far away. She tried to open her eyes or move, but nothing worked. She was stuck, and just wanted to slip away.

"Gabrielle. You have to open your eyes. Listen to me. Gabrielle."

The voice was getting closer and would not leave her alone. She just wanted to drift away.

"Open your eyes. Please."

Ouch, Gabby thought and tried to open her eyes. Her lids fluttered, but the blackness still surrounded her.

"There you go. Come on, Gabs. Open your eyes."

Gabrielle managed to blink, and the darkness began to clear. She blinked again. Chris was standing over her.

"There you go. You're almost back. Keep your eyes open."

Gabrielle felt the pain return to her shoulder and she winced. She tried to sit up but couldn't.

"Just relax. You're okay. Take some deep breaths," Chris said.

"Wh . . ." Gabby tried to talk, but her throat was too dry. She forced a swallow. "What happened?" she rasped.

"You were hit with a tranquilizer. They were planning to separate us and capture us one boat at a time. Like us, they sent a skeleton crew in. They may have a larger team waiting to take us out," Chris said.

"What? Where are we?" Gabby asked.

"Gabs, listen, you need to get up and start moving. There's probably another team en route. Paulo is still alive, but he refuses to talk. We are heading out now, on two boats. Sit up. Drink a Coke. It helped Trent," Chris said, and handed Gabrielle a can of soda.

She forced herself up. Trent was at the front of the boat on his computer.

"Okay, Kukua. Head out," Chris yelled.

Kukua pulled the first raft out and Chris followed. They were moving as fast as the boats would travel. Gabrielle's head pounded. She glanced at the jungle moving past, and instantly threw up. She watched behind the Zodiac as a school of fish frantically gulped at her vomit, and that made her throw up again.

Trent moved back and handed Gabrielle two quick-dissolve Benadryl. "We had a couple of these stashed. You'll feel better soon," Trent said.

"What happened?" Gabrielle asked.

"Paulo is working for someone else. There were only two guys in the crew that tried to trap us. That's why they wanted us to come in boat by boat. We don't know how they got there, but we're assuming the plan was to tranq us, then the two guys plus Paulo would drive our boats to the assembly point," Trent said.

"Where are we going?" Gabby asked, the fog of nausea lifting.

"We had to switch our plans. Paulo has somehow

been communicating with them, so they know our route. Chris also found a tracking device on Paulo, and we left all of his belongings back there. We are taking a different tributary, but we will have to go by land sooner than we wanted to," Trent said.

"How much sooner?" she asked.

"We'll have to get a few hours in just before dark, today."

"Ugh, my head is pounding."

Trent reached into his pocket. "Here's a Tylenol. You won't throw up anymore."

Gabby's palms were sweaty and the red 'T' on the white pills had smeared. She tossed them in her mouth, gulping them down with some more Coke.

"The tranq drugs are quick acting, and they'll be out of your system soon," Trent said, and started to move to the front of the boat near Chris. He stopped and turned back to her. "Gabrielle, I'm glad you're here. I knew that I made the right call bringing you."

What right call? Gabby thought, but her head hurt too bad to continue the conversation. *Did she make the right call coming?* Her head pounded with a ferocity she's never experienced. *Was it better to get killed quickly trying to help out, or to sit and*

wait to get sick, watching the world die around her?
She sipped on her Coke.

The jungle here was much thicker. It was darker under the canopy, and slightly cooler. There were so many shades of green, colors that she hadn't even known existed.

"We are getting close to a suspected indigenous tribal zone," Chris yelled over the engines. "These particular tribes made a conscious decision more than a hundred years ago to avoid contact with outsiders. They've had limited interactions. For the most part, they view outsiders as enemies that spread disease and famine and bring evil spirits with them. They're skilled hunters and use arrows and poisoned darts. I think they'll avoid us, but stay alert."

"Do you really think we could pick out a native hiding in their habitat?" Trent scoffed.

"Nope, I'm just letting you know where we're at. FUNAI has a surveillance post about seventy miles farther up. We're not sure if it's still manned, but we are not going to chance it," Chris said.

"I'll drive for a bit," Trent offered. "I have some intelligence files on the different tribes in this area, including the one we're looking for." He handed

Gabrielle and Chris a folder each. "These files have remained sealed until now."

Gabby opened hers and began to read:

The Javari river region is inhabited by Matsés. Portions of this indigenous group have had contact with the outside for nearly a century. Loggers, rubber extraction camps, missionaries, and military have been in and out of this region, bringing disease and war, forcing members of those groups either deeper into the Amazon to preserve their indigenous traditions [from here on out referred to as "Pure"] or to acclimate to modern ways of life [from here on out referred to as "Modernized"] with a small sector straddling the two worlds [from here on out referred to as "Blended"]. The Pure have gone to great lengths to preserve their ancient way of life, which means they view all ties to modernity, including other humans, as the enemy. This is our target population. However, in order to successfully make contact with Pures, the goal of this mission is to form an alliance with the Blended. A complicating factor in this operation will be the inter-warring between different groups. Rely on Kukulcan's expertise in this matter. Pures are thought to be high in the mountain region, whereas Blendeds live close to waterways in order to make transit between towns and settlements more efficient.

"When you're finished reading, throw those documents into the water. They will dissolve," Trent said.

"So, we're heading into the Andes?" Chris said.

"We've got some jungle to cross first, but yes. We wanted to take an easier way in, but that's not an option anymore. This is the most bio-diverse region in the world, and extremely difficult terrain," Trent said.

"What are we going to do with Paulo?" Chris asked. "We're not going to be able to keep him with us."

"I don't think we have many options. We can't risk this mission," Trent said.

"You can't kill him," Gabby said.

The boat remained silent.

CHAPTER 21

On Foot

IT TOOK THE TEAM LONGER to break down the boats than they had wanted. They had to conceal their ditched equipment while narrowing down their supplies to what they absolutely needed and could carry. Gabby's pack was the lightest at fifty pounds, while the others' gear packs were closer to ninety.

The onslaught of insectile bombardiers began to drive Gabby insane almost immediately. They were relentless, swarming clouds of torture. They flew up her nose, bounced around her eyes, and buzzed near her ears. Her scalp began to crawl. She scratched, but it just intensified the itching. Tiny bugs began sticking to the dewy beads of sweat on her skin. The bugs that had swarmed the boat were as gentle as a sleeping baby compared to what she now faced.

"Stop," Gabby said, frantically pawing at her scalp, "I can't take this. Please tell me that someone has bug spray."

"Here," Chris said. "Sorry, I thought you put it on before we started. Keep that bottle. You need to keep a thick coating of bug spray on at all times. These insects carry some terrible diseases."

"I know," Gabby snapped, grabbing the bug spray from Chris, "I forgot."

"One of the diseases will cause your face to fall off, like leprosy," Chris said.

"I KNOW," Gabby said as she sprayed the mist all over her body and her pack, gladly accepting any and all of the DEET magic.

They quickly returned to their jungle march.

"Snakes nearby," Kukua announced. "See tracks." He pointed to what looked like a windswept brush of fallen leaves.

Without the steady cloud of pests, Gabby was able to take in the beauty of the jungle in its many shades. There were so many colors, so many shades of green. From the almost fluorescent yellow-green moss that crawled along the jungle floor and up the mottled brown tree trunks to the emerald green fern leaves veined with jade. Pops of deep purple, stunning red and bright magenta, seemed to glow against the vivid green backdrop.

"Our luck," Kukua said, "this passion fruit." He picked off a purple flower from a large vine and followed the vine to an outcropping of reddish-brown fruits. He filled a nylon bag attached to his pack, then cut one in half and sucked out the jelly innards of the fruit. He offered the other half to Gabby. She had never tasted passion fruit like this—maybe it was her surroundings, maybe it was the overabundance of MREs, or maybe it just was that much better here. A citrusy sweetness melted in her mouth and gave way to the softest tart finish. It was delicious.

"We need to keep moving," Trent said.

Bob and Patrick quickly filled up their nylon bags. Kukua grabbed one more, cut it in half, and gave both halves to Chris. Paulo's hands were tied in front of him by rope that Chris had attached to his rucksack. The man's mouth had been taped, but Chris removed the tape so that he could eat one half of the passion fruit.

"The second you make a noise I will tape and gag your mouth again. Do you understand?" Chris asked.

Paulo nodded his head in agreement, then sucked down the passion fruit.

The march moved on. Soon, it was as if they were all in rhythm with the jungle. Gabby walked toward the back of the line, near Paulo, while Kukua and Chris took turns using their machetes to clear a path, when the trees became thick.

"Hey," Paulo whispered to Gabby, "do you know what you're doing?"

"You're not supposed to be talking," Gabby said.

"Do you know who you work for?"

"Who do *you* work for?" Gabby snapped.

"I work for all people. I work for the world, for Mother Earth," Paulo said.

Gabby just rolled her eyes at Paulo's righteous arrogance.

"Do you even know who you work for?" he asked again.

"I can't stand this empty, duplicitous righteousness. You're as guilty as anyone else and just as desperate for a treatment. Do you want your mouth gagged again? I'm not talking to you."

"You don't understand. You don't know what's happening. You work for rich. Ask Trent who is safe. Ask who will get treatment. You're only going to save the rich and you're going to steal innocent people to do it." Paulo spat.

"You're wrong," Gabby said. "You don't know what's going on."

"I work for Interfaith for Peace. We have leaders from every religion and more than 125 countries. We believe that all people must be treated fairly," Paulo said.

"You're insane. You don't know what you're talking about. Do you understand that we are on the brink of extinction?" Gabby said, immediately regretting sharing this information with him.

"You and me, yes. That's why these people need to be protected even more. You bring your disease and take them from their home to a ruined world," Paulo said.

"Don't you want the human race to survive? You're not here to find a treatment, just like we are?" Gabby asked.

"Not like this. Do you know what the price tag for your treatment is? Fifty million dollars," Paulo said.

"What?" Gabby asked.

"You didn't know this?" Paulo said. "Every person that goes into your safe housing units to wait for treatment must pay at a minimum fifty million. And, to make the treatment, they are stealing innocent people."

Chris heard the mumbles of their whispered exchange and turned around.

"Paulo," Chris snapped, and jerked the rope attached to his hands. "One more word and I will tape your mouth."

Gabby dropped back to the rear of the line and walked with Bob. *Fifty million dollars to buy in,* she thought. *Paulo has to be wrong. Chris's family is in a safe house.*

Bob grabbed a passion fruit from his bag, cut it in half, and handed both pieces to Gabby. She took this delicious distraction from the trek and her troubling thoughts.

It was such a strange-looking fruit. Its bright yellow, slimy innards, speckled with black seeds, looked more like something that should come out of your body than something going into it. Gabby took a deep inhale of its aromatic citrus smell and slurped it down.

Suddenly, Bob yanked her arm. She looked up and saw Chris. He had his hand up to stop with a finger over his mouth. Bob quickly taped Paulo's mouth, and Gabby moved up near Chris and Trent. They had spotted some sort of outpost in a clearing up ahead. A rippled tin roof was visible through a break in trees.

"Gabs, where's your handgun?" Chris whispered.

"In my pack. Why?"

"You're coming with me to check out the structure ahead."

"Me?"

"Kukua, Bob, and Patrick need to guard Trent and Paulo. If something were to happen to us, they are better suited to get Trent to his target."

Gabby swallowed the sting of being expendable, but grabbed her gun and strapped the holster to her leg.

Chris leaned in toward her and whispered, "Don't worry, we'll be fine."

CHAPTER 22

The Warrior's Ceremony

IT TOOK CHRIS AND GABBY several minutes to get through the thick jungle leading to the structure. It was a rough structure. Thin timber panels supported a tin roof.

Gabby and Chris approached from the back. They listened for sounds of movement inside, but heard nothing. Quietly, they moved around the structure toward the front. Openings cut out to be windows were covered in bug netting and had rough shutters that were barely cracked open. There was no sign of movement. Ashen remnants sat cold in a fire pit.

They took positions on opposite sides of the door. Chris silently counted to three, swung the door open, and stepped to the side. The assault was instantaneous—the odor that poured out was so ferocious they both stumbled back.

"Tie your shirt around your face and breathe through your mouth," Chris said. "We have to go in."

Even covered up and breathing through her mouth, Gabby felt like she was being choked. Right inside, near the door, were two bodies. Another lay toward the back of the hut. The bodies were covered in clotted blood and small wounds. Numerous visible marks crisscrossed the distended figure closest to the door.

Inside, there were four hammocks attached to the back wall, a small table with four chairs, and eight stacked trunks. There was an opened computer on a small table inside, still plugged in to a solar-powered charging station that indicated it was fully charged. Gabby touched a key. The solid blue screen flashed on with an empty square password login. She pushed the computer closed.

Behind the stacked chests, Chris found a fourth body. This one still had two spears buried deep into the abdomen. The dead were all men, and all wore light khaki pants with solid white tee shirts. There wasn't much Gabby could tell from the bodies; she roughly estimated that they had only been dead for twelve to twenty-four hours. Their skin was pale gray and had begun to expand, distorting their features. The only identifying feature that remained intact was their hair, all short brown hair in varying shades.

There was nothing in the stacked chests except basic supplies—extra clothes, dry food goods, and some creature comforts like shampoo. Chris grabbed a couple boxes of granola bars and they took the computer. There were no guns or weapons, not that they could find.

Once outside, Gabby gulped in fresh air. "Who do you think they were?" she asked.

"I don't know. Their clothes, the lack of weapons . . . maybe aid workers or FUNAI. Possibly scientists. Or, whoever killed them took their weapons and they could be military. Part of the unit tracking us. We need to get into that computer," Chris said.

"Obviously an indigenous group killed them, right?"

"It definitely appears that way, or was made to appear that way."

Gabby let out a breath of frustration, "Assuming

it was an indigenous group, do you think they're close? Are we in danger?"

"I don't know," he admitted.

Gabby stopped asking Chris questions, as it was not making her feel any better. The pair made it back to the group much quicker, as they took a direct path. There, they filled in the team, excluding Paulo.

"This bad part of jungle," Kukua said. "No like outsiders. Kill them."

"Then we need to get to the mountains as quickly as possible," Trent said.

"Mountains. No. No go there. Very bad spirits guard mountains," Kukua said.

"We will pay you more, enough to have everything you want for the rest of your life," Trent said.

"No. It . . . No."

"We will bring you back to America with us. You will have the best life possible," Trent offered.

"Bob and Patrick?" Kukua said.

"Yes, of course," Trent answered.

"Us talk, may be possível."

"Just think about it, but get us close for now," Trent said.

Chris said, "We need to find a place to camp. We

have just over an hour of daylight and need to move away from this outpost."

Kukua found a small, muddy stream. They followed that for about a mile, until the last rays of day were barely able to cut through the trees.

Kukua, Bob, and Patrick used their machetes to clear an area for camp. Chris tied Paulo to a tree, then he, Gabby, and Trent used their foldable buckets to gather water from the stream.

Gabby stepped on a broken trunk to get her footing as she bent with her bucket to the water. Suddenly, her foot and leg were on fire with a pain like nothing she had ever felt. She began screaming. What felt like electric shocks sent jagged shards of pain streaming through her veins. She collapsed backward.

Bob and Chris were the first to reach her.

"What happened?" Chris asked.

Gabby couldn't answer. She was gripped in pain, with waves of nausea and uncontrollable shaking taking over. Kukua made his way over.

Bob quickly reached down to her ankle, swatting a few insects off and stomping on them. He pulled one more off of her ankle and held it up for Chris to see.

"Is that an ant?" Chris asked.

The insect was black, about an inch long, with visible fangs and a stinger.

"Sim, ah, yes," Kukua answered.

"It's huge. Is she okay?" Chris asked.

"Her be okay. Hurt very painful and many bite Gabby. It bullet ant," Kukua said as Bob crushed the ant in his fingers. "Most painful bite of all insects. Warriors do ceremony with ants sewn into gloves that cover hands in stings. Your people say it get name, because sting feel like . . ." Kukua mocked a gun shot with his hand.

"A gun shot?" Chris asked.

"Sim," Kukua shook his head, "yes."

"Oh, bullet ant, got it."

"Ah," Gabby gritted, "I need something for the pain."

"Help me carry Gab up to camp," Chris said.

They picked Gabby up—she was still shaking.

"Put a mat down," Chris yelled. Kukua quickly grabbed a pack and rolled out a mat.

"Get my pack," Gabby gasped. "I need . . . anti-histamine and pain . . ." Her voice trailed off.

Kukua ran over with her pack.

"Hurt so much. Do ceremony. Pain go to bone," Kukua said.

"Gab, where's the medicine?" Chris asked.

"There's a black"—Gabby gritted her teeth—"zippered case." She was momentarily overtaken with shakes. Chris handed her the case. She took two pills out, but the crescendo of pain returned and she was shaking too badly to take them. During a brief respite, she tossed a Vicodin and Benadryl in her mouth and swallowed.

The pain continued to wax and wane, each wave worse than the previous. He body shook uncontrollably. The poison felt like it was attacking the bones in her leg, sending bolts of pain through her core. Her body was drenched in sweat as she lay there waiting for the medicine to take effect. The pain was so extreme, waves of nausea washed through her. She forced back the urge to vomit, desperately waiting for the pain meds to take effect.

Chris covered Gabby in her mosquito net and sat with her until she fell asleep. When she came to, the camp was set up and a fire was lit.

"Hey Gabs, hungry? We're eating MREs, again," Chris said.

Her pain had subsided and was now just a dull ache. Gabby felt groggy and disconnected. She guzzled down some water, anxious to get the narcotics out of her system. Though she wasn't hungry, she forced herself to eat. After moving into her tent with Chris's help, she passed back out.

She came to just as the sun broke through the thick canopy. Her head was clear and the pain was completely gone. Everyone else was already up. Chris brought Gabby a cup of coffee.

"Morning sunshine, feeling better?" he asked.

"Much. How much hiking today?" she asked.

"A full day. We need to cover as much distance as possible. Trent received a radio silence order from headquarters. He was directed to continue with the mission as planned, but to not attempt contact for the next two weeks," Chris explained.

"What does that mean?" Gabby asked.

"There's a suspected mole inside AmCorps, and they are relaying our location to another organization," Chris said.

"Other than Paulo?" Gabby asked.

"Presumably." Chris nodded.

"He's working for Interfaith for Peace," Gabby said.

"He told you that?"

She nodded. "He also told me that in order to get any sort of help or protection, people have to pay a minimum of fifty million dollars per person, and they only plan to treat those that can afford it."

"That's just to raise funds in order to get a treatment developed for everyone," Chris replied.

"Does that seem right?" Gabby asked.

"Doing whatever it takes to develop a treatment to cure everyone? That seems right to me."

"But—"

"Listen, these are unprecedented times. We need desperate measures in order to come out of this," Chris said.

Trent joined them for the first time since they'd entered the jungle on foot.

"How are you feeling?" he asked Gabby, as Chris moved up to the front of the march.

"So much better."

"I checked on you last night, but you were sound asleep."

"The pain meds knocked me out."

"That sting looked painful."

"You have no idea."

"Glad you're feeling better. Listen, did Paulo say anything to you?"

"Not really—he just thinks that what we're doing is wrong. He thinks we should just leave the indigenous people alone and that our treatment should help the whole world."

"Of course it's going to. What is he even talking about? These extreme groups are so uninformed, it's almost shocking that they have even managed to be a thorn in our side. We are also approaching the indigenous population as sensitively as possible."

"Yeah, I know," Gabby said, but something Paulo had said wasn't sitting well with her and the seeds of doubt had been planted.

"Sorry I haven't been more attentive," Trent said. "I just have so much on my plate."

She shrugged. "It's fine. I knew what I was signing up for."

"You're perfect. Thanks for coming."

Gabby smiled, and Trent resumed his position at the front of the line.

CHAPTER 23

Deep State

"DR. SABARA, you have an urgent call," a lab tech paged Dr. Sabara, who sat within a protected laboratory, staring into a microscope.

"I'm in the middle of something. I will call back," Lucien said without looking away from the computer screen that projected the slide of the microscope. Lucien was covered in full PPE gear. As he adjusted the microscope, the image on the screen became clearer.

"It is General Holton, sir, and he says that he needs to speak with you immediately," the tech replied.

"Fine. Tell him I will conference him in from my office right now," Lucien replied.

Lucien promptly made his way out of the lab,

stopping only in the decontamination unit. His office overlooked the lab through a series of polycarbonate windows. Lucien's office was completely soundproof. He woke up his massive desktop and linked in to the computer from the lab, then focused intently on a series of cells growing, dividing, and moving across the screen. Finally, he opened a window on his screen and saw a somber General Holton.

"I'm in the middle of something very important," Lucien said.

"This couldn't wait. There is at least one other mole. They are likely high-ranking and working at your lab," General Holton said.

"That's impossible," Lucien snapped.

"Interfaith for Peace has threatened to make this information public. They have detailed information about your plans—"

"Our plans," Lucien corrected.

"Yes, our plans. I only said 'your' because IFP has threatened to first alert the Brazilian government and then go to the press here," Holton snapped.

"What do they want?"

"They claim that AmCorps and the American government are practicing ethnic cleansing on a genetic scope in a way that dwarfs the Third Reich," Holton said.

"Imbeciles. What do they want?"

"They want a safe house to place a selection of people they choose, and they want to receive the treatment. They said that's the only way to get a fair representation to survive into the modern world." Holton snorted.

"What bullshit. Do those self-righteous pricks realize how ridiculous they sound?" Lucien froze. "Don't say any more. I'm going to call you back." He abruptly clicked off the channel, then shut the blinds in his office and pulled out a secure phone. Lucien turned it on and dialed.

"So, how are you going to handle this?" he snapped as soon as Holton answered.

"It's taken care of on our end, but you need to figure out who's the double agent inside your lab," Holton said.

"Obviously I will. How are you taking care of it?"

"We are using military force and treating them as the terrorist agents that they are. In fact, most have been taken care of or are being handled as we speak."

Lucien clicked his computer and a screen of cameras came on.

"I trust they wore their pandemic-level protective gear. Our military support will be essential as we move forward," Lucien said.

"Of course—and before you ask, no, it was not the extraction unit."

"Alright. We will talk again tonight." Lucien hung up the phone.

As he watched the cameras, he saw a female lab technician look at her phone, cover her mouth, and start crying. Lucien zoomed in on her mousy features, wet with tears. He picked up the phone.

"We have a lab technician that's in violation of our laws and must be disposed of," He zoomed the camera in on her name badge. "One-zero-seven-four-three-four-two."

Moments later, two guards walked into the lab and quietly grabbed one arm each. She tried to struggle, but there was nothing she could do. Her phone fell to the counter and Lucien was able to see the screen 'They're dead. All dead.'

CHAPTER 24

The Martyr

THE MAIN ISSUE OF THE MORNING was what to do with Paulo. Trent pulled Chris and Gabby aside.

"Obviously, we need to do something with Paulo," Trent said.

"We should just keep him with us," Gabby responded.

"That's not possible. He's a threat to our entire operation."

"He has information that could help us," she said, hoping her rationale would sway Trent. She'd seen enough death recently, and though Paulo had misled them, killing him didn't seem to be the answer.

"He's not talking," Chris said.

"Keeping him with us is a bigger risk than his information is worth," Trent said.

Chris nodded in agreement.

"No, it's not. He can tell us who's after us, how they're tracking us, and why," Gabby said.

"Fine. Gabrielle, you have five minutes to get him to talk," Trent said.

She made her way to Paulo, who was tied to a tree at the edge of their camp.

"Paulo, please talk to me. Trent and Chris gave me five minutes to get information from you. If you don't tell them what they need to know, they're going to kill you," Gabby pleaded.

"I am okay with that," the man said.

"Please—you already started to tell me some things."

"It won't matter." Paulo shook his head.

"Yes, it will."

"No, because you don't even realize what you're doing. You think you're saving the world, but you're just killing what small bit of humanity is left," Paulo said.

"The human race is about to go extinct. You think we should just let it?" Gabby asked.

"No, the entire human race is not going extinct. The indigenous people you are after are not—not unless you infect them."

"Your organization wants this cure as badly as we do, they just want it for themselves," Gabby reasoned.

"I fear that you're right. I'm finished." Paulo turned away from her.

"Please," she said.

"I've made my peace. I thank God that I will not be here to witness the horrors that you will unleash upon this earth. God has rewarded me," Paulo said, his eyes ablaze with a fervor she had not seen before.

As hints of his fanaticism came through, Gabby realized she would not be able to reason with the man. He was just another radical, a terrorist. Though terrorism was now only found in history books, Gabby remembered how it had ripped her family apart, that 9/11 horror that took her father and crippled her mother's mind forever. It made it much easier for her to walk away from Paulo now.

She picked up her pack and joined Trent, Kukua, Patrick, and Bob. They began the march while Chris stayed behind.

He executed Paulo with a single bullet to the back of his head, then quickly caught up to the rest of the group.

Gabby easily fell into the monotony of the jungle. It felt like she had been walking on the same path for months. The bullet ant sting seemed like a distant memory. If it weren't for the subtle ache in her ankle, she would've thought it had all been a bad dream.

"Trent," Gabby called, quickening her pace to match his, "did you find out who was at that station?"

"Not yet, but Chris has a decryption drive that I will try tonight," Trent replied.

"What's going on back home?" Gabby asked.

"It's bad—infections across the board were at the highest level ever. Hospitals have closed. Sick people are being urged to do their part for society and stay home in order to not infect others. But, on a high note, the first signs of the martial law order being effective are starting to show, and the safe house locations are proving to be effective. Chris said he explained a bit about that to you earlier."

Gabby nodded. "Do you know how my grandparents are?"

"They're fine. Their house is completely self-contained," Trent replied.

"How did people get into the safe house locations?"

"We just completed Phase One. The president and other critical individuals have been moved in. Now our first public group is in the pre-quarantine phase," Trent explained.

"How are people chosen to go in?"

"Our first group are our lab investors."

"Do people have to pay to get in?"

"No, but we have to honor our investors first before we can open up to the public, which is pretty far down the line. Then it will be based on a lottery system," Trent said.

"Water!" Chris shouted, and started jogging toward a stream up ahead.

Gabby looked up and saw the beautiful stream. A soft, ethereal layer of vapor floated just above the water.

"No," Kukua yelled, "stop. Water hot. Water kill you."

"What?" Chris asked, slightly slowing his pace.

"You smell," Kukua said.

There was the faintest scent of sulfur.

The creek wasn't just hot, it was boiling.

"Oh shit," Chris said.

"Us move fast now. Very bad spirits here, evil spirits," Kukua said.

"We need to hike through today, anyway," Trent said.

"Us stay together. Shapshicos here," Kukua said.

"What's that?" asked Gabby.

"Bad spirits. No like people. They take form of someone you know, trick you to follow. Then shapshicos eat—no, no eat, what word? Like eat, but no food . . ." Kukua paused to think.

"Consume?" Chris asked.

"Sim, consume and take away."

"Devour?" Gabby inserted.

"Sim, shapshicos devour your . . ." Kukua held a hand to his chest.

"Your heart?" Chris asked.

"No," the man said, and passed his hand over his entire body, then pounded his chest.

"Your soul?"

Kukua nodded. "Devour soul and take body. Make you do bad things till body dies."

Trent scoffed. "Kukua, you don't actually believe that ridiculous nonsense, do you?"

"Shapshicos true. Forest sacred. Here all rock, all tree, all animal have spirit . . . all have spirit. Us know, us live here, us see," Kukua said.

Trent rolled his eyes. "What you think you've seen can all be explained with science. It's amazing how primordial your thinking can be in this modern age. Have you heard of mental illness?"

"Us no stupid. Us know mental illness. Shapshicos different. See it happen," Kukua snapped, and pointed a finger at Trent. "Trent spirit sleep. Not all can see with eyes."

The conversation quickly fizzled out. They marched for hours and hours in silence. Metal bars made out of vivid green vines imprisoned them. Gabby felt like a little white mouse, running on a wheel but going nowhere. The monotony of the jungle started to get to her. She thought she heard things.

Suddenly, a tingle ran down her spine. She had an eerie feeling, like they were being watched. She heard twigs snap, but saw nothing. Her heart sank and caught in her throat, and she saw a face smiling at her from just behind the trees. She recognized the warm grin; it was her grandfather. Though she knew that was impossible, the prickles of panic spread from her core to her limbs. It took every bit of her will to continue to move forward and not towards her smiling pop.

As she forced the fear down, she slowly realized the face that she saw was nothing more than a play of shadows on bowing jungle leaves. Gabby felt silly, but relieved nonetheless.

Finally, the sun started to sink in the sky, and the jungle quickly darkened.

"Us close," Kukua said, "but need hurry."

The jungle was a very different place in the dark. The shadows that hid behind trees and rocks during the day seemed to move freely at night. It wasn't something that Gabby could explain with logic. She didn't dare mention it to anyone. Her brain told her that it was simply fear and boredom playing tricks on her mind, but deep down it felt like something else. The Amazon was full of life that existed on so many different levels, but there was also a darkness here. Something that Gabby didn't understand.

Finally, they made it to a small clearing near a stream. She helped Chris set up the tents, while the others gathered wood and lit a fire. Trent sat down on a few fallen tree trunks to try to break into the computer they found. Suddenly, he screamed, "Snake! Snake—it bit me."

Kukua got to him first. He still had his machete and was able to find and kill the snake. The creature was huge, at least six feet long. Gabby ran over with her medical kit. Based on the size of the snake, she thought it was a boa constrictor.

"No good. Snake bushmaster," Kukua whispered to Gabby.

"Is it poisonous?" Gabby asked.

"Sim. Bite give much poison."

Chris, Bob, and Patrick ran over. They carried Trent to the fire and laid him down next to it.

He was bit around his calf, just under the knee.

"Chris, hand me the sawyer pump, and get the constriction wrap ready," Gabby said. She quickly used the pump to extract as much venom as she could. Then she began to wrap Trent's leg just above the bite. She wrapped it just tight enough to apply some compression, but not impede the circulation.

"Can you get the IV ready, then start to reconstitute the antivenom?" Gabby said.

Trent was so pale, he looked gray.

"I'm going to throw up," Trent moaned, and began to heave. "I'm dying."

"No, you're not," Gabby said. "You have to stay calm."

"Where's the antivenom?" Chris asked.

"It's marked *Wyeth Crotalidae*. We have thirty vials. Just reconstitute the first two," Gabby said as she cleaned Trent's arm and inserted the IV needle. She quickly taped it in place.

"How do I reconstitute it?"

"You just have to break the seal, then shake it."

Chris handed her the first vial.

"Oh shit," Gabby said, "I have to do an intradermal skin test first. Hand me a syringe." Chris quickly handed it to her. She injected a small amount of antivenom into the skin on Trent's arm. His leg was swelling.

"What are you doing?" Chris asked.

"A lot of people are allergic to this antivenom—it can cause immediate anaphylaxis. I have to check his reaction first," Gabby said.

"What if he's allergic?"

"We're not there yet."

"Bushmaster kill many," Kukua whispered to Chris.

"No reaction. Good," Gabby said. She administered the first dose. "Someone keep track of the time. In ten minutes, we need to administer another."

There was no improvement in Trent's symptoms. He continued to heave, but only a whitish foam came out.

"Should I get an ice pack?" Chris asked.

"No." Gabby shook her head.

Trent began to lose consciousness.

"Trent," Gabby yelled, "you have to stay awake. Trent!" She felt his pulse. "His blood pressure is dropping. Give me the next dose, and ready the third. Set another timer for ten minutes."

"You still have three minutes," Chris said, and handed Gabby the vial.

"I'm pushing it," she replied, then inserted the second vial into the IV.

Trent's eyes fluttered opened. "My stomach. I have to—" he moaned as his bowels emptied.

"Gab, he's dying," Chris whispered.

"No, he's not. These are symptoms of the bite," she said.

Kukua, Bob, and Patrick began to chant over Trent.

"Next vial," Gabby ordered.

"That's three," Chris said.

After the third vial, Trent's blood pressure began to return to normal. Over the next hour, Gabby administered five more vials of antivenom. Trent's symptoms subsided, with the exception of severe pain at the bite site and tissue damage.

Chris helped him to get cleaned up downstream from their camp. He had to be careful to not get any water on the bite, as infections in this naturally bacteria-infested world were a common complication. Gabby was amazed at the tenderness Chris showed toward Trent; earlier today, the man had killed someone.

Trent was a mess. He was completely weak, covered in feces and a foamy mix of bile and spit. Chris gently held him while he washed himself off, then helped him out of the water.

After Chris got Trent settled in his tent, he joined the team at the fire.

"Where's Kukua and the crew?" he asked.

"They went to hunt something for dinner," Gabby said.

"We can't stay here. But I don't think Trent is going to be able to move."

Gabby sighed. "He thinks he'll be ready to go in the morning. But the tissue around the bite has been so damaged, I'm worried that it may need to be surgically removed."

Kukua, Patrick, and Bob returned. They had killed something, but it was too dark for Gabby to see what it was. Kukua also had something else in his hand, which he held up to her.

"Gabby," Kukua said, "this runa nushi. Put on bite . . . tie. Leave on when sleep. Change in morning."

"What is it?" Gabby asked.

"Plant. Trent lucky, us see. Runa nushi not easy to get. No one us know die from bite when have runa nushi," Kukua said.

"Thank you, Kukua," Gabby said, and made her way to Trent's tent.

Again, she heard leaves crackle and twigs snap. Gabby looked around, but no one was there.

Everyone else was gathered around the fire. Gabby quickly unzipped Trent's tent and sealed herself in. She realized that the tent was more of a security blanket than actual security, but regardless, it made her feel better.

Trent was asleep. His leg was still swollen around the bite—the tissue had darkened even more, and the skin around the site had started to blister and peel away. Gabby hesitated, looking at the leaves. They could contain bacteria that would further infect his wound. Yet there were therapeutic properties to the flora in the Amazon that science still understood little about. She knew his wound would not get better without some kind of treatment, so she felt she needed to trust in Kukua's help. Gabby gently placed a few of the dark green, waxy leaves over the bite.

"What are you doing?" Trent moaned.

"Kukua gave me some leaves that he said would heal your bite," she replied.

"Don't put that shit on me," he scolded.

"It's worth a shot. Without this, you will not be able to move for at least two weeks or longer," Gabby insisted.

Trent paused and seemed to consider that fact. "Whatever," he relented.

"How do you feel?" Gabby asked, but he did not reply, having already fallen back to sleep.

She finished wrapping Trent's wound and quickly made her way back to the group. Gabby froze when she got to the fire. Cooking over the open flame was a figure that had been skinned. It had a small head, two arms, and two legs. The figure appeared to be the size of a small child.

"Gabs," Chris said, "it's okay. I know it looks bad, but we have to eat."

"I . . . I don't know." Gabby started to gag and looked away.

"Good eat. You like," Patrick said as he turned the figure over the flame.

"Us thank forest for monkey us eat," Kukua said. "It blessing."

Gabby couldn't watch the monkey cook, but Chris was right—they had to eat. When the food was ready, he brought her some meat. It was dark and greasy, with a mild gamey flavor. The texture was a bit stringy, but otherwise tender. It didn't taste terrible, much better than Gabby expected, and she was hungry. As long as she didn't think about what she was eating, this campfire meal was good. The solid dose of protein was much needed. MREs, protein bars, and guava could only go so far. They all slept well that night.

The next day, Trent's leg was much better. The swelling was gone, but he still could not bear weight. A very small amount of necrotic tissue remained around the bite marks, but it had not spread since Gabby placed the leaves over his wound. To speed the healing, Gabby had to remove this tissue. The risk of infection was high, but since Trent wouldn't need stitches it was worth the risk.

There was a bit of dark, dry leathery tissue that was easy to remove. It was the layer of green, slimy, stringy tissue that proved to be more difficult. Gabby had to gently slice away each string of dead flesh within a fraction of the living side. She had to be careful not to draw blood. This was a slow and tedious process, although she found that practicing medicine again was a welcome break from the monotony of jungle life.

"Ouch. Fuck. That hurts," Trent snapped.

"Sorry," Gabby said, and sprayed a little more lidocaine on the wound. "How do you feel overall?"

"How do you think I feel?" Trent snapped. "My leg fucking hurts."

"What about your stomach?"

"Fine, I'm hungry."

"Do you have any tingling in your arms, fingers, toes? Anything like that?"

"No."

"What about headaches?"

"No, I'm fine, just hungry and thirsty. Will you get me something to eat and the computer, and ask Chris to bring me the decryption drive?"

"When I'm finished cleaning and dressing your wound."

"It's up to you to make me better by tomorrow. We can't stay here."

Gabby doused Trent's wound with a strong antibiotic and antiseptic, then covered it with the remaining leaves and wrapped it again.

"What is it with these fucking leaves? Don't put them on," Trent ordered.

"They're helping. In one night, your bite healed more than what is commonly expected to take two weeks. At least according to the manual in my med kit."

"I think it was the doctor." Trent smiled.

Gabby grinned back and finished wrapping his leg, then started to leave the tent.

"Wait, help me get out of here. It's too fucking hot. I can't sit in here all day," Trent said.

She helped him out and left him to sit on the log. Gabby was glad he was feeling good enough to be grouchy. The night before, she had read up on bushmaster bites and realized how close to death Trent had been. Although they were rare, victims that were lucky enough to survive usually ended up with amputated limbs and months of recovery.

PART 3

"Seeking to populate this otherwise sterile universe with living creatures, God chose the elegant mechanism of evolution to create microbes, plants, and animals of all sorts."

—FRANCIS COLLINS

The Language of God, 2006

CHAPTER 25

The Torrent

THE DAY CRAWLED ALONG with a sort of misery Gabby had never thought possible. At least while they were hiking, she had movement to distract her from the utter and relentless torture of the rainforest. Her skin crawled with bug bites and prickled with heat. She was hot, uncomfortable, and bored, a combination that eats away at the psyche with surprising speed.

"Gabby, come. Us look for food," Kukua called.

She jumped at the opportunity to do anything. For the past two hours, Chris and Trent had been consumed with deciphering the code to the computer found with the executed crew.

"Us gather, not know how to say in English . . . castanha," Kukua said.

"Mmm, I don't know," Gabby replied.

"Hard, trees grow but no fruit," Kukua said.

"Coconuts?" Gabby asked.

"No, mmm, little, hard." Kukua mocked a crunching motion with his mouth.

"Nuts?" Gabby asked.

"Sim. Us look on ground, for ball this big," Kukua held out his hand to about the size of a baseball.

As they walked away from camp, Gabby became so much more relaxed. She almost felt normal.

"Kukua, why did you leave your way of life, the jungle?"

"No want to, but home ruin. Land ruin. Take trees. Take food. Us get sick. Many die. Us no have choice," Kukua said.

Even though the man was young, had learned to speak English from SpongeBob SquarePants, and possessed what she saw as a primitive naivety or innocence, she found him wise. Kukua understood the world in completely different terms. Gabby was drawn to that—she respected it and needed it. Kukua opened something in her. She felt wonder again.

Sensing Kukua's sadness, Gabby changed the subject. "So, what are we looking for?"

"Big tree. We look under. Fall from tree and make big boom," he said.

"Can we get hit? Is it dangerous?"

"No, no. Fall already. Now us gather."

"Phew, okay."

"Know man killed by boom. Old man. He ready. Tree do favor."

"Do you miss living in the jungle? It seems really tough."

"Sim. Us lose much. Here, connected to earth, to jungle spirits. Now people give food, but food empty. You understand?" Kukua asked.

"I do, and I'm sorry," Gabby said.

"It not you. Gabby good people. Other bad people want too much. Want control everything."

Gabby nodded her head. Kukua was right.

"Here, us find," he said, and pointed to some large dark balls on the ground.

"Are you sure they're not some type of coconut?" Gabby asked.

"No coconut." Kukua took his machete and chopped the end off of one of these dark brown balls. Gabby immediately recognized what was inside.

"Oh, Brazil nuts! I had no idea that's what their shells look like."

"That what you call." Kukua laughed. "Fill bag. Stay close."

Gabby quickly stuffed her bag and heaved it on her shoulder.

"Us go. First thank Sachamama. Give seed back to tree," Kukua said.

He broke open a few pods and tossed the nuts around the base of the tree. Gabby bowed her head as her Catholic roots had taught her, and they began their walk back.

"Sachamama?" Gabby asked.

"Mae . . . ah." Kukua paused. "Mother spirit. Her no like Trent. Send snake. Us thank her and give seeds to ask her help us."

"She must not like me either then. Remember she sent the fire ants to me?"

Kukua grinned. "No, fire ant for warrior. You warrior."

"I think Sachamama might be a little confused."

Kukua laughed and sheepishly shrugged his shoulders.

"So, how do you know which way to go?" Gabby asked.

"You no remember way?"

"No," Gabby laughed, "it all looks the same."

"What?" Kukua mocked a shocked expression. "No. Every tree different."

"That's amazing," Gabby said.

Kuka suddenly froze, "Hear?" he asked, following a loud call of birds.

"The birds?"

"Piha, it warn. Something happen. Us hurry," Kukua said.

They made it back to camp in about ten minutes. Gabby was winded and hot, but otherwise fine. The birds had grown louder. Howler monkeys now added to the brutish orchestra of animalistic sounds. Trent and Chris were still by the computer. Kukua immediately ran over to Patrick and Bob; they appeared nervous.

"Kukua," Gabby asked, "what's going on?"

"No sure, but it no good." Trent and Chris looked up from the computer as Kukua's voice loudened. "Pack camp," he directed; Bob and Patrick had already begun to pack up.

Chris, Trent, and Gabby just stared at Kukua.

"What's going on?" Chris asked.

Gabby noticed the stream beside them seemed to be flowing a little faster. Suddenly, the rush turned into rapids—the water level had grown by a few feet. Gabby ran to grab her medical bag and her backpack. The stream washed away ten feet of their camp in seconds and continued growing.

"Run!" Kukua yelled.

"Get my equipment," Trent screamed. "Get my equipment!"

Bob, Patrick, and Kukua grabbed the lab equipment and as much of the supplies as they could. The stream overtook their fire and washed away three of their camp tents. Chris grabbed Trent and the computer, and they ran.

CHAPTER 26

Alone

GABBY GRABBED HER MEDICAL PACK and backpack and fled as well, plunging through the wild greenery away from the water. She tried to follow the team, but they disappeared into the leafy foliage and she soon found herself alone. Water still flowed in the distance.

"Hello," Gabby called. "Kukua . . . Chris . . . Trent!"

There was no response. Gabby froze. She felt her heart quicken.

"Chris? Trent!" she yelled.

Nothing. She started walking, but quickly realized that she could be moving farther away. She stopped and turned around, trying to remember which direction she came from. Having no idea, she began to panic. She heard twigs snap but saw nothing. She wanted to run, but didn't have a clue which way to go. Her heart pounded in her ears. She spun around and around, but was lost.

Another twig snapped and she spun toward the noise. A black jaguar stepped out of the shadows. It stared at Gabby and licked its lips. Hunger glowed behind the animal's cold eyes. There was nothing beautiful, just pure power coiled in its tight muscles. The animal's head was low, with its yellow eyes fixed on Gabby.

She had no idea where she'd put her gun. Gabby knew she couldn't outrun this beast. Gabby took a step back; the jaguar a step forward.

Suddenly, she heard a whoosh and felt something pass over her right shoulder. A dart stuck in the jaguar. It whimpered, spun around, and bounded off.

Gabby slowly turned. A bright red, painted face stared at her. A small, curved bone pierced the man's septum. He had what looked like long whiskers sticking out of his nostrils. His ear lobes were stretched and drooped down. He wore nothing but a loose loin cloth. He just stared at Gabby.

She stared back for a moment, then looked down and bowed her head, diverting her gaze toward the ground. She didn't know what else to do. The man bent down, so that he was in her line of sight. He cocked his head as if confused by her. Then a smile crept across his face.

As Gabby looked up, she saw two more men step out from behind trees. They said something in a language that Gabby had never heard. The painted man touched her face and laughed. He said something that made the others laugh too. Grabbing her face, he turned it from side to side. Then he motioned for Gabby to follow him. At first, she stood frozen. He took her hand and pulled her along. He was small, much smaller than Gabby. He smiled again. With nothing to lose, she followed them.

"Where are we going?" Gabby tried asking, "Adonde Vas?" Nothing. The men just looked at her.

They appeared happy and relaxed. They smiled at Gabby, then spoke to each other.

"I need to find my friends, mis amigos," she pleaded. but nothing. The group just smiled. The man that had saved Gabby from the jaguar grabbed her hand. He walked with her hand in his and continued smiling. The other two men walked behind Gabby and periodically patted her back.

They walked that way for over an hour. Then the trek suddenly became more difficult as they worked their way uphill. The three men watched Gabby closely. They were quick to help her up if she stumbled. They were very kind, but the farther they moved, the more Gabby started to panic. How was she going to find everyone? What if something happened to them? What if she never found them? What if these men were going to kill her? What if, what if, what if.

Gabby was quickly tumbling through a descent of despair. As the endorphins from the near-death experience cleared, she became physically and emotionally depressed. As a doctor, she understood that. As a human being, she was sad. Although she refused to cry, a few tears leaked down her cheeks.

The men wiped her tears in the most tender way. It was so gentle that it made Gabby feel guilty. The purity and kindness in these men was so sincere. She felt guilty that she had never been this innocent, this willing to help a stranger, this unafraid of the unknown, not even as a child.

Finally, pure exhaustion overtook Gabby and she sat down. She couldn't walk anymore. Her tears had dried. She was drained. One of the men sat down next to her. Only his eyes were painted red, and he had a design of black markings around his mouth. He had large, dark brown eyes, which seemed to smile at Gabby. Pulling out a couple leaves, he rolled a few up, chewed the roll a little, and showed Gabby how he stuffed it in the side of his cheek. Then he handed Gabby one and motioned for her to do the same.

She did. He motioned for her to suck on the leaves. Soon her whole mouth became numb and she started to feel better. Her energy returned and the utter despair lifted. She saw the beauty of humanity in these souls and through them she found hope—or at least whatever she stuck in her mouth made her feel that way. She smiled and they smiled back even bigger. She stood and started to grab her packs, but the men took them and insisted on carrying them for her.

The pace easily picked up. Gabby felt a need to move. The birds seemed to call in harmony and tree frogs chirped in rhythm. The guys with Gabby just kept smiling at her, and she smiled back. She had no idea what was going to happen, but at this moment, she didn't care.

Suddenly, the jungle opened into a small clearing. There were thatched huts covered in layers of brown palm leaves. Kids came running out first. They swarmed Gabby. Some had red paint on their faces, others had black designs that swirled around their lips and jaw, while some had unpainted faces but bright headbands. None of the children were clothed. They touched Gabby's clothes and laughed.

"Gabs," called Chris as he stepped out of one of the huts, "they found you. Thank God."

Then Kukua followed. "Gabby," he said, "us so happy they get you."

Kukua walked over to the guys who found Gabby. He spoke to them in another language, but slowly. Gabby could tell that they didn't speak exactly the same tongue, but were able to understand each other in bits and pieces. Kukua appeared to be praising her rescuers.

"What happened?" Gabby yelled to Chris through the throngs of kids. "Where's Trent and the others?"

"Everyone is here," Chris said. "When the flood came, we thought you were with us, but then we couldn't find you anywhere. It was crazy, like you just disappeared."

"How did you get here?" Gabby asked.

"When we were yelling your name and looking for you, they found us. Kukua saw them first and made contact. They were hunting. A few of them brought us here, while the others went to look for you." Chris reached Gabby and grabbed her hand, pulling her through the crowd. "Come in here, I'll fill you in."

Gabby followed Chris into the hut. Her things had already been brought in. It was cool inside, and it felt good.

"Listen," Chris said, "we were able to get into the computer. There is definitely another team after us. Paulo was telling the truth—it is headed by Interfaith for Peace. They must have some powerful backing. They also had some very detailed information on us," Chris said.

"Why? Are they trying to steal Trent's work?" Gabby asked.

"Yes, but the operatives here didn't seem to know

that. From what was in the computer, they think they are on some sort of ethical mission. It's a little confusing; we really didn't learn that much," Chris said. "They appear to be religious fundamentalists and terrorists."

"What's that mean? Are they still after us?"

"There's no way to know. I'm sure they will try to send more people in, but it's hard, so we should be ok for now. Trent wants to run the DNA of these natives as soon as possible, then figure out what to do."

"So, we're staying here for a while?" Gabby asked.

"Probably a few days. Trent is setting up his lab in another hut."

"Who are the people that saved us?"

"Kukua said that they're jaguar people. He said that they're very mysterious and that other groups don't know much about them, because most of the indigenous peoples avoid this area of the jungle. They think it's inhabited by bad spirits," Chris said.

"Chris, Gabby," Kukua announced from the entrance to the hut, "mmm, need talk."

"Of course, Kukua, come on in. What's up?" Chris asked.

"Chief Ëpë, this his village, say, to stay, must do ayahuasca tonight," he said.

"What's that?" Gabby asked.

"It drink, shaman make. Hard to say to you, mmm, open you to see other world," Kukua said.

Chris explained, "It's a hallucinogenic drink that's used in a ceremony here. It's said to pierce the veil between the physical world and the spirit world. Let you delve deep into your psyche, heal you. Tourists were into it a few years back."

"Wait, what? I don't want to take a hallucinogen. I've seen a few people in the emergency room that used them and became mentally ill, permanently," Gabby said.

"Chief say must see spirit if Chief let you stay," Kukua said.

"Gabs, it's not like eating ten tabs of acid. You'll be fine, it's mild. Some people don't even hallucinate," Chris said.

"Do we have a choice?"

"No." Kukua shook his head.

Chris asked him, "Did you tell Trent?"

"Sim, say fine," Kukua said.

CHAPTER 27

Ayahuasca

THE NIGHT CAME QUICKLY. Gabby, Chris, Trent, Kukua, Patrick, and Bob were taken to a large, circular, thatched hut. The sides of the space were open, framed with rough timber, and a heavy palm branch roof covered the patio space. Small torches softly lit the gathering.

The chief sat on a platform across from the entrance. He wore a bright headband with a plume of tan and white feathers. His eyes were painted red, his ear lobes so stretched out that they grazed his shoulders. He had several whiskers that stuck at least six inches out of his nostrils. The shaman stood next to him. The shaman's eyes were shaded black and he wore the head and skin of a jaguar over his own head and body.

"I don't want to do this," Gabby said.

"You can," Kukua said. "Us do many times. You okay."

Mats of soft woven vines had been laid out in front of the chief and shaman. For a minute, they just stared at one another. Then they said something, pointing at Gabby. They spoke to Kukua and gestured toward her again.

Kukua looked at Gabby. "Chief say you chosen by were-jaguar," he said.

"What?" Gabby asked.

"Warriors tracking were-jaguar when find us. Say jaguar brought to you."

"They did save me from a jaguar," Gabby agreed.

"What?" Chris asked.

"A jaguar was about to attack me, and they saved me."

"No jaguar, were-jaguar," Kukua said.

She squinted. "What's a were-jaguar?"

"Some elder become jaguar when he die," Kukua explained.

"Enough," Trent said. "Gabrielle, I'm so glad you're okay, but we need to get on with this."

Kukua said something to the chief. The shaman

walked to each of them, chanting and touching each of their heads. Then he carried around a bowl made out of carved wood filled with a brown liquid. He scooped out a cup of liquid with a coconut shell and worked his way down the line.

The liquid was thick, almost starchy. It tasted awful. It was bitter and left an aftertaste of rotting wood and dirt. For a minute, Gabby thought she was going to puke, but was able to keep it down.

They all sat there in perfect silence. Kukua, Patrick, and Bob closed their eyes. Trent lay down and looked like he had fallen asleep. Gabby looked around from person to person and noticed the chief just sitting there, watching her. The shaman lit a pipe and walked around the group. He chanted and blew smoke over them.

At least forty minutes had passed, and Gabby started to relax. Maybe she would get lucky and nothing would happen. Then she became even more relaxed, then so relaxed it felt like time had slowed down just so she could sink into a comfortable state. She looked around and still nothing had changed. Then she lifted up her hand and moved it across her face, revealing a fan of ten of her hands or more.

Time had definitely slowed down, or she was able to see things at such a fast speed that it appeared slow. Either way, Gabby was happy to take it in.

In this moment, she realized that it was starting, but she didn't feel scared. She felt almost giddy. It seemed like the veil of time had been peeled back for her to get a better look, and she laughed. Gabby felt more aware than she had ever been.

When she looked at the chief, he began to change— he was no longer human. His eyes grew big and round, the headband of feathers that he wore grew to cover his whole body, his nose curved into a small beak, and he became an owl. Still this didn't scare Gabby—she felt like she could see how connected humans were to the natural world around them.

She looked at Chris but saw a big bear. She knew it was Chris; the bear had his big, kind brown eyes. He slowly looked at Gabby and smiled. As his lips pulled back from his snout, she could see a mouth full of fierce teeth.

Gabby smiled back, amused by all of this. She looked at Kukua; he flashed a playful smile, then howled at the moon. As he threw back his head to howl, his mouth lengthened and his hair grew to cover his body, turning Kukua into a wolf.

When Gabby looked at Trent, he sat with his head bowed. He was perfectly still and covered in shadows. He looked up at Gabby with piercing yellow eyes. The shadows closed in on Trent, turning him into a cobra. The glossy black scales shone on the massive snake. He bowed his head toward Gabby and she smiled back.

Soon the shaman stalked toward her and sat in front of her. He had become a jaguar, and he blew smoke on her as she heard the words in her head: *Soul to soul, spirit to spirit.* The shaman motioned for Gabby to follow a path outside of the gathering. As Gabby looked toward the path, it became illuminated.

She stood, her head and upper body feeling like she was floating, but her legs felt completely grounded in the earth. Gabby walked away from the group, following the glowing path. It took her to a large tree that glowed with radiant veins, stretching from the roots to the highest branches. She knew she was waiting for someone, but didn't know who. She felt a breeze brush her face, and then her mother and father walked out from behind the tree.

"Sweetheart, we are so proud of you," her dad said.

"Dad, Mom?" Gabby was stunned.

Her dad looked so handsome and young. He was strong and muscular, dressed in his favorite jeans and Quiksilver tee. His eyes were bright, the bags from years of working long days vanished. His smile, though, was unchanged. His full grin, and the happiness behind it, was Gabby's favorite memory of her father.

Her mom was young too. Gabby was struck by just how beautiful she was. Her thick, dark, wavy hair flowed as it had before her mental breakdown caused her to chop it off. She wore a sinuous floral dress. Her arms were open, waiting for Gabby to run into them as she had so many times when she was a kid.

"Yes, my love," her mom replied.

"It's been so long. I miss you so much," Gabby cried.

"Yes, but we are always with you," her mom said.

"At first it was hard to get used to this omnipresence, but we haven't left your side," her dad said.

"Your grandparents have done such a wonderful

job, and you've become such an incredible person," Gabby's mom added.

"But sweetheart, listen, we don't have much time. Don't let her bite the apple. When Eve bit the apple, it wasn't knowledge that she sought, but control."

"What?" Gabby asked.

Her mom shook her head. "We were created with free will, not meant to be controlled."

"I don't understand," Gabby cried.

Her dad explained. "Control is an illusion. We can't seek to control."

"What do you mean?" she pleaded.

Her mother took a step forward. "My love, the greatest gift in life is allowing free will to guide you toward the path of love. That path is what we were created for. Not to control through fear, science, or commandments."

"I don't understand," Gabby cried. "I don't understand. What are you telling me?"

"You will . . ." Her dad's voice trailed off.

Mom's voice also began to turn faint as she spoke. "Sweetheart, don't let her bite the apple. You have to stop this."

Out of the earth crawled a creature made of

black, knotted vines with red fiery eyes. Claws made of crooked tendrils began pulling at Gabby.

"Dad," she pleaded, "Mom, help me, please, help me." She cried, but they just bowed their heads. They looked at her with concerned eyes, and then her mom blew her a kiss.

Darkness engulfed Gabby and the demonic vines pulled her down. She screamed and screamed, then called out, "Chris!"

"Gabs, I'm right here. Open your eyes. You're safe. You're fine. I'm here," he said as he hugged her.

Gabby opened her eyes. Time had returned to a normal speed. Everyone was around her. The shaman blew one more puff of smoke then did a sort of clearing gesture as he fanned the smoke away from her.

Chris was holding her. Trent was sitting just to her left and Kukua to her right.

"Are you alright?" Trent asked, and grabbed her hand.

"I—I had the weirdest . . ."

"We all did," Chris said.

Gabby sat up and looked around. The sun was starting to come up. She was on a mat near the back of the patio space. Patrick and Bob were helping the shaman clean out the space. Gabby stood up. She felt okay—exhausted, but okay.

"What now?" she asked.

"Kukua is going to talk to the chief; we are staying for the time being. I would like to do some testing as soon as possible," Trent said.

"I need a nap first," said Chris.

"Yeah, that's fine," Trent replied, "Gabrielle, I'm going to need your help collecting samples this afternoon."

"Okay," Gabby said, noticing again just how striking Trent's golden eyes were. "What did you see last night?" she asked.

Trent paused as if trying to recall. "I don't think I can explain it. At first, I could look at you guys and read your genetic coding. Then something was after me. It was a strange trip, but nothing more. Don't put too much stock into what you think you saw," he cautioned.

"What about you?" Gabby asked Chris.

"I *think* I saw angels. I don't know. I was raised very Catholic; it was weird. It was like I was watching a movie. Then there was a war, but . . . I don't know. I can't explain it," Chris said.

He stood up and rolled up his mat, and so did Trent. Neither asked Gabby what she saw. They both seemed a little shaken by the experience. She could understand that; she felt that way herself. Gabby grabbed her mat.

They made their way back to their huts. The temperature here was very comfortable, especially inside the rough shelters. Gabby found a hammock, lay down, and was out instantly.

CHAPTER 28

Testing and Samples

"GABRIELLE," TRENT CALLED, "wake up. Gabrielle, come on."

"What time is it?" she asked.

"It's almost one," he said as Chris let out a snort and rolled over in his hammock.

"I need Tylenol," Gabby croaked—her head was pounding.

"Here, I came prepared." Trent handed her two tablets and some water.

She forced her legs over the side of the hammock. The room was spinning.

"Is there anywhere we can get a cup of coffee around here?" Gabby asked with a pained smile.

"Kukua is getting us some, but we need to hurry

up. I want to get a few samples processing today," Trent said.

He was like a different person, excited and happy. Gabby stood and stretched, feeling like she had been run over by a truck. She put on her boots and prayed that the Tylenol would kick in soon.

They found Kukua by a round, communal firepit just outside of their huts. He had made a pot of coffee, a tradition he'd quickly come to love after modernizing. He had poured cups for two of the men who had rescued Gabby. When they saw her walk over, they jumped up and their faces beamed with huge smiles. Gabby smiled back and happily took the coffee Kukua passed to her.

"Gabrielle, while I finish setting up the lab, I want you and Kukua to collect at least six samples, though I'd prefer eight. Half female and half male," Trent directed. "As soon as you get the first two samples, bring them to me."

Gabby nodded and Trent retreated to his lab with his cup of coffee.

"So, Kukua—" Gabby began, but was interrupted.

"Gabrielle," yelled Trent, "here's your pack with the test kits." She jogged over to meet him. Her headache was gone. When she returned with the canvas tote, she picked up her coffee. "What was I saying?" she asked Kukua.

"So, Kukua," he repeated.

"What?"

"So, Kukua," he repeated again.

"Oh, right." Gabby laughed and rubbed her head. "So, Kukua, how should we do this?"

"Talk to friends already. Them waiting," Kukua said.

"I didn't know you knew people here. Are you from around here?"

"No."

"How do you know people here, then?"

"Us here. Talk to friends." Kukua looked at Gabby, puzzled.

"Oh, *new* friends?"

"You okay?" Kukua asked. "Here, eat." He handed her a couple passion fruits and a knife to cut them with.

"Thanks." Gabby smiled.

They finished their fruit and coffee, and Kukua brought Gabby to their first stop, a large hut on the outskirts of the settlement. It was near a small field with rows of small, green, leafy shrubs. There were a few women tending to the field, but the area was otherwise empty and quiet.

Inside the hut, there were generations gathered and just lounging. The youngest hopped between the laps of the oldest. They warmly greeted Kukua and Gabby. A young man and woman stepped up to meet them. Kukua said something that Gabby couldn't understand, and the couple smiled, looking at each other and laughing.

"Gabby these friends, they say they give you spit," Kukua said.

Gabby smiled. She pulled out two kits and handed one to each. As they filled their small test tubes, they couldn't stop laughing at one another. Gabby couldn't help but giggle as well. She labeled the test tubes and then they headed back to give them to Trent.

When she came out of Trent's lab, Kukua had vanished. Gabby waited by the firepit and had another cup of coffee.

"Gabby," Kukua called, "Chief call to me. Him say tomorrow take us to Cloud Village meet king."

"Really? There's another village?" Gabby asked.

"Yes. Chief say they guard Cloud Village and king."

"That's weird, right?"

Kukua nodded. "Sim, not know any village that guard other village with king."

For the rest of the day, the two of them collected more samples.

The villagers seemed to be in awe of Gabby. They stared at her and smiled, gathering in groups to watch her walk by. She chalked it up to her unusual clothes.

That night, a family in the village prepared dinner for the crew. Kukua picked it up and they ate in front of the firepit. Although, it was just Gabby, Kukua, Patrick, and Bob. Chris opted to sleep through dinner, and Trent stayed in the lab to work.

Kukua handed Gabby a coconut bowl filled with a smooth, mild, slightly sweet porridge. She was starving. The creamy porridge was topped with something that tasted like a combination of peanuts and eggs. Gabby figured that it was some sort of unusual fruit or seed, but it was delicious.

"What are we eating? It's amazing," she said, after she had finished most of her bowl and her ravenous hunger was quelled.

"Root, they grow in field," Kukua replied.

"I thought so. Is it cassava?"

"Sim. Not know what you call," he replied.

"Were those crunchy things nuts or seeds or some type of fruit?"

"No," Kukua said, and his eyes widened with a bit of a mischievous grin.

"What?"

"It baby insect," he said.

"What?"

"Mmm, live ground, under rocks, it grow to be insect."

"I just ate grubs, didn't I?"

"It crawl like this . . ." Kukua made a crawling motion with his pointer finger.

"Yep, those are grubs. I'm glad that I was finished eating before I asked." Gabby laughed. "I'm going to bring Trent his. Tell the family thank you, it was delicious."

She could hear the busy hum of machines even before she walked into Trent's lab. Inside, she was momentarily struck. His eyes bulged when he looked up from the microscope. His hair was a mess; she'd never even seen a strand out of place on his head before this. He smiled. Jumping up, he kissed Gabby, picked her up, and spun her around. She barely managed to keep Trent's dinner from spilling.

"You're happy," she said.

"Every sample that I've run so far has had a fully active, *functioning* EVE-0 gene." Trent beamed.

"Wow, that's great!"

"It's better than great. I'm going to save the human race," he said.

"Now what? How do we get out?"

"I will call for our extraction soon."

"Will they pick us up here?"

"Here or somewhere nearby," Trent replied.

"Are you bringing back saliva samples?"

"What?"

"Are you bringing back saliva, or do you need blood? How are you bringing back the active EVE-0 genetic material?" Gabby asked.

"Oh, right. Yeah."

"Should Kukua and I gather more samples?"

"I want to go to the, what is it, the Sky Village—"

"Cloud Village," Gabby corrected.

"Right. We will gather a few samples there tomorrow. I want to identify the best samples to bring back."

"Alright, I will leave you to work. We'll have to be up really early tomorrow," Gabby said.

Trent's focus had already shifted back to his lab, and he didn't notice as Gabby left.

.

CHAPTER 29

The Cloud Village

"RISE AND SHINE, SUNSHINE," Chris called.

It was cool to the point that Gabby wrapped herself in a blanket. She was perfectly comfortable for the first time since coming to Brazil.

"What time is it?"

"0400."

"I'm tired. I didn't sleep twenty-four hours straight like you."

"Somebody's cranky," Chris joked. "Here, I grabbed some coffee."

"I feel like I've been living on coffee," Gabby said as she forced herself to sit up and grab it.

"You're welcome," Chris mocked.

Gabby smiled. "Thank you," she said, and rolled her eyes. "Where's Trent?"

"He's outside, waiting."

"Is everyone ready?"

"Yep, waiting on you."

"Why didn't you wake me up?" Gabby said as she got up.

"I did." Chris smiled. "But relax, we leave in twenty."

"Do I need to pack anything?"

"Just bring your med kit and one change of clothes. Trent has the collection kits."

"Okay, I'll be right out."

"Oh, also, wear pants and bring a sweatshirt."

It was still dark out. Everyone was gathered outside, including the chief and the trio that had found Gabby.

"Gabby," Kukua said, "this Aru, Zeca, Gavião. Find you."

"Yes, they saved me," Gabby said, and hugged the men. They laughed and said something to Kukua, and he laughed as well. She recognized them based on their face painting, though today they all wore rough-sewn, loose pants and shirts. As did Chief Ëpë, though his garments seemed slightly nicer. They were tailored to his body and dyed a deep yellow-gold.

"Are we ready?" Trent asked.

The sun was just starting to peek over the trees, but the jungle remained dark. Gabby couldn't see anything, yet the locals seemed to be able to traverse every root, rock, and stump with their eyes closed. While the jungle was pitch black, it boomed with noise. From high-pitched bird calls to the baritone call of howler monkeys, the jungle hummed in every octave as it woke. Soon, Gabby was able to at least see her feet in front of her, and she was able to fall into a rhythm.

As the sun came up and lit the way, the path only became more difficult. The terrain was steep, and slippery. It was difficult to find solid footing among the thick, loose layer of dirt, leaves, rocks and debris. Gabby's knees quickly became covered in mud. She was exhausted, but the team kept moving and she didn't want to be the one to slow them down.

While her legs ached, she forced herself to continue. *I think I can, I think I can* echoed in her mind and she remembered her dad reading that book to her when she was little.

Finally, they stopped for a short break. Aru gave Gabby a handful of the grubs she'd eaten the night before. In the light, she could clearly see the plump shape of the larvae. She closed her eyes and tossed a couple in. The crunchy shell gave way to a soft-boiled egg consistency. She actually liked the taste— it reminded her a bit of a homemade pork rind.

"Chief say not far," Kukua announced. Although they had been moving and Gabby was tired, there was a definite chill in the air, and she was glad that she had a sweatshirt.

"How much farther?" Trent asked.

"Chief not use time in way you use . . . maybe one or two horas," Kukua said.

The chief said something in his language and stood.

"Chief say next part very hard," Kukua announced. Aru walked over with a long, hand-braided rope. The chief tied it around his waist, then Aru and Zeca wrapped the rope around their waists. Kukua, Patrick, and Bob were next, followed by Trent, Gabby, and Chris. Gavião brought up the back of the line.

The pace picked up immediately, as did the grade.

Their hike soon became a climb. All of a sudden, out of nowhere, the group was wrapped in a thick cloud of fog. So thick that Gabby couldn't see Trent just two feet ahead of her. She couldn't see anything. Grabbing the rope a little tighter, she tried to just put one foot in front of the other.

They climbed like that for the next hour, or so Gabby guessed. As quickly as the fog came on, it cleared. It took a moment for her eyes to adjust. The sudden brightness forced her lids shut. Once her vision adjusted, she was in awe. The scenery was not what she'd expected.

They were in a mountain valley, surrounded on all sides by high peaks. Where there had been jungle, there were now fields of emerald grass, dotted with a rainbow of wildflowers. The valley was surrounded by steep walls of rock that shot up to majestic, snow-covered peaks.

"Where are we?" Gabby wondered in a slight whisper.

"We must've crossed into Peru—this has to be the Andes," Chris said.

"It's beautiful. I wasn't expecting this," Gabby said.

The chief stopped briefly to untie and gather the rope. He said something to Kukua.

"Us here," Kukua announced.

They looked around but didn't see anything.

The chief motioned for them to follow. They traced the valley just a little farther as it became narrow and snaked first east, then west. Then it opened wide and they saw the Cloud Village.

Carved into the side of the mountain was a palace that spilled out to a series of stone buildings. A small wall surrounded the buildings. The palace stood at least six stories tall. Ornate pyramids were carved into the stepped walls.

"Oh my God," Chris said.

They could see people moving through the village paths in brightly colored, heavy-knit sweaters and matching, wide-brim hats. They moved through the village in small groups. Some tended to several gardens spread through the village, while kids played in open fields. Just past the walled village was a turquoise-hued lake. It was mesmerizing. The vastness of the sugar-coated mountains, set against an emerald valley and turquoise lake, was the most beautiful natural setting Gabby had ever seen.

"Chris," Trent asked, "will our extraction team be able to get into here?"

"I haven't been briefed on our extraction plan, but a heli may be able to get up here, or we'll hike back down," he replied, looking at the mountains and the fields as he assessed the situation.

It took them another ten minutes to get to the gate into the village. Though the wall was low and easy to hop over, there was a large archway that stretched at least twenty feet high, with double doors made of a heavy carved wood. Its deep hue suggested a mahogany. There were twenty one-by-one-foot squares carved into the doors with elaborate scenes on each. Some seemed to depict battles, while others featured flowers and trees. It was beautiful.

At the threshold, the chief simply pushed the doors open. They were not locked or latched. No one was guarding the entrance or waiting to greet them. Inside was even more spectacular. The gardens were filled with many different types of plants, flowers, and trees. Orange trees grew next to azalea bushes, apple trees next to grape vines and honeysuckle bushes. Lemon trees stood near almond trees, with orchids growing at their base. It didn't seem real.

Chief Ëpë led them in and along a winding, shaded path. Gabby noticed that Aru, Zeca, and Gavião had left the group. As people walked by, they greeted the Chief with warm familiarity.

The people of this village looked different than Gabby had thought they would. There seemed to be several different nationalities inhabiting the small area. There were black, white, and brown inhabitants with a combination of blond, brown, and red hair, along with blue, green, and brown eyes. There was not a single unifying characteristic that would indicate an indigenous group. Gabby also started to notice that each person who passed was strikingly attractive, regardless of age.

"Wow," Trent said, "they're perfect."

"Yeah," Chris said, "it's kind of freaking me out."

"Why are there different nationalities here?" Gabby asked.

Trent suggested, "My guess would be that this was some sort of trading post in the past and was somehow forgotten."

"That doesn't make sense—with such a small population group, those defining characteristics would have blended together throughout the generations," Gabby argued.

Trent shrugged. "Not necessarily. Maybe they have some sort of division in place that prohibits interracial mixing."

"I don't know," Gabby said.

"Exactly," Trent said, "we don't know anything about them. Besides, if there was any inbreeding, we would see physical clues and abnormalities. The people here are perfect." He stared at a dark-haired, olive-skinned girl walking by who looked like she may have just stepped off of an Italian film set. She smiled at them but didn't seem affected by their presence there at all.

As they approached the palace, they walked up a flight of perfectly carved stone steps. The palace was perfect. Each angle lined up. Every line was flawless. Although it was man-made, it fit seamlessly into the cliff and mountain it was carved from.

As they approached, the door swung open.

Chapter 30

King Adão and Queen Hawa

THE CHIEF WALKED THEM to the door, but didn't go in. After they entered, he closed it behind them. Inside was an arcade of vaulted arches that led to an open courtyard. There were seats made of mahogany set about the courtyard. While it seemed impossible, a layer of thick, soft, jade-colored grass coated the courtyard floor

In the middle was a large, weeping willow tree with vines of bright pink climbing rose clinging to its trunk. Magenta Mandevilla vines wrapped each column surrounding the courtyard.

Gabby was so in awe of this palace that she didn't notice anyone else join the group.

"Please, sit. Make yourselves comfortable. Can I

get you anything?" Gabby spun to see a woman so beautiful that words failed to capture her exquisiteness. Her long black hair, worn in a loose braid over one shoulder, fell to her waist. A thick gold band rested on the crown of her head. She had big, round brown eyes lined with thick black lashes, and high cheekbones accompanied by a strong jaw and full, pink lips. Her skin was radiant though she had no makeup. She wore a long, white dress and natural wool sweater loose over her lithe, elegant frame.

"Are you thirsty? Would you like water? Something to eat, perhaps?" she continued as the group just stared at her.

"No, thank you. We're fine," Trent said as he moved closer to her. "I'm Dr. Trent Martins."

"Yes, I know. We've been expecting you. I'm Queen Hawa, though the 'queen' is mostly a formality."

"Isn't Hawa an Arabic name?"

"Indeed, it is." Hawa smiled.

"Are you Islamic?" Gabby asked.

"We don't practice religion in the way that you have come to understand it."

"How do you know how to speak English so well?" Chris blurted out.

"We speak many languages here." Hawa smiled.

"What is this place?" Gabby asked, no longer able to contain her wonder.

Hawa looked at Gabby and smiled. "We will get to that, I promise. But first, can you tell me why you're here?" She motioned for the group to sit.

"Why didn't you tell me our guests had arrived?" boomed a voice from the darkened arcade.

Hawa smiled and moved to join the man as he stepped into the courtyard. He was as beautiful as Hawa. His thick black hair formed neat, glossy waves. His cheekbones and jaw looked like Michelangelo himself may have chiseled them. His tan skin sat in contrast to his icy, blue eyes. A tall, muscular frame shone through the gauzy white shirt and pants he wore.

"I couldn't find you, my love," Hawa said as she took the man's hand and led him to their guests. "Please allow me to introduce King Adão."

Kukua jumped up and bowed, while the rest of the group followed suit.

"No, no, please sit. We don't follow those traditions here. We're very informal," Adão said.

"I was just asking them why they were here," Hawa said, looking at Adão, "and what we can do for them." She said directing her attention back toward the group.

Trent stepped forward. "Much of the human race is on the brink of extinction," he began, and went on to explain how they ended up at the Cloud Village. He included every scientific detail, which, to Gabby's surprise, Hawa and Adão seemed to easily grasp.

"And what do you think caused the EVE-0 gene to deactivate?" Adão asked.

"We're not entirely sure, but most likely a combination of the over-use of antibiotics and aggressive vaccinations, and there may have even been a viral component," Trent said.

"How are you testing for an active evolution gene?" Hawa asked.

Trent reached into his bag. He pulled out a test collection kit and showed it to them. "It's easy. I just get a collection of saliva in these prepared test tubes."

As he held up the test kit, Gabby looked at the label: *APP-L3*. It hit her all at once—she couldn't believe that she didn't see it before. *APP-L3. Apple.* She remembered the words clearly: *Don't let her bite the apple*. She felt as though she had just been hit in the stomach. Was this what she was meant to stop? This, that she almost died to find?

"Then, what do you do with the saliva?" Hawa asked.

Trent pulled out the small, portable processing machine that he brought with him.

"I run it through this machine and get the answer in a couple hours," he replied.

"Don't let her bite the apple," Gabby mumbled.

Trent looked at her. "What?" he asked. She looked at him.

"Gabrielle, do you feel okay?" Hawa asked.

"Yes, I'm sorry. I—I just need some water," Gabby replied.

"Why don't we take a break? I prepared lunch for us," Hawa said.

Gabby caught a glimpse of anger from Trent as he turned his attention from her to Hawa. He smiled and said, "Yes, that would be wonderful. We had a very difficult hike this morning."

"Perfect timing," said Adão. "I'm starving."

"Me too," smiled Chris.

"Lovely, follow me," Hawa said.

They followed the queen out of the courtyard and down a hallway, which quickly turned into a cave. Although Gabby couldn't see a light source, somehow the cave was illuminated. Hawa and Adão made a sharp turn into another cave. They walked a little farther till the cave widened into a huge cavern.

There was an intricately carved balustrade where the cavern opened up to overlook the village. A long wooden table was piled with fresh fruit, yogurt, cheese, nuts, dried fruit, hardboiled eggs, and bread. It was a feast. The table looked like it had been plucked from a Napa Valley winery advertisement.

"Please, make yourselves comfortable," Hawa said, as she took her seat next to Adão.

Trent positioned himself right across from Hawa and Adão. Gabby sat between Trent and Chris, while Kukua, Patrick, and Bob spread out around the table. The plates and bowls were brightly colored, hand-painted pottery which looked like fine art set against the natural wood table.

"This tableware is beautiful," Gabby said.

"Thank you," Hawa said.

"Hawa, tell them," Adão beamed. Hawa just

smiled and attempted to brush him off, so he continued, "She made the plates and bowls herself."

"Oh wow, beautiful," Trent feigned.

"They're really beautiful." Gabby smiled at Hawa, but she couldn't help but think how weird this whole situation was. Suddenly, they were at a lunch party, socializing as if they were at home.

"Thank you, but please, eat. You must be starving," Hawa said.

"Yep," Chris said, and immediately began piling food on his plate.

The food was delicious. The apples tasted like apples, the cheese like cheese, the bread like bread, but everything just had more flavor. It was so familiar, yet so delicious it made Gabby feel euphoric. This strange, yet familiar feeling just stoked the unease in the pit of her stomach.

"This is incredible," Trent said. "Thank you so much."

"You're very welcome," Adão said with the slightest tinge of sarcasm. "So, let's get back to how we can help you with that evolution gene of yours?"

"Ah, okay. How much do you know about genetics?" Trent asked.

"We are well versed in all forms of science, though granted, our understanding is different from yours," Adão said.

"We have a strong science collective here," Hawa added. "We have a thorough understanding of genetics."

"Does that include the EVE-0 gene?" Trent asked.

"We do not have an evolution gene in our DNA," Adão inserted.

"You do. If you're human, you do. This gene interprets information from the environment and tells our body how to adapt and evolve. Every living being has it," he said.

"We refer to that portion of our DNA coding as our connection genetics," Hawa said.

"Alright, whatever you call it," Trent said with a slight eye roll, which Adão zeroed in on. "We have been dying at unprecedented rates. If we are not able to reactivate this gene, the modern human race will be extinct within a few years," Trent said.

"No, not extinct. We are doing very well, and so are our friends that brought you here," Adão inserted.

Gabby looked around the table. Chris was staring intently at Adão; his military training had him at the ready. Kukua, Bob, and Patrick had their heads bowed as they sat perfectly still. She looked back to Adão, who was no longer attempting to hide his disdain.

"You can save billions of lives, without leaving your palace. Don't you want to help?" Trent replied.

"Help?" Adão laughed. "Help perpetuate a population that has destroyed itself and much of the planet, so it can ruin us as well?"

"You have absolutely no idea how difficult it is to care for populations of billions of people that live closely, that need to eat, that need to be healthy, that want to have children. It's easy to pretend you're perfect from your tiny world completely isolated from the reality of what it means to be a human being."

"You know nothing about us," Adão snapped.

"Gentlemen, there is no need for hostility," Hawa said.

"As always, you are right," Adão said as peace returned to his tone and expressions. "Unfortunately, I must excuse myself, as I have a great deal of work to return to. My queen, I leave this to your judgement, and please show our guests the utmost hospitality."

"Of course," Hawa said.

Adão got up from the table and began to leave the room.

"Maybe King Adão is right," Gabby spoke up as Adão paused to listen. "Empires collapse. The human race isn't doomed. The Matsés, Adão, Hawa, they can save . . ."

"Gabrielle," Trent snapped. "Yes, they can save us, but let me explain the situation to them."

Adão quietly left the gathering.

"No," Gabby explained, "this may be a time when we let nature run its course."

"That's very hypocritical of you as a doctor that has prescribed antibiotics. But, for the sake of this discussion," Trent seethed, "we can't just cross our fingers and place our hope on a group of people who have chosen to live separated from the rest of the world and modernity. I don't mean to be offensive, but we would lose thousands of years of science, technology, art, and humanity. Please, Gabrielle, just stop talking."

"Trent, come on man," Chris said.

"All opinions are welcome here," Hawa said, and smiled. "Gabrielle, I appreciate your input."

"Yes, I'm sorry." Trent let out a breath. "We are getting ahead of ourselves. We don't even have an understanding of your genetic makeup yet."

"Ah, so you'd like to run my DNA on that machine of yours?" Hawa asked.

"Yes," Trent replied.

"Okay, we will talk more this evening. You must be exhausted, and it is our afternoon meditation. I will show you to your rooms." Hawa stood, then led them to a small, spiral stairwell that climbed to a hall of rooms.

"Take any room you like. They all have bathrooms and they are stocked with plenty of clothes. Help yourselves to anything. We will gather for dinner back in the Great Hall," Hawa said, and vanished back into the spiral stairwell.

Kukua, Patrick, and Bob were like little kids. They went skipping down the hall, darting in and out of the rooms.

"It so nice. Us never stay nowhere so nice." Kukua beamed and disappeared into a room toward the end of the hall.

"Neither have I," Chris said as he headed toward

the closest room. "A bed sounds really nice right about now."

"Gabrielle," Trent said and grabbed her hand, "I'm sorry about that, we are just so close. I know this has been tough on you and you're not thinking clearly. Get some rest. You'll feel better."

Trent pulled her in and gave her a kiss, then took her hand and led her to a room.

"Sleep well." He left Gabby at the threshold. "I'm going to do a little work before I nap, and I don't want to keep—"

"Okay." She quickly closed the door and collapsed on a heavy leather armchair.

She didn't want to be around Trent. A bit of alone time sounded wonderful.

Gabby looked around the room. It was huge. There was a massive four-post bed made of intricately carved dark wood. A plush mattress was piled with pillows and blankets. A light wood armoire, with horses carved into the paneling, appeared completely stocked. Gabby found a cream silk night gown hanging there.

The bathroom was as exquisite as the rest. There was hot running water, working toilets, candles, and lavender-scented soaps. Gabby filled the clawfoot tub and added some dried flower petals. The warm water wrapped around every sore muscle in her body. The dried flowers and candles filled the room with delicate notes of lilac and jasmine.

An uneasiness began to creep into her thoughts. How much stock should she really put into a hallucination based on something her grandfather had said in a dementia fog? This whole situation was so strange, but in this moment, Gabby felt so relaxed. Those dark thoughts quickly faded on the soft scent of flowers. Utterly and completely relaxed, Gabby pulled herself from the warm tub. She collapsed into the impossibly soft bed and fell instantly to sleep.

When Gabby woke from her nap, she found a pair of soft linen pants, a thick cable-knit sweater, and a pair of wool slides. The hallway was empty as she found her way to the Great Hall. She paused just outside the door, where she could hear Trent's voice. From the door, she peeked in without making herself known. She could see that it was just Trent and Hawa—they were sitting on a deep sofa in front of a soft fire just beyond the entrance to the Great Hall.

Gabby stepped back and listened. Their conversation carried easily over the quiet of the castle.

"You can save the entire modern human race," Trent said.

"I want to help you, but I'm part of this place. I'm needed here," Hawa replied.

"Here you help, what, a few hundred people? If you join me, you can save billions. You will, quite literally, be the mother of the modern human. You'll be a goddess."

"A goddess?" Gabby could see Hawa's shadow lean in toward Trent.

"Yes, you will save the world. People will follow you anywhere. They will do anything for you. You will have complete control. People will write about you, say prayers to you for thousands of years. You will be the most important human to have ever lived. You can create a world better than this."

"Will I have a say in how the world moves forward, in policy initiatives, environmental and government terms?"

"Yes, of course. You will be the single most important voice in the world. You have my promise. You will have complete control."

"How are you so certain that it will work?"

"I know it will work. We can even test it here, before you commit to anything. Here—fill this up with your saliva and I will run some tests, then we can go from there."

Gabby looked in and saw Trent pull out a test tube. He held it up for Hawa to see.

"This is it. It's so easy," Trent said.

As he held up the tube, Gabby could see the logo again, and she made up her mind.

"Stop," Gabby yelled from the door. Hawa and Trent turned to see her. "Don't do it."

"Gabrielle, what is wrong with you?" Trent shouted, his voice scathing.

"Wait, why shouldn't I?" Hawa asked.

"It's just not right. I was warned," Gabby pleaded.

"By who? What are you talking about?" Trent said.

"My grandparents and my parents. They told me to not let her bite the apple."

"Your grandparents have dementia, and your parents are dead. I don't think you're well, Gabrielle. You should go back to your room," Trent ordered.

"I can't explain it, I just know it's wrong." The sting of tears began to well up in Gabby's eyes.

"Go back to your room," Trent said through clenched teeth.

"Gabrielle," Hawa interrupted, "I need a more concrete reason. Why shouldn't I save your people? Isn't this what you came here for?"

"I . . . I just know it's wrong."

"I need more than that. I'm sorry Gabrielle, but I want to help you and your people. Trent"—Hawa took the test tube from him—"I just fill this up with saliva?"

Trent nodded his head, while Gabby could no longer hold back her tears. Hawa placed her lips around the test tube. She wanted to scream or say something, but couldn't. When she opened her mouth, no sound came out. The room began to spin and blur. Gabby felt nauseous. Blackness began to close in on her until the room went dark.

CHAPTER 31

The Tree of Knowledge and Control

WHEN GABBY OPENED HER EYES, her head was pounding and the light was blinding. As her vision focused, a thatched roof came into view. The sun cast light shades of pink and orange on the tan ceiling.

Confused, Gabby sat up. She soon realized that she was back in the ayahuasca hut. She could clearly remember every detail from the past the two days, except how she got back to the hut. It appeared she was alone; the village paths were empty. Lying back down, Gabby tried to figure out how she got there.

"You're finally awake," Chris said, startling her.

"How did we get back here?" she asked. Sitting

up she was quickly overcome with nausea. Chris quickly handed her a bowl and she threw up.

"What?"

"From the Cloud Village?"

Chris just looked at her for a moment. "Here." He handed her a water bottle. "Drink some water. You need to get the ayahuasca out of your system."

"What day is it?"

"You're just waking up from the ceremony." Chris was becoming frantic.

"Really? It was so realistic. I can remember every detail. I . . ."

"Okay. Listen. We don't have much time. Everyone is still sleeping. The effects wore off really quickly. When I came out of it, I had this urge to go through Trent's computer files. I asked him for his passwords and he told me, but he was totally out of it. He didn't remember doing it . . . I don't think."

"This is so weird. We've been here? We didn't go to the Cloud Village?" Gabby wondered.

"Gab, there's no Cloud Village. You haven't left this hut. Focus, this is serious. Trent lied to us. He's not collecting genetic material. There is a military crew ready to come in and take twenty villagers."

"What? Take them where?"

"The extraction team has a plane, with sterile holding units. They are basically four-by-four cages that are completely sterile and self-contained. This plane is meant to bring back fifteen females and five males with active EVE-0s, by any means necessary. They just have to be alive."

"Are you sure? Maybe that was part of the aya-huasca too?"

"I'm sure. It barely affected me."

"Where is everyone else?"

"They are in their huts, sleeping. I've been checking on you all night. I wanted to wake you up, but the shaman wouldn't let me."

"How sure are you?"

"I bet my life on it."

"What about your family?"

"They wouldn't want to be saved like this."

"He's coming," Gabby whispered.

Their conversation abruptly halted.

"Were you here all night?" Trent asked.

"Yeah, I just woke up," Gabby said, adding a little extra inflection of grogginess.

"What about you?" Trent asked Chris.

"I got up about twenty minutes ago. Gabby wasn't in her cot, so I came to look for her," Chris answered.

"Did the ayahuasca do anything to you?" Trent asked.

"Yes," Gabby said. "I . . . I—" She paused, trying to find the words to describe her night. "It was very real, and vivid. What about you?"

"Not really. We have a lot to do today. I want to collect samples from as many people in the village as possible. I'd like to have our specimens identified by tomorrow and then get out of here as soon as possible," Trent directed.

"We're leaving soon?" Gabby asked.

"We should be able to, as long as today goes well."

"Wow, really? Are they picking us up here?"

"I'm not exactly sure—we haven't worked out the schematics. Let's just focus on collecting the samples. Get a sample from everyone who appears under thirty-five. Take a picture and log it with their sample."

"A picture? Why?" Chris asked.

"For our specimen records," Trent replied with an incredulous crinkle of his brow. "Split up and bring five samples at a time to me. I want at least fifty to choose from. The collection kits are in my lab." Trent got up and left.

"Trent, wait," Gabby called, following after him. "What are we going back to?"

"We have places reserved for us in the safe house."

"What about my grandparents?"

"I didn't want to upset you, but a virus hit their assisted living facility. They became sick soon after we moved them and both died within hours of each other. I'm sorry. It was fast, relatively painless. Their existence was miserable, anyway."

"But . . ." Gabby stumbled over her thoughts and paused.

"It's better that they died like this. Forgetting how to breathe is a horrible way to die."

"When did they die?"

"I'm not sure—a day or two after I told you that we moved them."

"You should've told me."

"I didn't want you to be distracted."

Tears began to roll down Gabby's cheeks.

"I wish I had known."

"Don't be selfish; they're not suffering anymore.

Pull yourself together. Get some breakfast, then start collecting samples."

Trent left her and disappeared in his lab. With tears stinging her eyes, Gabby saw Chris motion for her to follow him. They took a path that wrapped back into the jungle. When they were a safe distance from the village, out of eye sight, Chris stopped and waited for Gabby to catch up.

"Gabs, I'm sorry about your grandparents. I know how important they were to you."

"Thanks, but Trent's right. They had been sick for a long time, and this world . . ." Gabby's voice trailed off.

"Still, you have the right to be sad and mourn them." Tears filled her eyes and Chris hugged her, just for a moment. Then he pulled back, still holding her arms. "But, listen, what Trent's doing is wrong."

"I know," Gabby said. "I don't know why I know. I can't fully explain it, but I know it's wrong."

"Do you understand the implications, if we are able to stop this?" Chris asked.

"What do you mean?" Gabby asked.

"We will be stuck here indefinitely." He paused. "And people back home might die because of us.

We'll find a way to bring a treatment back eventually, but it could take a while."

"If I tried to explain this to you, you'll think I've lost my mind, but it's—"

Suddenly, they heard a gun cock. They looked up to see Kukua step out from the tree cover.

"Kukua, what the fuck man?"

Patrick and Bob stepped out behind him.

"Us sorry. No want hurt you. Trent take us to good place. Us not hungry no more. Us have good place to sleep. Life hard here. No food, bad people. You no understand."

"No, Kukua," Gabby said, "you don't understand. This is wrong. The world they've created is wrong. They are going to rip families apart. They are going to take people like they're animals."

"That good. Them lucky. You not know. Life too hard here." A look of disgust flashed on Kukua's face. "No more talk." He thrust his gun out and Patrick and Bob surrounded Gabby and Chris. They jabbed their own guns into their backs. The innocence that Gabby admired in Kukua was gone.

"Where gun?" Kukua yelled. Chris slowly moved his arm toward his waist. "No," Kukua said, and fired a warning shot in the air. "No move." He took three steps toward Chris and aimed his gun at his head. "Patrick take gun."

"Okay, be easy Kukua," Chris cautioned.

Patrick kept his gun jabbed into Chris's back, and with his other hand he took the two guns from the gun belt, then tightly tied his hands behind his back.

"Kukua, don't do this," Gabby pleaded while Bob secured her hands behind her back.

"You do what Trent want. Us go to America. Us get good life . . . us be friends there," Kukua answered.

"It's not that simple," Gabby said.

"No talk," Kukua snapped, and jabbed his gun barrel against Gabby's back. He had a firmness in his tone that Gabby hadn't heard before.

Patrick jabbed Chris with his gun to start walking. Gabby followed with Kukua, Patrick, and Bob close behind. They marched back in complete silence as each passing second dragged along. Dread combined with despair, and any hope that Gabby had for the human race was quickly sinking.

The gathering villagers stared with obvious confusion as they passed. Gabby realized she had failed them. These innocent mothers, fathers, sons, and daughters were now nothing more than caged rabbits in AmCorps's lab. She watched a mother clean the remnants of breakfast from her daughter's face, then hug her and send her to play in the dirt with her friends. Completely happy with nothing but a twig and her comrades.

Suddenly, Gabby's heart felt like it flipped in her chest. Then it condensed, filling her with sadness. Whether she had been naïve or just stupid, Gabby realized that the world she knew was already dead—there was no saving it. And, like the dumb little fish, she had happily gobbled down the bait, proud that she was a hero as she swallowed the hook.

Now she mourned the death of her motherland, and began to see Trent as the architect that he was. This made her want nothing more than to stop him. Her pulse quickened as sadness boiled to rage.

Trent was behind a makeshift desk, typing furiously on two different laptops.

"Great, you found them," he commented with a complete lack of emotion.

"What the fuck do you think you're doing?" Chris snapped.

"We're very close to the finish line, Lucien decided

that it's better to have you sit this part out," Trent snapped.

"What are you talking about?" Gabby asked.

"Gabrielle, you're the only person that I've ever loved. I knew that this part of the mission would be hard for you to handle. Once we are back, you will understand why we had to do this."

"Trent, no. This is wrong," she pleaded.

"You'll come around," Trent said with a madness Gabby had never seen before, "when we're back and your head is clear, you'll come to your senses. We're an ideal genetic match; the children we'll have will be perfect. Especially after a few minor improvements, so they will never get sick."

"I'm done, I'm not part of this."

"You're already part of this. You saved my life. You got me here. We have been handed the perfect opportunity—you just can't see it yet. Nature is doing an incredible job of cleaning up the population. When we get through this, there will be no more disease, no more racism or sexism, because now we are able to truly make all races and sexes equal. The human race will be cured of everything that has troubled it."

"What are you talking about?" Chris asked.

"We have identified genetic markers for virtually every disease. We have also isolated genes such as intelligence, emotion, drive, propensity for addiction, athleticism, and several others that we can adapt. We can balance these characteristics—you know, less emotion, higher intelligence—so that equality can actually exist. For the first time ever, all men, and women, will be created equal."

"Fuck you. You're insane. You can't do that," Chris said.

"That's exactly what I'm talking about. You can blame your predisposition, but if you had better control of your emotions, you could have been more practical about your plan to stop this. Instead, you're tied up."

"You're sick. This is illegal—you'll never get away with it."

"We've already started, and we've been supported along the way. In fact, the first round of genetically modified racial embryos were implanted just before we left. This round is experimental, because we still do not have an active EVE-0, but it's very promising."

Trent said, with his shoulders back and head high, clearly proud of his work.

"You're using a disaster to erase humanity. You're trying to turn the human race into photocopied robots in a lab? You're fucking insane," Chris yelled through clenched teeth.

Trent raised an eyebrow and tilted his head back to look down at Chris. "This isn't science fiction, imbecile. We are gently coaxing the better qualities of the human race to bear their gifts on the masses, while negating those characteristics that imprison them in low-quality existence."

"They are imprisoned because of the hand they've been delt by an unjust system," Chris said.

"Oh God," Trent snickered, "tomato, tomahto. Haven't we finally put nature versus nurture to bed? Resiliency is a genetic trait that we have included in the profile of desirable characteristics. Everyone will be equal. This is evolution. Can't you grasp that?"

"Stop," Gabby interrupted, "you're not listening. You can't go through with this. It's wrong."

"How is it wrong? We are saving mankind. We are saving billions of lives and creating equality. Isn't that what the world has been crying for, practically, since the dawn of humanity?" Trent asked with wide eyes and sincere confusion.

"Not like this. Not in a lab, and not by stealing innocent people from their home," Gabby pleaded.

"How do you know that?" Trent asked.

"I saw everything," Chris said. "We know about the extraction team. You're not taking samples. You're taking people."

"How. Do. You. Know. That?" Trent slowly repeated, completely calm.

"It doesn't matter how we know," Gabby insisted, "it's wrong. These are human beings."

"Are you that naïve, or are you just stupid?" Trent spit, his shoulders crouched and his entire demeanor flipping. "Sacrifices have to be made. It's not pretty, but this small handful of people will save the modern world and the countless human beings that will emerge from it better."

"That's not your choice to make," Chris said.

"Oh, but it's your choice to condemn them to death? The millions of people fighting to protect their families. Sacrificing everything just to survive," Trent snapped.

"You're not saving them. You're saving the billion-aires that bought into your safe houses," Gabby said.

"Sweetheart, unfortunately great scientific discoveries are expensive. If you are able to summon some logic, you may be able to understand that by preserving the wealth of the world, the benefits will flow down much quicker than starting from the bottom and clawing our way up."

"Don't talk to her like that," Chris snapped.

Trent flashed him a cold glare of pure hatred, then took a breath to regain his composure. "You're right. I'm sorry," Trent said, "I forget that this is all new to you. I knew that this would take you some time to process. I know this is a hard pill to swallow; it took me a while to accept."

"Rest assured, we already have a team preparing a plan to disseminate the treatment to survivors outside of the safe house as soon as it's ready. And the people we bring with us will be well taken care of. Their lives will be so much better. This is war."

Trent paused, reconsidering his statement. "No, this is worse than war—this is survival. Sacrifices have to be made, but we are doing it in the kindest way possible. We are doing it to create a better world for everyone."

"Not like this. The people here are not your lab rats; they're human beings, and they shouldn't have to pay for our mistakes," Gabby said.

"The entire plan is fundamentally wrong. Where's the line you will draw with your experiments?" Chris snapped.

"Line?" Trent cackled. "This is science. Actually, it's creation. You have to think outside of lines."

"You're not God," Gabby said.

"True, and Gabrielle, you know that I don't believe in God," Trent said with an eyebrow raised, "but this is the closest thing that the world has ever actually had. Nature couldn't have created a better situation. It's literally doing the dirty work and handing us the keys to create a perfect species." A smile slowly crept across his face. "But right now, we have a lot to do. The extraction team will be here in a few hours." Trent looked back at Chris. "You've already lost, but thanks for your help. Couldn't have done it without you." Trent winked at him.

"I won't let you do this," Chris said.

Trent ignored him. "Gabrielle, I still love you. I

know this is difficult to process, but I know your intelligence will see you through. Look, as a woman, you are prone to overly emotional reactions—it's in your genes. You'll come to your senses. Kukua." Trent nodded his head toward the door, then returned his focus to the computer screens in front of him.

"Wait," Trent stopped them, "I was waiting to tell you, but you know that you're likely to develop Alzheimer's. We've finally perfected the cure. You will never have to suffer like your grandparents. It's so simple, an easy edit on one single gene in the brain's nerve cells that will stop the over-production of beta-amyloid. It took us almost ten years to perfect, but we have. I'm going to do it for you as soon as we're back and in the safe house."

"What?" Gabby asked.

Trent nodded and smiled wide-eyed at Gabby. Then he turned his attention back to his computer screen, and Kukua marched them out.

Chapter 32

Exit from Eden

KUKUA MARCHED CHRIS and Gabby back to their hut. He tightly bound their legs and arms with a rough, hand-woven twine. Then he gagged them with a tight cloth tie made out of a cut-up tee. The gag made it hard to swallow.

Gabby began to panic; she felt like she was slowly drowning in her own saliva. She tried to scream, but all that came out was a high-pitched gurgle. Bob stayed back to guard them.

While Gabby's panic continued to rise, Chris remained stoic. He sat still—all that moved were his watchful eyes. In utter terror, Gabby's gaze frantically darted around the dark hut. Bob refused to look directly at them. He kept his eyes low and toward the door. Chris caught her glance. His steady look calmed her. He gave her a slight nod and motioned deep breaths, through his nose. Gabby followed and her mania began to subside.

With her physically bound, her mind began to race, tortured by hindsight. Why hadn't she asked more questions in the meeting? Why didn't she demanded more explanation for Patient 12, the patient in D-Wing that started this for her? How could she have gone into this so stupidly and blindly? How could she have lived with Trent for so long and not known what he was doing?

Is this it? Gabby suddenly had a vision of sterile classrooms of emotionless, unsmiling children. No love, no hate, no feeling, just pure intellect. *Is that the future? This couldn't actually happen, right?* she thought. But, here she sat. Bones aching, tied up on a hard mud-floor hut, while Trent gathered untainted specimens. The threat of unchecked science unleashed on a village that had never experienced running water, toilets, electricity, or even basic clothing loomed heavily.

Gabby tried to moving her hands, squeezing them out of their binds, but the rope was tied too tightly.

Her fingers had gone numb. She could feel the rope cutting into her wrists as she struggled to free them, rubbing a layer of skin off with each twist. Gabby began twisting her entire body, trying to find a more comfortable position. Bob looked over at her, and she caught his eye. His gaze quickly darted away, filled with shame under a concerned brow.

Gabby shuffled her body again. When Bob looked back, she jutted her chin out and crinkled her brow, gesturing for him to take off her gag. He shook his head no, immediately looking at the floor. This time, Gabby shook her body as violently as possible and made a grunting plea.

Finally, Bob got up and made his way toward her. He suddenly stopped—his eyes fluttered, and he stumbled, then collapsed. Gabby looked at Chris, who crinkled his brow and shook his head. He was as stumped as she was. A moment later, the jaguar warrior who had rescued Gabby peeked in, Zeca. He rushed over and began to cut away the ropes that bound and gagged her.

When the gag came off, Gabby took a deep breath and stretched her sore jaw. Soon her hands were free, though her wrists were bloody and raw. She tried massaging her hands, but the pins and needles were too intense. Next, he freed her feet.

Gabby wanted to stand up and stretch her sore body, but her feet were completely numb. She tried to stand, but felt like she was trying to balance on stilts. She collapsed and lay flat on her back. Stretching out her arms and legs, she gently wiggled her fingers and toes. *Shavasana, dead man's pose,* popped into her thoughts with a dark sense of irony. It had been years since she had gone to a yoga class; gyms and fitness studios had been among the first businesses to permanently shutter due to the pandemics.

Once the feeling returned, she sat up. Chris was free, massaging his hands and feet. Zeca covered his mouth to tell them to be quiet. He pointed at Bob and mimed a sleeping position. Then he gestured for them to stand and move toward the door, but not leave.

They stood there, waiting for something. Zeca cocked his head to listen. Soon, they heard a bird's call, and the warrior grabbed Gabby's hand. She flinched in pain. He smiled up at Gabby, loosened his grasp, and gently but quickly guided them out of the hut and to a nearby forest trail.

They wove from path to path, walking quietly in the growing heat. Bugs swarmed the oozing rope burns on Gabby's wrists. She knew that they would be infected soon if she wasn't able to clean and dress the abrasions. The warrior looked back often, urging them along at an exhausting pace.

"What's happening?" Gabby whispered to Chris.

"I don't know," he replied.

The warrior looked back, smiled, and hurried them on.

The mid-day heat began to wear on Gabby. Flashes of the ayahuasca burned through her thoughts. It had seemed so real. She could clearly remember Hawa, Adão, and every detail from their conversations. She could remember how their lunch tasted. Most importantly, she could remember, "Don't let her bite the apple."

It was so strange. Her logic couldn't explain it. Well—unless, Gabby mused, her hallucination was based on what her grandfather had told her the last time she saw him. But what were the chances the DNA collection kits would be marked *APP-L3*? She was filled with so much doubt and exhaustion. Maybe . . . maybe Trent was doing the right thing.

Gabby tripped on a twisted black root that had torn its way through the hard jungle earth, skinning her knees as they broke her fall. Her vision went black. She blinked her eyes and when she opened them, she was back in that classroom. Blank faces sat perfectly still. Hawa was teaching the class. She blinked her eyes again and was back on the jungle trail. Zeca and Chris helped Gabby up. Zeca urged her to continue.

"Are you okay?" Chris asked

"I'm just tired, and I think the ayahuasca is still in my system."

The warrior quickened his pace. Gabby's legs burned, and a stitch began to creep its way into her core. If they didn't stop soon, she might collapse. Finally, they came to the edge of a clearing and the warrior paused.

As he started to step into the clearing, Chris quickly pulled him back.

"We can't go through the clearing. There may be people looking for us," Chris said.

Gabby immediately remembered the intel unit that Trent talked about. The warrior just stared, not understanding.

"People," Gabby said slowly. "In the sky." She pointed up. "Looking." She mimed using binoculars with her hands and searching down. "For us," she said, touching her chest and pointing at Chris.

The warrior cocked his head. He raised one eyebrow and crinkled his forehead. He clearly didn't understand. Then, with his spear, he pointed across the clearing at a massive, umbrella-shaped tree. Chris nodded and gestured walking with his fingers on his hand and pointed at the very edge of the clearing, then gestured a curving motion with his hand.

The warrior somehow understood and took off. They hugged the tree line as they made their way to the other side of the clearing. It was farther than Gabby expected. The long grass brushed her ankles, causing tremors of itchiness too deep to scratch. Her wrists had turned into a full-blown throb, each explosion of pain worse than the prior.

As they approached the tree, it was even bigger than it seemed from across the clearing. The trunk had to be twenty feet around. Gabby felt like a miniature figure from a doll house next to it. She dragged herself the last ten yards and collapsed on a large root that curved out from the trunk.

Zeca bowed in front of the tree, said something in his language, then sat down with Gabby and Chris. He looked at them and just smiled. He seemed to find them amusing. Gabby was so tired, and suddenly so comfortable—there was a soft layer of dry moss in the crook of the root Gabby was sitting in, and her eyes began to flutter shut. She fought to keep them open, but they were just so heavy. She let them rest.

Gabby had a dream she was falling, and jumped. Her eyes shot open just in time to see several more people approaching.

She saw Chief Ëpë and the shaman, with a group of men that she didn't recognize. They were dressed in a mismatch of torn jeans and camouflage shirts, their faces covered with bandanas. Most of the men also donned tribal touches, while others wore military gear. Their heads were crowned with beaded, woven bands, decorated with patterned red and white feathers, similar to the headbands she saw in the village. Just one of the men wore a tactical boonie hat with a patch that had jaguars baring their teeth. Each man had a gun tucked into his jeans.

The shaman walked over to Gabby, opened a pouch he had tied around his hips, and pulled out a few leaves. He wrinkled them in his hands and scratched their surface so that liquid oozed out, then wrapped them around her wrists. The throbbing fires that had steadily grown around her wrists cooled immediately, and the pain dulled to a slight ache.

"Thank you," Gabby said.

The shaman paused for a moment, looking at her, then pulled her forehead to his before leaving and joining the chief.

Chris stood, but he hadn't approached the group yet. Gabby stood next to him. She could see his muscles tighten under his shirt. He was nervous. The group gawked at them, deep in a conversation she couldn't understand.

All at once, the entire group approached in unison. Gabby wanted to back up, but forced herself to stay. The men pulled their bandanas down. They looked to be in their thirties. The softness of their youth had been replaced with a toughness. Though their skin was smooth, an unmistakable sadness lined their faces. The man with the hat stepped forward. He had high round cheeks and a strong jaw accompanying dark eyes. Up close, Gabby saw a rough scar that covered his neck. He touched his chest. "Rodrigo."

In return, Chris touched his own. "Chris." Then he touched Gabby's shoulder and announced her name.

"Speak little English." The man paused. "Family . . ." He paused, then mocked slicing his neck.

"Killed?" Chris asked.

He nodded. "White man kill. Take tree. Take food. Kill." He motioned around the group.

"Everyone?" Gabby asked.

He nodded, but frustration began to cloud his expressions.

"Falo português?" Chris asked.

"Sim," Rodrigo said, every feature on his face lifting.

"Eu entendo mais do que eu falo, mas vá devagar" Chris replied.

Gabby was shocked. She hadn't heard Chris speak Portuguese once the entire time they had been in Brazil.

They talked for what felt like an eternity to her. Each of the five men took turns talking, then translating to the chief, shaman, and warrior.

"Sorry Gabs," Chris finally said as the group paused their conversation and turned to her. "I was trying to keep up."

He explained that Rodrigo and his crew were from a few different nomadic indigenous groups that moved throughout this area. They knew Chief Ëpë and the Jaguar people. His group respected them; Rodrigo would come here and do important ceremonies. When Rodrigo was fourteen, loggers came through his camp and killed almost everyone from his tribe. First, they unleashed dogs that attacked anyone they could. He saw his uncle torn apart. Then they set fires to their camps, burning everything. Anyone that was left after that, they shot.

Rodrigo was initially taken in by FUNAI, before he went back into the forest. He found many others like him, and they formed this makeshift army to protect his people from outsiders. Rodrigo trained at the Brazilian Jungle Warfare School and had built a small army. He said he had almost fifty of his guys coming here to help, and that they'd have weapons.

Gabby looked at the machete hanging from his belt and the old gun handle sticking out of his jean pocket. "Did you tell them about what's going on?"

"My Portuguese isn't good enough to explain the genetic component, but I told them about the extraction team coming to take some people."

"Did you tell them who they're up against?"

"I did."

"How do they possibly stand a chance against the most elite soldiers, with state-of-the-art weapons and no rules?"

"I think it's our only option. They've already located the extraction team's runway. They said there are about twenty people. At first, they thought loggers were back after not seeing any for almost a year. But AmCorps must've taken over a deserted site."

Gabby looked up. The entire group was watching her, apprehension filling their wide-eyed stares. "The extraction team is already here?"

Chris nodded. "This is our only option."

Gabby looked at him, then back at the group. She nodded her head yes, and a wave of relief washed through the gathering.

CHAPTER 33

Evol

"TRENT, IT'S GREAT TO BE ABLE to speak with you again," Lucien said over a secured and encrypted digital signal from his new apartment in the AmCorps Labs safe house headquarters. It was an exact copy of his apartment from AmCorps. The main difference was that the lab here was much larger and had units for EVE-0 active specimens.

Just like in Lucien's old apartment, there was a large, wall-sized window that looked out over the lab. However, the facilities here were ten times as large. The lab space was the size of three football fields laid next to each other. Thick plexiglass dividers sectioned off certain areas, and steel ventilation units and duct work ran across the exterior.

Much of the space was dark. There were a few techs moving throughout the lab, but it was otherwise quiet.

"Yes, agreed. How are things going in the safe houses?"

"Exactly as planned, just ahead of schedule."

"Perfect. Where is the extraction team?"

"Unit 1 is building a runway near the village you're at to bring the jets in. They will be ready in seven hours. Unit 2 is set to take off at 0100. Have you identified our targets?"

"I've found and marked three ideal genetic specimens, and identified four more that are getting marked as we speak. I'm running five samples, so I will have those results very soon. I have ten samples waiting and a team currently collecting more."

"Will you be ready for tonight?"

"Definitely. Seven out of the ten samples I ran this morning were ideal matches."

"Great. What about your team? You still have a guard on them, right?"

"Yes, of course."

"Do you want the extraction team to bring them or dispose of them?"

"Bring them. They will come around."

"Okay. Well, that's it for now. Keep this line available. I will check in again when Unit 2 is three hours out. Be near your computer at 1600."

Lucien would feel better as soon as the specimens were here. Right now, he wasn't in complete control of the situation, and that put him on edge. The bright note was that the genetically modified embryos had all taken and were developing extraordinarily well. The pregnant women were housed in apartment units just below the lab, with an attached obstetrics department.

All important politicians, artists, and intellectuals had cleared quarantine and were now placed in the safe houses. The final investors were in the quarantine process, and would be moving into the safe houses in the next couple weeks.

However, until Trent and the specimens were here, the survival and evolution of the human species was not secured. Standing on the precipice of such groundbreaking work was much more difficult than Lucien had anticipated. Until this point, only nature (or God, if that was what you believed) had managed to control the development of the human species. Lucien would be forever known as the father of the modern human, creating a perfect species. But, right now, he was stuck, waiting, and things were completely out of his control.

Lucien's phone rang.

"Yes," he answered.

"Where do we stand on the treatment?" General Holton asked.

"The specimens should be here within forty-eight hours."

"If we don't get a treatment soon, there will be no survivors left to treat."

"That's not necessarily such a bad thing."

"We need survivors to know that their government saved them."

"Everyone will know that the United States saved the world, don't worry."

"No, I am worried. We need outside witnesses to document their salvation. There will be other groups that survive, and we need them to witness Americans from all backgrounds getting saved as we share our treatment around the globe."

"You mean low-income."

"Yes. We don't need a ton of them, but we definitely need a few pockets."

"We are moving as quickly as possible."

"Move faster. The president is getting impatient."

Lucien hung up the phone. Politics infuriated him. Politicians were the scum of the earth, as far as he was concerned. They could care less about actually saving anyone; they just wanted to be perceived as the heroes. Helping out the poor on camera, while executing them behind the scenes. Everything had an ulterior motive.

Survival of the fittest was the only theory that actually made sense from a sociological perspective. If people didn't want to work to improve their condition, others shouldn't have to bear their burden. Let them kill each other, let them die of disease. Let the stronger of the species rise to the top. That was simply a fact of life, true to virtually every species that had a somewhat-developed brain. Why stupid people wanted to deny this fact confounded Lucien. However, this was precisely why AmCorps, only now, had the opportunity to equalize the race.

Lucien clicked open a hidden screen on his computer. The computer camera did a retinal scan, then he entered a PIN. The screen showed a grid map named *Vale do Javari*. The map was green, spliced with blue veins.

He zoomed in on an area between two thick blue veins, and three flashing dots appeared. He watched them move around the small area. A fourth dot appeared, then a fifth. Each pulsing speck on the computer screen was a step closer to making history. Each glow sent an electric pulse of adrenaline down his spine to his groin, where it buzzed. He began to unzip his pants, aroused by his own greatness, when the secure digital line on his computer rang.

Irritated, Lucien quickly zipped his pants and answered. Trent's face flickered on the screen.

"We have an issue," the man said as he wrung his hands over the keyboard.

Lucien took a breath, the buzzing of excitement suddenly condensing to stone. "What?"

"Chris and Gabrielle are missing."

"What?" Lucien said again, shaking his head with obvious disgust.

Letting out a defeated breath, Trent explained, "I had them detained ahead of the extraction process in order to prevent any potential issues."

"You told me that," Lucien snapped.

"They were being guarded. He doesn't know what happened. Another one of my guys found him, knocked out with a dart in his neck, when they were switching shifts. Gabrielle and Chris were gone."

"Did someone help them escape?"

"I don't know. I can't imagine that's possible. No one in this village speaks English, or any modern language."

"What about your guys?"

"No, definitely not. They're very upset; they want to get out of this hell hole as bad as I do."

"I need you to do better than that, if you want me to come up with some sort of solution."

"Chris is extremely industrious—he must've gotten them out. That's the only thing that makes sense."

"So, you think it's only two rogue agents that we have to contend with?"

"Most likely."

"What the fuck does that mean?"

"I have no way to be 100% certain, but it's highly unlikely that they've had any help."

"I'm alerting the extraction team. I'm having Unit

1 lock down the village. No one comes in or out. I'm also directing them to terminate the rogue agents."

"No, not Gabrielle."

Stunned, Lucien's head swung back. "Do you understand how important this is? We will be the first human beings in history to have played a role in the creation and salvation of homo sapiens."

"I know, but I . . . I—" Trent paused, unable to continue. He put his head down.

"Gabrielle will come around, Chris may even have her captive."

"Don't screw this up. Get the specimens marked. Now. I'm alerting the extraction team and deploying Unit 2 ahead of schedule." Lucien clicked off.

CHAPTER 34

Guerilla

"WE HAVE TO TRY TO CAPTURE Trent and the crew first. Once the full extraction team is here, it's too late," Chris said, pausing to translate into Portuguese.

"What are you going to do to Trent? You're not going to hurt him, are you?" Gabby asked.

"Gab, I can't promise anything. He's going to realize that we're missing any minute and call in backup. We have to move quickly."

Chris spoke more to the group in Portuguese. They nodded and the warrior, chief, and shaman quickly left along with two of Rodrigo's crew.

"They're going back to the village," Chris explained. "Trent has been marking his specimens, I'm not sure how, but I'm assuming GPS, as a way for the extraction team to identify and grab them. They're going back to watch Trent. We're meeting at the ORP in two hours."

"What's the ORP?"

"Objective Rally Point."

"Where?"

"I'm not sure. Rodrigo is taking us there. The rest of crew is meeting there too."

"Then what?"

"I don't know. It depends on the intel the chief gathers."

"What are you thinking?"

"We need to somehow throw the extraction team off of their mark."

"Vamos," Rodrigo urged.

Chris nodded. "It's—"

"Let's go," Gabby interrupted. "I know. It's the same in Spanish."

Rodrigo headed toward a wall of jungle that looked impenetrable. Massive hardwood trees with thick, heavy trunks created the foundation. Tall, thin palms with matted trunks jutted up in between, fighting for their share of sunlight. Shrubs sat below that, filling every space that a drop of light squeezed through. Vines winded their way up and down, left and right, creating a braided curtain to keep them out.

Rodrigo ducked behind the curtain, disappearing into the heavy layers of green. One by one, they vanished into the thick jungle. When Gabby crossed the threshold, the air was so heavy and thick with oxygen and dew, she felt as if she might drown. However, her body adjusted quickly. The oxygen invigorated her and made her feel almost euphoric.

They moved over thick roots, fallen trees, and tangled vines with ease. The staccato song of forest birds lifted their spirit. They had a purpose, and each knew that what lay ahead mattered. It was bigger than them.

For the first time ever, Gabby wasn't thinking about herself, or planning for her future. She thought back on all the stress she'd created—over school, over work—and thought how insignificant that seemed now. She marveled at nature's wonder in a way she had never done before. She saw nature at work on so many levels and realized how important every bug, every leaf, every animal was.

"Gab," Chris said, breaking the human silence. "Rodrigo told me that the spirits told the shaman that you are the savior."

"What?" Gabby replied.

"They said you're special. The spirits brought you here. You're the savior."

"You must've misunderstood. That's crazy."

"I'm not that great at speaking Portuguese, but I understand it very well. You're special."

"Why did you tell me that? That's ridiculous," Gabby snapped.

"No, it's not. It's true. I feel it too, there's something special about you." he said, his eyes so wide she thought she could see his soul. In that moment, Gabby was inextricably drawn to him, but immediately felt guilty for betraying Trent.

"Stop. That's ridiculous. This isn't about me. Don't put that pressure on me."

"I'm sorry, but they look up to you."

"Are you kidding me? Stop," Gabby pleaded, at the crossroad of desperation and anger.

"Okay, okay," Chris said with a huge smile, then paused, becoming serious again. "When we go in to stop the extraction team, you need to stay back."

"No," Gabby said, "absolutely not."

"Then you stay with me."

"Fine. Ouch," she said as a hard, unripe fig

bounced off her shoulder. Gabby looked up to see a howler monkey. The monkey announced itself with a wide-mouthed, loud, eerie howl that turned Gabby's skin to gooseflesh.

One of Rodrigo's guys answered back, and the monkey quickly swung out of sight as the crew laughed. They were as amped up as a marine squadron getting ready for war. Chris knew this mood well.

Soon, Gabby could see a clearing ahead. It wasn't completely open; there were still large trees covering the space. The high canopy kept the area well shaded, but the smaller trees and brush had been completely cleared. In its place, a patchwork quilt of tents and huts had been set up. There were several dark green and tan frame tents that looked like they may have been part of a military operation. Gabby figured that they must've been taken from an illegal logging operation.

There were also a few traditional dark blue camping tents, stamped with the F.U.N.A.I. marking, that lined the perimeter of the camp. Two large huts made of a thin timber frame and covered in dried palm leaves sat at the center of the camp.

As they approached the camp, Rodrigo's crew

rushed out of their tents to meet them. There were many more than Gabby had expected. Most of the crew were men, but there was a small team of six women as well. Everyone was dressed in modern clothes, although Gabby was surprised by some of the logos they donned on their tee-shirts and jeans. It was as if the fashion from her middle school hallways that had vanished decades ago had suddenly reappeared in the middle of the Amazon. Gabby wondered how brands like Stüssy, the upside-down Guess triangle, and Airwalk had found their way here.

It quickly became clear to Gabby that they were nervous. Though she couldn't understand the words, the hurried chatter that carried through the group exposed the anxious energy. Rodrigo went running over, as a single man still dressed in the style of the Jaguar people emerged from a tent. Chris followed.

As the group spoke, Rodrigo yelled commands out, only pausing to converse with Chris. Suddenly, the camp began buzzing with action. Weapons were gathered and organized in the center huts. Everything from old shotguns and semiautomatic rifles to bows and arrows and spears were neatly placed inside the palm-covered shelter. A few guys jumped on dirt bikes and took off on worn paths.

After a moment of quiet observation, Gabby walked across the camp to where Chris and Rodrigo were talking to the jaguar man.

"They realized that we were missing much quicker than we'd hoped. This is Dunu—he lives in the lower section of the village. He was in a tree, gathering mangos, when a group of men dressed in all black moved in. Kukua translated and said that they were there to protect them, and to do so they needed to gather the entire village and have them wait at the ceremonial promenade, outside of Trent's lab."

"Dunu said that Kukua told them that the white man and woman, obviously us, are trying to hurt them with evil spirits, and that only they could protect them. They said this would be over soon and their lives would go back to normal. Dunu didn't trust them, so he stayed in the tree until they moved out, then he came here."

Gabby put her head down.

"We're done—they moved too fast."

"Don't say that. I have a plan."

Chapter 35

Orders

"UPDATE?" LUCIEN BARKED.

"The villagers have been centralized and secured."

"Why do I still only have seven marks on my screen?"

"We had to secure the village first. I have three more females ready to be located and marked. Then my team will start collecting samples again."

"You're falling behind," Lucien said through a clenched jaw.

"Your pick, Chris, is screwing things up."

"Don't worry about that. Just get the fucking specimens identified and marked. Let the extraction team handle the natives."

"It's not as simple as you think—they are very superstitious and sensitive."

"They don't wear clothes and carry spears; we have guns. That's as simple as it gets."

"It's easier to get my job done when they're happy and willing to cooperate."

"I need twenty living specimens. I don't give a fuck about the rest."

"Understood," Trent relented as Lucien's office phone buzzed. He switched over and picked up the receiver.

"What's going on? Why did you order Unit 2 to deploy now?" the gruff voice of General Holton growled through the receiver.

"It's under control. There was a minor disturbance and I wanted to get the specimens out as soon as possible."

"What minor disturbance?"

"Lt. Christopher Silver and Dr. Gabrielle Gale went rogue."

"Why wasn't I alerted?"

"I didn't deem it necessary. It's under control."

"Where are they?"

"They're being located now."

"What do you mean? You don't know where they are?"

"Not exactly, but—"

"Then the situation is not under control. I will handle operations from here on out."

"That's not going to happen. Unit 1 has secured the village. Unit 2 will be there to assist and get the specimens out in five hours. Silver and Gale can't do anything. They have no weapons and are alone in the jungle."

"I want them found and disposed of."

"I already issued a kill-on-sight order for them. There is a team combing the jungle for them as we speak."

"From here on out, I want to be included on every decision that's made until this operation is successful."

"I will do my best to keep you informed," Lucien said, and slammed down the phone receiver.

His pulse quickened. He didn't take orders. If it weren't for him, no one would be here. He watched the pulsing lights on his screen and calmed himself. The movement of the seven dots had subsided. They sat close together, now. He could imagine those dull-witted natives, huddled like sheep. Perhaps Lt. Silver and Dr. Gale actually did him a favor and they would move things along much quicker.

Suddenly another pulsing light came to life on his screen. Then another, and a wave of relief washed over Lucien. They were back on track. Unit 2 would have no problem identifying their targets when they were gathered in a small area. *It's funny how things just work out*, Lucien thought.

Then another light came on, and another. Then three more. *This is going too fast.* Then he watched as a string of ten lights right in a row came on. Lucien knew something was wrong as panic surged.

He opened the encrypted box to Trent.

"What?" Trent answered still behind his desk.

"How many specimens have you marked?"

"My team just marked the three females I told you about."

"That's it?"

"Yes, I'm running the samples. I can't go any fucking faster. We have time," Trent snapped, momentarily flashing an angry glare at Lucien's face before going back to his work swabbing the samples and smearing the small, paper-thin, glass processing screens.

"Something's fucking wrong. I just had ten marked specimens show up on my screen in succession."

"What?" Trent said as he clicked open his tracking screen. "That's impossible."

"Go figure out what the fuck is going on."

Trent jumped up and left his makeshift lab for the first time since the extraction team had moved in.

CHAPTER 36

Trinidad Guppies

RODRIGO DREW A ROUGH MAP of the village in the dirt outside of the huts. Gabby and Chris had been through the upper and lower sections of the village, but there were three more offshoots that Rodrigo just circled in the dirt.

"There are about three hundred people that live in this settlement," Chris explained to Gabby. "As you know, there are around a hundred living in the main village where we stayed, but there are another two hundred divided between these smaller offshoots."

"Are they part of Chief Ëpë's village?" Gabby asked.

"Yes, different kin but part of the same village umbrella."

"Did you ask Rodrigo if they've been affected by any of the pandemics?"

"Yes—he said that they have not. They've heard of some diseases spreading through the big cities when they go into town for supplies, but they've been fine."

"That's good, strange, but good. Three hundred people is much larger than I thought."

"It's much larger than anyone thought. It's incredible that such a large village has lasted out here, Rodrigo said that the indigenous populations have actually come back over the past few years. And, it will help us. We are going to use these offshoots as the base of our operation. Do you see how they form a triangle around the main area of the village?" Chris said, drawing the shape in the dirt.

"Yes, but how do you know the extraction team won't be there?"

"In order to be efficient, the extraction team needs to herd as many of the villagers as possible into the centralized section and guard them there. They will do one or two phases where they clear and condense those outer sections. We are going to use those to get more of our guys into the village. A few are already headed over to find out how they are marking the targets and disrupt whatever they're doing . . . if they can."

"And what do we do? Sit here and wait?" Gabby asked with obvious irritation in her tone. Between the need for Chris to translate everything and being left out of the planning, she felt like a third wheel.

"No, but I'm sure they have a search party looking for us, so we have to be smart about what we do and when we do it."

"Okay, so what exactly is it that we are going to do?" Gabby asked, frustrated with Chris and his apparent lack of direction.

"Look, Gabs, we have to put our trust in Rodrigo's planning. This is his territory, this is what he does best. I'm not making decisions—I'm listening to him and providing intel where I can."

"I just want to know what's going on."

"I'm trying to explain it to you."

"It doesn't sound like you actually know what's going on."

"We're going to set traps and strategically lure the extraction team to different points tonight. You will be with me and Rodrigo."

"I need to talk to Trent," Gabby blurted out.

"That's not going to happen," Chris ordered, his military background showing in his tone.

"I can get through to him."

"Gab, I'm sorry, but I think he would kill you for this mission."

"I'm willing to risk it."

"I'm not. It's not going to happen. That's final."

Gabby opened her mouth to let Chris know where he could shove his orders, but then just clenched her jaw. She knew nothing she said would get through to him. She would have to find her way to Trent on her own.

"Are you going to help us? We need to organize and count our weapons."

"Yes, Sir!" Gabby clicked her heels and saluted Chris, then spun and stomped off to the newly ordained weapon's hut.

Inside of the hut, weapons were tossed everywhere. There were bows resting on top of semi-automatics, spears thrown across hand guns, rifles and arrows and ammunition strewn everywhere. Gabby was shocked by the arsenal that had been amassed so quickly and the mess that it was in.

She didn't waste any time. Gabby began by shoving the huge pile tighter toward the center of the space, creating an aisle around the perimeter. She neatly stacked handguns and rifles in one corner, automatics and semis in another, bows with spears, and all ammunition together.

Seeing this many weapons unleashed a swarm of collywobbles in Gabby's stomach. Each of them possessed the ability to take a life with little effort, yet here they lay in a messy pile. How would they ever match up to the extraction team?

Gabby spent the next two hours organizing. She was so deep in focus that her mind was clear. It was cathartic. Every weapon was laid out by type, lined up by size, and placed so perfectly that she started to think that maybe they stood a chance. Their cache of weapons was surprisingly impressive for a ragtag crew of jungle progenies.

"Gab," Chris called from the door, "this is incredible!"

"Thanks, I'm pretty impressed myself. It looks so much better when it's organized." She spun to see Chris as he walked inside the hut. "Whoa, look at you." She was stunned by Chris's camouflage transition. He was covered head to toe, even his face painted different shades of green, gray, and black. He tossed Gabby some of her own gear.

"We're going with Rodrigo to set some traps, but I need to put camo on you first."

"Turn around," Gabby said as she stripped to her underwear and pulled on her camo. "Traps?"

"Yeah, they've already got some pretty gnarly ones set up, they just need to be engaged. Then they are going to add some strategic pits."

"What kind of traps?"

"You'll see. Can I turn around?"

"Okay."

"Sit down," Chris said as he sat and spread out some shells with different shades of paste in them. He painted Gabby's face to match his.

"I wish I could see what I look like." Gabby smiled.

"You pull it off, don't worry." He laughed.

"Are you scared?" she asked, suddenly serious.

"Of course. It's good to be scared—it heightens your senses. Fear is good. Panic, on the other hand, gets people killed."

Gabby just nodded.

CHAPTER 37

Specimen 317

TRENT MARVELED AT HIS microscope. Specimen 317 was absolutely perfect. Trent had found his Homologous recombination mediated gene editing—Activating repair—Wild type—Aa allele pair, or HAWA.

Using the CRISPR method, EVE-0 would be solved using a basic copy and paste, the inactive gene simply replaced with the active version using a viral vector. This would create a double-strand break in the DNA chain, which would activate and repair the EVE-0 gene. The specific substitution in this process would be the Wild type Eve-0, or the original, natural form of the EVE-0 gene.

Each human genetic trait had two alleles, including

EVE-0. The active EVE-0 gene could be one of four allele pairs, depending on inheritance from the parents. The $A\alpha$, $A\beta$, $E\alpha$, and $E\beta$ alleles were all codominantly expressed and performed virtually the same function. However, in chimp studies, the $A\alpha$ pair had the most robust immune response, and therefore the most evolutionary aptitude.

The active EVE-0 was also found well within the nuclear center, where inactive EVE-0 mutations had moved to the outer periphery of each cell. HAWA-317's EVE-0 was perfectly placed in the center of the cell's nucleus.

It was really quite simple and could've been done almost ten years ago . . . if they'd had an active human EVE-0. Now, Trent had found his perfect specimen.

"Hey," Trent yelled to the extraction officer guarding his lab.

"Yes sir?" the guard quickly stepped inside. He was dressed in all-black tactical gear. He wore a lightweight helmet and his eyes were shaded by dark glasses.

"Find Kukua and send him to me now."

The man nodded and vanished into the bright afternoon sun.

"Call to me?" Kukua asked just moments later as he walked into the lab.

"Yes. I need you to find specimen 317 and bring them here." Trent handed Kukua the paper he had with his collection of 317. Kukua had taken notes on it in his language, though to Trent they looked more like doodles.

Kukua looked at the paper. "Sim, yes, know where her is. Us get." Kukua quickly left the lab.

Trent opened up the secure chat window on his computer and rang Lucien.

"Do you have something good to tell me?" Lucien said through a squinted glare.

"Yes," Trent beamed. "We have our HAWA."

"Where is it?"

"I'm having Kukua bring the HAWA into the lab to wait for extraction here. I've already stationed guards."

"Call me back when you have it secured." Lucien abruptly clicked out of the conference.

Just moments later, Kukua entered with the specimen. HAWA-317 was a young girl. Her voluptuous figure showed that she had recently entered her child-bearing years. Her round, soft features shone with youth and beauty, and her deep set black eyes were stunning. Trent stared in awe at his perfect specimen.

The electric buzz of instruments terrified the young girl. She clung to the wall near the entrance.

"Wow, she's perfect," Trent marveled. "Why is she scared?"

Kukua said something to the girl, to which she replied with one whispered word: "Macumba."

"Black magic," Kukua translated. "Her not know electric."

"Can you explain it to her?" Trent softly smiled.

As Kukua spoke to HAWA-317, Trent reengaged his conference with Lucien.

"She's here." Trent beamed.

"Let me see her," Lucien ordered.

"Kukua, can you bring her over here?"

Kukua guided the hesitant girl to Trent's computer. He was gentle, but had a firm grasp on her arm and elbow. She was shaking.

Trent turned his computer screen so that the camera faced the girl. When she saw Lucien, she immediately began crying.

"She's perfect," Lucien said with wide eyes. "Why is she crying?"

"She's never seen electricity or computers. She'll be fine."

The girl was so scared that tears now covered her face and she was visibly trembling.

Trent pulled out a Hershey's chocolate bar. He broke off a piece and handed it to Kukua, then smiled and handed the girl a piece. The last piece he put in his own mouth. Kukua said something to the girl and she reluctantly took a small nibble. Her eyes widened and she took a bigger bite.

Lucien just watched.

"Trent, don't introduce too many modern products. We want her to be untainted," Lucien quietly said while staring in wonder through his computer screen.

"I know, I just needed to calm her down."

"Don't let her out of your sight. Do you understand?"

"Yes. I have her."

"Don't screw this up."

Lucien turned his camera off, but continued to watch his HAWA-317 as she softly started crying again.

"Her want her mamae e papai," Kukua said.

"Kukua," Trent said, becoming very serious, "tell her that she is special. She has been chosen to be a queen—no, a goddess."

Kukua began to speak to the girl. She stopped crying and looked at Trent. Her full lips tightened and her eyes narrowed in mistrust, then she said something to Kukua.

"What did she say?"

"Her say." Kukua paused. "Her why."

"What?"

"Ah, no, her say . . . why her."

"Tell her my people are in trouble. They need a savior. She can save them, then rule over them. She will have anything she wants—money, gold, jewels, chocolate. Anything."

The girl's face began to soften as Kukua spoke. She looked at Trent, then back to Kukua, then between them. She said something to Kukua with her hand on her hip, and all the attitude of a typical teenager.

"Her not know how her can give help to you people." Kukua shrugged.

Trent gently took the girl's hand with both of his. Then he opened her palm and touched the center of it. "Tell her my people are very sick. They're dying.

She holds the cure," Trent said, brushing his finger along her palm. Then he smiled. "Tell her the cure is in her spit." Trent spit in his own hand, held it up, made a silly face, laughed, and wiped his hand on his pants.

The girl giggled. Her smile was fleeting, though, and she quickly looked down at the ground while mumbling something to Kukua.

"Her ask why her mamae can't come."

"Tell her that there isn't room for elders, but I promise we will come back for anyone that would like to come. Kukua, remind her that she will be a queen and will have anything that she wants. She will be able to take care of her entire family and give them food and safety."

The girl's face remained somber. She placed her head down, but nodded in agreement.

Chapter 38

Hide and Seek

IT WAS HARD TO KEEP UP with Rodrigo. He moved through the heavy underbrush so quickly and quietly, while every thorn seemed to catch on Gabby's clothes and every twig snapped under her foot. Rodrigo kept looking back and gesturing for Gabby to be quiet, but there was nothing she could do. Finally, he whispered something to Chris, and Gabby knew it was about her. Her cheeks, sticky from the camo paint, burned hot.

"Hey," Chris whispered, "Rodrigo said that you're stomping through the jungle like a bull." He smiled sheepishly, which Gabby returned with an unamused glare. "He said that if you keep your weight on your toes and step quickly and lightly, you'll conserve energy, and move faster and much more quietly."

Gabby wanted to tell Chris to shut up, but he was right. Even Chris, who was actually built like a bull, moved through the jungle softer than she did. So, she bit her lip and gave it a shot. Suddenly, she felt like a gazelle. Everything felt lighter—it was amazing. Rodrigo looked back and gave Gabby a thumbs up, which Chris saw and followed with a wink. Both made her smile.

Moving through the jungle, for the first time with ease, Gabby marveled at how incredible the human body's ability to adapt was. When she'd first arrived in Brazil, just breathing onboard the *Marlow* was a Herculean task. Now, it almost felt normal.

The human body was amazing, like all living things, but the human mind was in a class of its own. No other living creature had an intellect that could even remotely touch the human mind. Capable of abstract thought, combining seemingly unrelated concepts, generative computation, and symbolism; the human mind was virtually limitless.

However, here they were—that incomparable intellect murdering their own bodies. Now AmCorps's cure was threatening to remove emotion from the human psyche; the one commonality we share with many other living creatures, as anyone who's ever had a pet will tell you. Gabby knew that this was wrong.

Suddenly, Rodrigo lifted his right fist and everyone froze. He raised his pointer finger, rotated it in circles, then put his hand flat, and everyone immediately crouched. Gabby followed.

"Keep your head down and don't move," Chris whispered.

Gabby could feel herself begin to panic. Was the extraction unit nearby? She slowed her breathing, forcing her panic down. Closing her eyes, she listened for any signal as to what threat they were about to face. Soon, she heard a mechanical buzz in the distance. It was a sound she recognized, though she couldn't immediately place it. Suddenly, it clicked . . . a drone was coming toward them.

She remained frozen as she listened to it fly closer and closer. Then Gabby heard a screech in the distance. Through the corner of her eye, she saw a while plume of feathers and massive wings swoop down, grab the drone from the sky, and disappear.

"Anjo da guarda." Rodrigo breathed a sigh of relief.

"What was that?" Gabby whispered to Chris.

"It was a harpy eagle."

"It was huge."

Rodrigo flashed them a quick glare, and silence once again overtook the march.

This was the first time that Gabby felt like she was moving with the jungle, not against it. That was, until she ran smack into the back of Chris's pack. Rodrigo had both fists up, and the crew had stopped. He lifted two fingers on each fist and fanned them down twice. Then Rodrigo looked directly at Chris and Gabby. With his eyes wide and fierce behind the black camouflage paint, he motioned for them to be absolutely silent and still.

The rest of the crew quickly pulled back a large carpet made of leaves and grass, completely indistinguishable from the forest floor. Under the rug lay a latticework of thin wood slats. As the crew removed the wood slats, Gabby saw a wide, deep hole with thick spikes that shot up at different heights. Gabby estimated the pit to be about twenty feet long and five or six feet wide. It was huge.

They quickly spread the rough wood planks around so that they looked like a natural part of the jungle floor. Then they pulled the carpet back over the trap. Rodrigo circled his hand above his head and the unit moved out in formation.

They spent the next four hours maneuvering through the jungle and setting traps. They set whip traps, with bent bamboo tied around heavy tree trunks that sent spikes at a hundred miles-per-hour into the unlucky target. They also set cartridge traps with ammunition in small holes that would fire up into the target's foot, often leaving the foot so mangled it was barely there.

The last traps they set were overhead. Large planks with spikes through them were weighted with heavy stones and rigged to fall when the target breeched the trip line.

When they finally made it back to camp, the late afternoon sun had begun its descent. The surveillance team had returned, though not all of them made it back.

"What's going on?" Gabby asked Chris.

"Three from the surveillance team didn't make it back. They're okay, but they're trapped in the village. The chief and the shaman are also trapped."

"Trapped how?"

"The extraction team is behaving exactly how we predicted. They've formed a perimeter around the village and moved everyone into the main square. Now, we have a few guys on the inside, which is great. Well"—Chris paused—"as long as they're not discovered."

"Are we going to get them?"

"We've also received intelligence that a second and much larger unit has just landed at the airstrip. They have two very large planes with them."

"Have they started loading anyone in the planes yet?"

"No."

"What are we going to do now?"

"We have to wait, rest and eat. We have a couple hours till it's dark enough for us to move in."

"So, we just do nothing? What if they load up the villagers and leave before we can stop them?" Gabby was vexed.

"Rodrigo has eyes on it. You and I have to keep a very low profile. They are looking for us."

"We're sitting ducks here. If they're looking for us, this is a pretty easy place to find us."

"No, it's not. It looks big and obvious from the

ground, but Rodrigo has spent years camouflaging this camp and has remained undiscovered. At one point, there were several groups looking for him. We're safe here."

"Safe and useless."

"Would you rather be captured and dead? Then we'd really be helpful." Chris rolled his eyes.

Gabby walked away. She understood why he felt this way. But if she could just get to Trent, she knew she could change his mind. Though, she didn't dare sneak off into the jungle alone. She had no other option but to get comfortable and wait.

Waiting . . . there was nothing Gabby hated more than waiting. She tried to convince herself that she should appreciate this time. She should be calm, she should relax and eat something or take a nap. Instead the anxiety planted its seeds and began to grow. Each second felt like an hour, watering the fear and allowing dread to grow strong roots in the pit of her stomach.

Finally, Gabby couldn't take it any longer and set out to find Chris. There had to be something she could do to pass the time.

She checked every tent and hut, but Chris was

nowhere to be found. She became furious. He had blatantly lied to her just to keep her away so he could do things his way. As embers of fury began stoking flames of full-blown rage, Gabby decided she wasn't going to sit there and wait.

She took a handgun from the weapons stash, which was still fully stocked. The amount of weapons still there seemed weird, but she had made up her mind that she wasn't sitting around and waiting while Chris decided how things were going to go.

When she stepped out of the weapons hut, it dawned on her that she had no idea which way the village was. Gabby froze, and tried to remember which way they came into the camp from. It all looked the same. Then she saw a group of Rodrigo's guys walk out of a hut and across camp. She decided to follow them. They were so deep in conversation that they didn't even seem to notice that she was there.

They crossed the perimeter of camp and disappeared into an outcropping of large palms. Gabby followed them and found another tent. A makeshift command center had been set up inside. Rodrigo and Chris were deep in conversation, as Rodrigo's guys quickly joined in. There was no technology, no blinking lights showing radar locations, no computer screens, no high-tech radios. Instead, large, quickly sketched maps littered the tables.

Gabby just stood there unnoticed for a few moments, as Rodrigo's guys seemed to update what she presumed were the enemy location and numbers. She couldn't understand what they were saying, but she got the sense of what was going on by the changes Rodrigo made to the map. Finally, Chris glanced up and saw her.

"Gabs, I didn't see you come in. I thought you were taking a nap."

"I couldn't sleep, and then I couldn't find you. I thought you left me behind."

"You really thought I would do that?"

Gabby just shrugged, and he caught a glimpse of the gun handle sticking out of her belt.

"You grabbed a gun?" Chris asked, putting the pieces together. "Were you going to try and get back to the village?"

"I—I—" Gabby stammered over her words. "I was really mad. I thought you left me, and I was going to look for you. Then I saw Rodrigo's guys leave the camp and I followed them here."

Chris stepped out from behind the table and walked over to her.

"Thank God, you didn't take off into the jungle."

"I have a gun."

"So?" Chris asked, and easily took Gabby's gun from her. "I will arm you better for tonight." He tossed the handgun to Rodrigo. "You forgot to load your weapon."

"I was going to. I was just really mad when I—"

"Anger clouds your thinking," Chris interrupted. "You'll need your mind completely clear and on point tonight." Gabby nodded in agreement; she knew he was right. He gave her a hug, then pulled her back, still holding her shoulders. "I would never leave you. Can I fill you in?" Chris asked.

A thin smile cracked at the corner of Gabby's lips. "Judging by the map, it looks like the rest of the extraction team has arrived and started their full extraction operation."

"Very observant—I'm impressed."

"It also looks like they've split into teams. It looks like one team is stationed inside the village, one team is working the perimeter, and a third team is . . ." Gabby paused and cocked her head. "I don't know."

"You're exactly right." Chris beamed. "We don't have eyes on Team 3, but we're presuming they're searching for us. Here, come over to the table."

Rodrigo's guys cleared a spot for Gabby as Chris continued, "By tonight we're hoping to have four teams with about ten guys on each, plus our team." Gabby nodded, feeling better with each moment that passed. Chris pointed out where they were, where the runway was, and where the village was. He then pointed out where each trap had been set and explained their plan for the night.

Gabby was amazed. She had never considered the amount of strategy that went into planning a combat operation. She had, quite stupidly in her opinion, assumed that they would grab guns and go out to look for the AmCorps extraction team. However, it was so much more than that.

"We can't compete on a weapons or technology front, but we have something better. We have Rodrigo. This is his land, and he knows how to defend it." Chris smiled. "What do you think?"

"What do I think?" Gabby repeated the question only because she was unsure how to answer without sounding completely green.

"Yeah, do you feel better? You seemed upset when you came in."

"I feel much better. The plan is smart—there's much more strategy than I imagined."

Chris gave Gabby's tense shoulder a quick, friendly rub and checked his watch.

"Já estava na hora. Você está pronto?" Chris said to Rodrigo.

"Sim. Vou reunir os caras e encontrá-lo nas armas," Rodrigo replied, then disappeared with his crew in tow.

"It's time," Chris translated for Gabby. "Rodrigo is gathering up his guys. We're meeting at the staging point for our mission brief."

"What?" Gabby asked.

"The weapons hut. Everyone is meeting there to go over the plan for tonight."

CHAPTER 39

Taking Sides

"PATRICK NO HERE." Kukua burst into Trent's lab.

"What do you mean? No, he's not in the lab," Trent asked through gritted teeth.

"No. Patrick gone."

"Did he go somewhere?"

Kukua just shrugged, as fear creased his brow.

"When was the last time that you saw him?"

"Patrick go to give shot mark to go to America."

"You can't worry about him right now. I will send some of our soldiers to find him. I need you to physically locate the specimens and bring them here one at a time," Trent ordered, and handed Kukua a piece of paper. "This is the most updated list with their pictures."

He took the paper and looked at it.

"Go," Trent demanded. The list had grown to fifteen specimens, and he had ten more samples cued.

HAWA-317 sat quietly in the corner of Trent's lab. She hugged her legs as she watched him work. He would occasionally look up and smile at her. When he did, she quickly diverted her gaze. Trent wished Gabby were here; he wished that she had had time to process this. He knew she'd come around. He just needed to get her back.

The conference screen on Trent's computer flashed as Lucien's face came onto the screen.

"You were supposed to give me an update twenty minutes ago," Lucien barked.

"I'm busy," Trent flatly replied.

Lucien took a deep breath. "Have you found your rogue agents?"

"Not yet, but there is a team locating them now."

"So, they're still out there?"

"Yes, but they can't do anything."

"What about the specimens? According to my data, you've marked sixty-two for extraction."

"We are physically gathering the specimens. It is no longer an issue."

"How many have you secured so far?"

"I've identified fifteen."

"That's not what I asked. Where *are* they?"

"They're in the square—Kukua is pulling them now."

"Let me know when you have them physically secured."

Lucien abruptly clicked out of the conference screen, then flashed back on. "Just to fucking remind you, without our specimens we are nothing."

"I know how"—Lucien once again clicked out of the conference window—"important they are." Trent's voice trailed off. He looked up and caught HAWA-317's eye; she looked concerned and just stared at him for a moment. Trent attempted a smile, but again she quickly looked away.

An alarm in Trent's lab chimed, and a report was spat out by the printer. Trent grabbed it—two more specimens had just been identified.

Trent printed out the new specimens' identifying info. Then, suddenly, he heard a loud bang, followed by the shuffling of footsteps and muffled cries. He jumped up, then froze, remembering that he needed to stay close to HAWA-317.

Trent tried to smile, but couldn't hide his concern. With terror spilling over to tears, HAWA-317 jumped up and tried to run to the door, but Trent blocked her. Then Kukua came in with a bleeding lip, rubbing his chin and dragging two of the specimens behind him. An extraction team member brought up the tail.

The two specimens were both male. They were strong and young. HAWA-317 looked at them with tears streaming down her cheeks. They tried to walk over to her, but the guard forcefully stepped in between them.

"Sir, where would you like them?"

"I want two guards stationed next door and one guard directly outside of my door. Keep the girl in here, but start placing all the specimens next door."

"Yes, sir." The guard started dragging the two specimens out.

"Do not hurt them," Trent ordered.

"You have my word, sir. I'm being gentle."

"Them do bad," Kukua added.

"What do you mean?" Trent gestured for the guard to wait with the specimens.

"Them know where Patrick go to."

"What did they tell you?"

"No talk."

"Then, why do you think they know something?"

"See them talk to man not from village."

"What?"

"More man here, not live in village."

"Are you sure?"

Kukua nodded his head.

"Bring him here for questioning," Trent ordered.

The guard grabbed the two specimens and started to walk out. Kukua accidentally stepped in front of them, causing the guard to stumble.

He angrily shoved Kukua, yelling "Get the fuck out of my way."

Kukua fell to the ground, dirt caking on his already bloody lip.

"Hey," Trent scowled, "he's on our side."

"Right sir," the guard replied through a squinted grin as he vanished from the lab.

Trent sat there, staring at HAWA-317. Once he was able to see past the rudimentary trappings of her culture, she was beautiful. Her skin glowed with warm caramel tones, her narrow dark eyes were piercing, filled with the ferocity of a caged animal.

Her full lips began to curl ever so slightly, as Trent could see her fear turn to anger. He was completely enthralled. He smiled, she scowled.

Trent took out a granola bar. Taking a bite, he smiled again, then offered one to HAWA-317. At first, she looked away. Trent moved to sit on the ground in front of her, then opened the package and gestured for her to take it again. She reluctantly accepted the granola bar, and took a very small bite. Her eyes widened at the sugary sweetness, and then she devoured the bar, licking the crumbs off of her fingers.

As Trent stood to go back to his desk, the mood in the lab now just a bit lighter, Kukua returned with the guard and a male villager. The villager looked to be somewhere in his twenties, though he had a few scars on his face that made him look harder than he should.

"Him not live in village." Kukua announced.

"He looks like he does to me," Trent replied.

"I agree. He belongs here and he was talking with a group that looked like his family in their language," the extraction guard added.

"No. Him no live here." Kukua then said something in a different language and the villager just looked at him. He remained completely expression-less and unaffected, as concern grew in HAWA-317. Kukua looked at HAWA-317 and said something to her. She picked up a rock and threw it at him.

"Kukua," Trent ordered. "Tell me exactly why you think that he doesn't live here."

"Him"—Kukua held up his hands pointing to his nails—"too smooth. Him cut."

When Kukua said that, Trent caught the villager glance at his nails. This struck him as odd. Could he possibly have understood Kukua?

"Do you speak English?" Trent asked the man.

He didn't reply. Instead the man looked at HAWA-317 and said something in their language. Kukua yelled at them.

"Him tell girl, no trust you. Him say you bad."

"Get him out of here."

"What should we do with him?" the extraction guard asked.

"Dispose of him quietly."

"Yes sir."

Out of the corner of his eye, Trent thought he saw the man mouth something to Kukua.

Trent looked at the man. "What did you just say?"

The man just looked at Trent and cocked his head, seeming to not understand.

"Put more guards on the specimens. I agree with Kukua. Something doesn't feel right."

"With all due respect, sir, we are on top of this. We are a unit of elite soldiers with the best weapons and equipment. We have this operation well under control. A few natives, with bows and arrows, and a rogue *chairforce* asshole . . . I mean, come on, sir."

Kukua pounded on the guards chest, yelling, "Make him take you to Patrick."

The guard pulled his gun and held it to Kukua's head. "Touch me one more time, fucker."

"Hey," Trent yelled, "He's helping us. I don't think you realize what's at stake here. Do not take this lightly. If you talk to him like that again, I will have you dismissed and rejected from our safe house."

"I'm sorry sir. I didn't mean—"

"Just shut up and do your job."

"Yes sir."

"Kukua, I need you to secure the specimens as quickly as possible. I don't want you to do anything else."

"Sim, yes. After us get specimens, us find Patrick."

"Yes, you have my word."

The guard dragged the mystery man out as Kukua followed. Just as quiet was overtaking the lab once again, Trent's conference screen flashed.

"What was that about?" Lucien snapped.

"What?"

Lucien just rolled his eyes.

"Were you listening?" Trent asked.

"So?"

"Kukua thought that one of the villagers wasn't really a villager because his nails were smooth."

"Well."

"I don't think there's any credibility to it."

"Where are the specimens?"

"They are in the hut next door."

"How many?"

"Two male specimens so far."

"That's it?"

"If you would stop bothering me, I could finish."

"Kookoo is starting to become a hinderance. One more issue, and he's done."

"We are not dealing with an intelligent group here. *Kukua*'s team let the villagers get ahold of the microchipping device, that's all. We need Kukua to help us communicate with them so that this is as easy as possible."

"You missed that opportunity. You don't have to worry about *communicating* with a dead villager. I'm directing the extraction unit to take out anyone that gets in their way, including Kookoo. As long as Lt. Silver is out there, this entire mission is in danger. We don't have time to worry about making this easy for the natives."

"Do not underestimate Silver's threat. I want him and Dr. Gale killed on sight. I'm issuing those directives now."

"No, not . . ."

Lucien abruptly cut Trent off, completely ignoring his plea.

A notification pinged and the printer spat out the final complete list of marked specimens. Trent studied the list. It was perfect.

"Hey," Trent called the guard outside.

"Yes Sir?"

"Have any more specimens been secured?"

"Several, Sir. It's going very well. They have all been gathered up here so it's easy to move them to the guarded hut."

"Great. Here's the complete list. Give it to Kukua."

"Yes, Sir." The guard quickly made his exit.

Trent stood and moved close to HAWA-317. She still sat huddled in the corner. Trent brought a couple pieces of paper and a marker over with him. Though they had very limited resources, he had printed everything he needed, and could now spare some.

Trent started to doodle; he was actually quite talented at drawing. He drew a simplistic portrait of the girl and some flowers around her. It was a bit cartoonish, but HAWA-317 was mesmerized. Trent handed her the paper and marker. She began to draw. A huge smile grew on her face. Trent returned to his desk, leaving her the slight stack of paper.

Suddenly, Kukua came storming in.

"Have you gathered all of the specimens?" Trent asked.

"Sim ... yes," Kukua hurriedly said as panic showed in his tone, "no find Bob."

"What?"

"Bob no here. Take Patrick. Now take Bob."

"When was the last time you saw him?"

"Bob help find rest specimens."

"We'll find him. Don't worry. Guard," Trent yelled.

"Yes, Sir?" he quickly appeared.

"Have you seen Bob?"

"Who?" the guard asked through an indignant frown.

"Kukua's helper."

"I don't know." The guard rolled his eyes.

"Can you help him find him? Kukua finished what I needed him to do, so now get someone to help him find his friends."

"Oh, you're finished with Kukua?"

"What?"

"You have nothing else that you need him to do?"

"No, why?" Trent scowled. He looked at Kukua, who appeared to be fighting back tears.

"I have orders that supersede yours. Come on, Kukua." The guard roughly grabbed Kukua and started to drag him out.

"No. No." Kukua pleaded through tears as the guard dragged him out of the lab.

"Stop. What the hell do you think you're doing?"

"Sir, go back in the lab. I have orders that I have to follow."

"I'm giving the orders here. Stop."

"Go back in your lab, Sir." The guard pushed Kukua down, pulled out his gun and in one swift motion, shot him in the back of his head.

"No. No."

"Go back in your lab, Sir. This will be over soon and you will be back home."

A round of gunfire exploded nearby. Two nearby extraction agents took off in that direction. The guard that had just executed Kukua guided Trent back into his lab, then anxiously took up his post just outside the door.

Trent slinked back to his desk and collapsed in his chair. The only solace he had was HAWA-317.

"Hold tight, Sir. We're heading to the extraction point soon." The guard yelled from his post just outside the threshold.

CHAPTER 40

This Is It

AS THE WEAPON HUT FILLED UP, Gabby couldn't believe how many had come ready to serve. Rodrigo and his team handed out armaments as groups of warriors descended on the small encampment. There had to be close to a hundred men and women. As the space became cramped, the crowd began to gather around the open exterior.

Chris leaned into Gabby. "Rodrigo just told me that the women here are called the Viragos. They've all had children or husbands or both murdered. He didn't think they'd get the word to come, but they did."

"That's . . ." Gabby couldn't find the right words. The emotion of seeing all of these people gather so quickly to protect this one small village began to overwhelm her. The sting of tears burned at the corner of her eyes. She fought back her sentiments with a few deep breaths—this was not the time or place to become emotional.

"It's great, but this is too big of a group to keep hidden for long. Rodrigo!" Chris yelled and gave the universal finger twirl gesture for "let's wrap this up."

With that, Rodrigo let out an ear-piercing whistle and the room went silent. He then began to address the group in Portuguese. They let out a brief howling cheer, then went silent as he introduced Chris. The crowd listened intently. Although Gabby couldn't understand what he was saying, she got the gist of it. Chris was trying, as best he could, to explain what was going on in the rest of the world and why they were there.

Gabby struggled to remember the last time she had been gathered in such a large group. Gatherings of more than twenty-five had been illegal for years, even with masks on. Her initial reaction was to panic, but then a strange comfort washed over her. The warm arms of nostalgia held her tight, and it felt normal. It felt good to be with people again.

Was she robbing the innocent survivors of this chance? She couldn't help but doubt her choice. It was made in such haste. Just twenty lives held the potential to make things normal again. To give millions to come the chance at life. Humans had been taking what they wanted, what they needed, what they coveted since the beginning of time. It might simply be human nature.

"Gabs," Chris said, urging her out of her thoughts. The crowd was staring at her. "We're introducing you. Can you stand up and wave?" He smiled.

Gabby stood and looked out at all the faces. In that moment she still wasn't sure that what she was doing was right for the world, but it was right for these people. Their entire lives had been ripped apart by others taking whatever they wanted from them without thought or care. She had to choose a side, right or wrong—or both.

Gabby smiled and held her hand up in a half-wave, half-pledge gesture, and the crowd whooped. The energy was infectious, and she was glad that she'd chosen them. Now, she just needed to get through to Trent.

Rodrigo yelled out a few more directives. Gabby

had no idea what he was saying. She pretended to listen because she was now aware of all the curious eyes on her. Rodrigo pulled out a list that he read from as the crowd began to move. The large gathering formed into smaller groups.

Rodrigo yelled something and everyone started howling, no longer sounding human. Gabby even joined in. The feeling was electric—it sent a bolt of animalistic energy thundering through her core.

Chris looked at Gabby with wild eyes. "Ready?" he asked. She nodded through a primal leer.

He handed her an M-16 assault rifle with a bag of ammo. "It's old, but in good condition," Chris said. "Remember where the safety switch is?" He quickly pointed to it. "Safe, semi, auto."

"Got it," Gabby said.

"Throw it over your shoulder—you'll only use it if we get caught in a heavy situation. Here's a holster and hand gun; this is the gun you'll want at the ready."

Gabby positioned her guns, then pulled out the handgun and did a quick check, just like Mari had showed her, which felt like an eternity ago.

The teams quickly dispersed, disappearing into the

thick jungle until just Gabby, Chris, Rodrigo, and four of Rodrigo's guys were left. The sun was quickly sinking, filling the camp with shadows. It had become so quiet so quickly. It even seemed like the normal dusk chorus of animal sounds had gone.

"Chris," Gabby called, "don't kill Trent, okay?"

"Gabs, I don't want to hurt him, trust me. I wish we didn't have to hurt anyone, but this is wrong. I—" Chris paused, struggling to find words. "I just know that I was put here, on this mission, to stop this."

"That sounds pretty cliché. How can you be so sure about anything? What if what Trent is doing is what's right for the world?"

Rodrigo whistled and gave a slight toss to his head.

"It's time," Chris told her. "I don't know what to tell you, Gabs. To me, cliché or not, this is an obvious decision. I can't explain it, but I just know."

"Really? I mean for argument's sake. War after war has been fought for reasons very much like this. When we want something we don't have, we take it. Maybe it's just part of human nature and it will always be like this, until we alter the species. I mean look at us." Gabby held up her gun.

"That's insane. Free will is what makes us human. Why would you want to take that away?"

"I don't. I'm just making a point. There's not always a clear-cut right and wrong."

"You're wrong. There are complicated situations, but this isn't one. Let's even take a step back—you were right when you said when we want something, we take it. That is wrong, it's always been wrong, and it's wrong now. That's what I'm fighting for—forget about what might come."

"I—" Gabby began, but she was interrupted by Rodrigo.

"Nós temos de ir agora," he snapped.

"Gabs, we have to go now."

"I'm ready," she said through a scowl.

Chris tossed her the final piece of her gear, a military camouflage helmet. He helped her adjust it so it fit snugly.

"So you know, I agree with you," she said. "I—"

Chris cut her off. "I know."

Rodrigo moved quickly. He was out of camp and deep into the jungle in just a matter of minutes. It was difficult for Gabby to follow. Physically, she was fine, she felt strong. There was a cool breeze, and by normal standards it was a beautiful evening. However, the fading light soon began to play tricks on her eyes. The shadows seemed so substantial that she continually stepped over things that weren't there and tripped on things that her eyes missed.

After a while of stumbling through the shadows, Gabby discovered that it was much easier to visually rely on the feet directly in front of her. It was difficult at first to convince her mind to not trust her eyes, but she got the hang of it.

"We have about forty more minutes till we're in position," Chris whispered to Gabby. "We just crossed over into enemy territory." Just as he finished speaking, a barrage of automatic fire tore through the jungle.

They quickly dropped to the ground, soon realizing that the gunfire wasn't aimed at them when the rounds were answered back. Rodrigo crawled over to Chris. Gabby couldn't understand what they were saying. To her, the gunfire sounded like it was in the distance, though that made it no less frightening.

"The enemy's been engaged," Chris said.

"I figured that." Gabby scratched her forehead, considering that she might be missing something in the military speak, but that seemed pretty obvious to her.

"Rodrigo and I estimate the gunfire to be about two to five miles away, which would put them at the lower-perimeter traps which means that we probably snared some as they were patrolling for us."

"That's what we wanted, right?"

"Yeah, we're heading toward active fire now, so be very alert and don't panic or jump when you hear it. We need to move as quietly as possible."

Gabby nodded. It had become nearly pitch black; she couldn't see anything.

"I can't see," she whispered to Chris.

"Alright," he said, and went into his backpack. "Here, I have NVGs."

"What?"

"Night-vision goggles—technically, they're ENVG-Bs. They attach to your helmet. They're binoculars too, so you'll be able to see much better." Chris quickly helped Gabby put on the NVGs, then adjust and focus them. She could definitely see better, but it was such a strange sensation. It felt like she was in a virtual reality world. Her head started to spin.

However, as they began to move, her eyes adjusted,

and then her mind. It was far from perfect. They still needed Rodrigo's innate knowledge of the jungle terrain to move as quickly as they were, but it helped. She could at least keep up.

Soon her eyes began to notice the incredible amount of life that moved through the trees under the veil of darkness. The jungle was crawling, slithering and teeming with movement. It was oddly mesmerizing. Tingles began to creep up the small of Gabby's back. A blast of gunfire ripped through the trees and seemed much closer. Gabby dropped to the jungle floor, but Chris quickly pulled her up.

"It's not coming our way. We're almost in position. Just keep moving," he whispered.

Gabby managed to keep her legs moving, though panic was threatening to spill over. She wanted to run away, a want that was so deep it was more visceral than anything. Her preservation-of-life instinct was becoming increasingly hard to ignore.

Suddenly she heard a loud rustle directly to her left and swung around, just in time to see someone crash through the thick brush. As her eyes focused, she could see that it was one of Rodrigo's guys. He was hysterical—he just repeated the word "morto" over and over. Dread quickly took hold in the base of her stomach, leaving a hollow pit in its wake. As Gabby's eyes focused more clearly, she could see that he was covered in blood, and the left side of his clothing looked like it had been burned.

"Corre, corre." The man began crying as he got up. Rodrigo placed a hand on his shoulder, which calmed him momentarily. He said something to Chris.

Chris turned to Gabby, pushing her. "Run!" he ordered. As she stumbled back away from Chris, a small mortar round exploded, tossing her back. The world around her flickered for a moment, but the loud buzzing in her ears pulled her back. As she blinked her eyes, trying to focus, flames shot up. She didn't see anyone. She tried calling for Chris, but got no answer.

Gabby began moving her legs and arms—they ached but were otherwise alright. She did a quick body check to make sure she hadn't sustained any injuries; she seemed to be okay. The ringing in her ears was subsiding and her hearing was returning.

Gabby tried getting closer to the blast, but the fire was too hot. She called for Chris again, but nothing.

She couldn't see anyone, couldn't even get close enough to look for their bodies.

Suddenly, with all the pain and surprise of a sucker punch, Gabby realized that she was alone.

There was no panic, no tears. Gabby was angry. She felt betrayed and abandoned. She was absolutely lost. For a moment, she considered just sitting down and giving up.

She tried recalling the map, but it was all a blur. Gabby took a deep breath; what she knew was that the trail was taking them south of the village to the western perimeter. If they had been twenty minutes away from their target before the blast, Gabby estimated, then she should be able to cut directly north and come to the village.

Gabby took a step toward the jungle, looking for some sort of trail or break in the trees. She couldn't see anything, and realized her night-vision goggles had been knocked off during the blast. Frantic, Gabby looked around where she had fallen, but they were gone.

She heard more gunfire, which sounded like it was coming almost directly north of her.

Gabby began feeling her way back along the path,

but soon tripped on something and tumbled to the hard ground. She rolled over, let out a huff of frustration, and picked herself up to her knees. Feeling around for what she had tripped over, she discovered it was her night-vision goggles. She let out a breath of relief, put on the goggles and refocused them. "Thank God," she muttered to herself. She could see again.

As Gabby began to reacclimate, she suddenly saw a large pair of bright eyes staring at her. A jaguar stood just one pounce away. Terrified, she shuffled herself back until her spine slammed into a hard trunk. The jaguar took two slow steps toward Gabby, then turned away and bounded off of the path. She let out a slow breath and began to pick herself up.

As she got to her feet, the jaguar reappeared. The animal stepped back onto the path, paused, and looked at Gabby. It slowly turned, took two steps back into the jungle, then stopped again, looking at her.

She began to get the strange feeling that this animal was waiting for her to follow. After quickly weighing her options, she shook her head in disbelief and started to follow the deadly animal.

Gabby stepped into the jungle behind the jaguar, realizing just how large and strong this creature was. It could kill her in a second, and yet here she was, blindly following it into the thick of the jungle. She felt incredibly stupid, all alone and following an animal, a very deadly one. A thorny vine caught her shoulder, drawing a small amount of blood. *Stupid*, she thought. *What am I doing?* She ducked under the vine and realized that the jaguar had led her onto a path.

The animal began to move quicker. Gabby was able to follow easily. The path was clear, but had a low-hanging cover that barely allowed her to walk upright. It must be a game trail, she figured.

They stayed on that trail, their pace increasing. The gunfire in the distance became louder and more regular. Each shot sent her pulse rate higher, adrenaline firing through her system.

The jaguar suddenly stopped, and Gabby saw a bright light through the trees. As she moved closer, she saw that the light was from a small fire burning in the village. She quickly recognized the location. It was where she had been staying—the main section.

She saw a group of soldiers around the fire, lining

up a small group of the villagers. Gabby realized that these must be the villagers that AmCorps was taking. A barrage of gunfire exploded. She took a small step back in reaction and realized that the jaguar had disappeared. She was alone.

Gabby counted five soldiers around the line of villagers. As gunfire mounted, they hurriedly pushed the line of villagers out. They vanished to the north of the village, opposite from where Gabby watched.

She had to do something. Gabby heard yelling, but couldn't make out what was being said. A soldier ran out of the hut that had been Trent's lab. Could he still be in there?

Gabby sprinted out of the jungle. The gunfire was constant now, but she didn't stop. Her legs moved as fast as they possibly could. She made it through the clearing and onto the dirt path that cut through the village, not pausing until she was outside of Trent's lab. *Please still be here*, she thought as she hurled herself inside of the hut.

"Stop," Trent ordered, as Gabby saw that he had a gun locked on her.

"Trent." Gabby tore off her helmet and night-vision goggles. "Don't shoot."

"Gabrielle." Trent threw his arms around her. "I was so worried about you. I didn't think you'd make it back."

"I thought you were gone," Gabby cried, emotion momentarily overtaking her.

"No, but we're leaving soon. You made it back, just in time."

Gabby suddenly noticed the village girl, quietly sitting in the corner of the lab. "Who's that?"

"She's our HAWA."

"What?"

"It's just an acronym. She's our perfect specimen."

"No, what did you call her?"

"H-A-W-A, HAWA-317."

The name swirled through Gabby's head, and it instantly reminded her what side she stood on. As her mind raced, she grasped for anything that could explain her vision of Queen Hawa. She knew this was a coincidence that she simply could not explain away.

"You can't go through with this," she pleaded. "It's wrong."

"I promise you that they will have better lives."

"Do they have a choice?" Gabby asked, looking at

HAWA-317 as she quietly hugged her legs in the corner of the lab.

"Gabrielle, the survival of the human race depends on this. It's not an easy decision, but I swear to you we will be kind in how we approach this."

"But, where does it stop?" Tears streamed down Gabby's face. "Modifying the race to fit into what you've deemed to be good qualities? That's not right, that's not human."

"You're looking at that wrong. We've tried to create equality, to have a system that provides equal opportunity to all. It doesn't work. They only way we will ever have equality is when all humans are truly equal. And what we're talking about are such slight changes, they will be imperceptible. Imagine a life without disease, our species as it is right now, could never handle that empowerment, that freedom. If we want to end disease, we have to improve the human condition."

"You're taking away free will."

"We're not. And, Gabrielle, we are not the first scientists to genetically modify embryos. It's been done for at least the past ten years."

"It goes against nature."

"No, it doesn't. This is the natural evolution of

the human species. We are driven by intellect. It's what makes our species so unique, and it's what will improve the human condition."

"Stop. Listen to yourself. Using science to change the human species is not natural. Stealing these people from their home is not right." Gunfire continued to tear through the night.

"Gabrielle, you have to look to the future. This will save the human race."

"No—these people will save the human race."

"Think of everything that will be lost if we let that happen. Antibiotics, art, literature, science. Think of how much the human race will suffer if we do nothing."

"Look what's happening here, right now. People are dying."

"Not because of us."

"*Yes*, because of you. All they want is to protect their home and their family."

"That's just it, Gabrielle. I want to end war and hate; I want to end the sort of irrational thinking that brings such suffering."

Gabby hung her head in defeat. "I can't explain it in words anymore, I just know that this is wrong.

Some force in the universe is telling me in ways I can't explain."

"I think the jungle is affecting your mental state." Trent stepped closer and hugged her. "Gabrielle, you have to trust me. You're the only person that's ever loved me. I didn't know that love was even a real thing until I met you. I still remember the way you looked at me, the first day of class." Trent rubbed a tear out of the corner of his eye.

"My father hated me, somehow blamed me for my mother's death. He was mean and irrational. Every time he looked at me, I saw disgust. Then I met you and saw how much your grandparents loved you and how you loved me, and I swore that if I ever found a way to remove people like my father from the world, I would."

Gabby recalled the many nights they lay in bed; she moved her finger over the many scars that Trent had, but never spoke of. She grabbed Trent's face, wiped his tears and kissed him. She loved him.

"I know, and I do love you, so much. But, you have to stop this."

"I can't."

"Sir," a voice called from outside of the lab, "it's

time to go." A soldier, dressed from head to toe in black, rushed in. "Sir, step away from Dr. Gale," the soldier commanded as he saw Gabby.

"No, Dr. Gale is returning with us," Trent ordered.

"Step away now, Sir. I have direct orders from POTUS to kill Dr. Gale on sight, no exception."

"They're wrong. She's coming with us."

"We don't have time for this. We have to leave now, we are having trouble holding our position on the tarmac. Step aside, Sir."

The soldier lifted his gun and fired. Trent simultaneously pushed Gabby back and jumped in front of her, taking the bullet in his chest. It happened so fast, Gabby didn't even realize that Trent had been shot until his legs gave out.

"What have you done?" she screamed at the masked soldier. He stood there frozen for a moment, then lifted his handgun and aimed at Gabby.

Fire erupted from the door of the lab and the soldier collapsed forward. Someone rushed in, but Gabby's focus was on Trent.

"I'm sorry," she cried, "I'm sorry. I love you. Hang on."

Trent's face had gone completely pale, and blood dripped from the corner of his lips.

"It's okay," he whispered. "I love you too."

"Just hang on," Gabby frantically cried, looking for the bullet wound, but there was so much dark blood.

"I'm sorry, I got you into this." Trent coughed.

"Don't apologize. Don't talk. I will save you, just hang on."

"Gab," Trent coughed, "you saved me in more ways than you will ever know. I lo—" He gritted in pain. "I love you. Th—thank you. Your parents say to save the queen . . ." Trent's eyes fluttered shut.

"What? No, Trent, please hang on," Gabby pleaded.

Trent's eyes fluttered as she ripped his clothes off, trying to stop the fountain of blood that poured from him. Gabby kissed his head, his chest exhaled, and then he stopped moving. She dropped her head and just cried.

"Gab," came a voice from behind her. Chris grabbed her shoulders. "Gab, we have to go. We took the village, but they need support at the airstrip. We have to get there now."

Gabby pushed the arms away.

"Gabrielle, I'm so sorry," Chris said as she looked up for the first time.

"Chris?"

"Yeah, I'm here."

"I thought you got killed—everything was on fire."

"I thought you were killed too. Somehow the blast separated us."

Gabby began to lie down next to Trent's body.

"Gab." Chris pulled her up. "I know you're sad. We will come back, but right now we have to get out of here. They're on their way here for Trent and the girl. We need to go."

"The queen." Gabby looked at the scared young girl.

"What?"

"The girl, HAWA, Queen Hawa." Gabby pulled herself up. She had never felt a sadness this deep; she knew she would be forever changed by it. This was a scar that would be here to stay, if she even survived.

As Gabby stood, she noticed that Rodrigo and two of his guys were also in the lab. They were talking to HAWA-317. Gabby looked down at Trent's lifeless body. He was so beautiful, he could've been a model, but he'd chosen a life of intellect instead. Gabby wanted to collapse next to him, to fall asleep and wake up in another world.

Chris put his arm around her shoulders.

"One foot in front of the other, Gab. You just have to move forward."

Unable to lift her head, she followed Chris out. She wasn't afraid anymore. She didn't care if she died, but she didn't want Trent's death to be in vain. Gabby realized that in his final moments, he'd chosen to save her, and for that reason she needed to finish this fight. As gunfire rang out, Gabby lifted her head, grabbed her gun, and rushed toward the sound.

One of Rodrigo's men cut them off—he had been waiting in the cover of the jungle. He quickly spoke to Rodrigo and Chris, then took off.

"He said," Chris whispered to Gabby, "we have them pinned. They think that they've held us off, but our second wave is about to attack. That's who we're going in with."

"Okay. I saw them take villagers with them. Where are they?"

"They're on the plane."

"Rodrigo's guys know not to hurt them, right?"

"Of course," Chris reassured her. "Stay right next to me, okay?"

She nodded. Then she saw Rodrigo nod and lift his gun in the air. It was still dark, but without the cover of the jungle canopy, the moonlight was bright. Chris lifted his gun, Rodrigo howled, and the jungle erupted in a voracious choir of howling. Rodrigo and Chris broke out into a run and Gabby followed.

An explosion cut through the air followed by a loud series of pops.

"Plane tires," Chris yelled to Gabby.

Gunfire quickly filled in. They were getting close. It was so loud. Gabby could see flashes of light. Rodrigo and Chris stopped; they could clearly see the runway through the thick jungle cover. They positioned themselves behind a low outcropping of rock and tree roots. Flood lights were trained on the surrounding jungle. The smell of burning rubber made Gabby's throat burn.

The bulk of the extraction team surrounded their planes. Short, small bursts of gunfire periodically rang out from different directions. Gabby saw an extraction agent take a heavy-gauge bullet to the chest; it knocked him back a step, but then he returned fire. There was a small jet on the runway in front of a much larger plane. The front end of the small plane was smoking, and it had been pulled over to the far side of the makeshift tarmac.

Chris leaned over to Gabby. "It looks like they're trying to ditch the small plane. Just stay right behind me, okay?"

"Yes, I know," Gabby yelled over the gunfire.

Chris turned and looked at her. "I thought you were dead. I don't want to—"

Gabby cut him off. "I know." She shook her head, not wanting Chris to say any more; she couldn't handle any more emotion.

"Ready?" he asked.

She nodded.

"You're loaded with armor-piercing rounds. We're going to shoot, then duck and cover."

Rodrigo let out an ear-piercing whistle.

Then, all at once, gunfire erupted from every direction. Gabby joined in. She aimed her large, high-power rifle at a group of extraction agents. The initial kickback blasted her shoulder, and she dug her feet in and pulled off another round. She wasn't sure if it was from her gun, but three of the agents collapsed. Those remaining ducked down.

Chris and Rodrigo ducked and lay on the ground, but Gabby pulled off another round.

"Down," Chris yelled, pulling at Gabby as a bullet ricocheted off of a nearby stone.

"I think I killed someone," Gabby said.

"It's possible," Chris yelled over the gunfire. "Don't think about it. If you don't shoot them first, they will shoot you."

"Pronto!" Rodrigo yelled.

"Get ready for round two," Chris yelled to Gabby.

"Agora." Rodrigo jumped up, followed by the two of them. Gabby held down her trigger—this time, she was ready for the kickback.

There were only a few black-clad agents still standing outside of the two planes. A large blast struck the front end of the small jet, catching it on fire. A handful of bodies scattered the runway, but most of the agents had already taken refuge inside of the large plane.

"Down." Chris pulled Gabby down as a blast took out a tree nearby. He slowly peered over their rock cover. "They're retreating inside the plane. Nos temos de ir agora." Chris stood. Rodrigo let out another loud whistle. Gunfire unleashed on the planes.

"Come on." Chris pulled Gabby up. They made their way to the very edge of the clearing and paused. For a moment, she felt like she was on the set of a movie. The extraction team's flood lights cast unnatural shadows throughout the clearing. Everything seemed so surreal.

Gabby's ayahuasca experience had felt so much more tangible than this moment. Even the hard steel gun in her hand seemed more like a toy.

"Ready?" Chris was bouncing up and down. "In three . . . two . . . one . . . GO!"

Chris, Rodrigo, and a line of men and women charged out from the jungle's cover, rushing toward the plane. Gabby was in such awe of this small force of ragtag jungle warriors that had come together for this tiny, ancient village that she forgot to run. Her legs began to move, but her mind was still focused on the scene, and she tripped over some fallen tree trunks.

Extraction agents moved out, forming a circle around the plane, and began firing into the crowd. Gabby saw several jungle warriors fall. She picked herself up and ran as fast as she could. She kept her focus on Chris and Rodrigo. The plane's engine suddenly kicked on as a bullet tore through her sleeve. That was too close.

Looking up, she saw an extraction agent directly ahead, his gun aimed at her chest. She pulled her trigger first and the bullet exploded through his armored chest plate.

Chris slowed and quickly glanced back, looking for Gabby. This brief pause was all she needed to catch up. The extraction agents that had been outside of the plane fled inside or lay dead on the ground. As Gabby got closer to the plane, she had to step over several bodies from both sides. She felt nothing; her emotional spigot had run dry. She wasn't scared, she wasn't sad—she was just there. Moving forward one step at a time.

Chris, Rodrigo, and a handful of warriors had gathered under the plane, while others tried to save their wounded. The gunfire had stopped and a strange quiet took over.

"Are you okay?" Chris frantically began checking Gabby.

"What?"

"You're bleeding." He checked Gabby's pulse and began to pull her shirt back. Confused, she looked down.

"Oh." She ripped the shirt where the bullet had sliced through her sleeve. It must've grazed her arm. The wound was a bit deeper than she'd expected, but the blood had already begun to clot.

"I'm fine."

"When we go in, I want you positioned out here."

"No, I'm going with you."

"Fine, but you won't be able to see anything. Get your handgun and hold on to me with your other hand."

Gabby hung her automatic rifle over her shoulder so it rested on her back, then took out her handgun. Rodrigo's guys had positioned ladders up to the front and back doors to the plane. The ladders were broken, so it took extra guys to hold them in place. The extraction team tried to destroy them before they barricaded themselves inside the plane.

Gabby heard the plane's engine struggle to life, and the craft suddenly inched forward, sending Rodrigo's guys tumbling to the ground.

"Mover! Mover!" Chris said as Gabby noticed

that they had managed to attach something to the door frame. Rodrigo's guys grabbed the ladders as they hurriedly moved out of the plane's way. Chris pulled Gabby toward the far side right before two loud explosions sent the plane's doors tumbling to the runway.

Rodrigo's team split into two and quickly formed a base as they held the ladders in position. Bullets rained down on the warriors. They answered back as best they could, but they were pinned.

"Agora! Agora!" Chris yelled.

Two warriors stepped out from under the plane and fired wildly into the doors. One of the extraction agents tumbled from the door. His body made a loud splat sound on the hard dirt runway. He was dead before he even hit the ground.

Then Gabby saw a warrior just a few yards from her shooting into the plane take a direct hit to his face from a high-caliber round. His features seemed to collapse in on themselves. His nose disappeared first, sucking in his eyes, then his lips, till nothing but a gaping hole was left. It happened so fast, yet every nanosecond had been permanently burned into Gabby's memory. It was the most inhuman sight she had ever seen. His body collapsed as blood pooled underneath him.

With that, every emotion Gabby had ever felt came flooding through. Glad that it wasn't her, then sad, guilty, angry; everything poured through her till she vomited.

Without hesitation, another warrior took his fallen comrade's place and started firing into the open doorway. Two more extraction agents tumbled from the plane, dead.

"Vai . . . Vai," Chris ordered as four more warriors ran out. With all the strength and accuracy of professional athletes, they each pitched something about the size of a beer bottle inside the doorways. Gabby heard a loud pop, followed by a slow sizzle.

"Todos nós entramos! Agora!" Chris directed. Rodrigo repeated this, then let out a series of high-pitched whistles.

The warriors positioned the ladders as close to the blown-out doors as possible. It took a team of four just to hold each ladder up. Rodrigo was the first one up. He quickly disappeared into the plane as two of his guys followed close behind.

"Ready?"

Gabby nodded; vomit still burned the back of her throat.

"Stay right behind me. You won't be able to see in there."

Chris was first, and he paused halfway up, waiting for her. As Gabby started climbing the short but difficult ascent, a quick burst of gunfire rang out. Dread set its anchor in the core of her being. Gabby wanted this to be over—she didn't want to go inside the plane, but forced herself to keep climbing. Chris quickly vanished into the thick fog within.

As Gabby struggled up the last two broken rungs and into the plane, Chris reached his arm out to help her. The smoke was so thick inside that Gabby couldn't even see him a few inches away. She reached out for him, finding his hand. He squeezed in return, then directed her back toward him as they inched deeper inside the plane.

"Lt. Christopher Silver," a voice boomed through the metal interior of the military plane, "this is not how I pictured our reunion, brother."

"Rob?" Chris asked, speaking into the air, as he had no idea where the voice was coming from.

"Yeah, man. What the fuck are you doing?"

"This is wrong—you have to let these people go."

"I have orders, Chris. Let me finish my job."

"I can't let you take them."

"These specimens are the only way we will survive this. We're taking them."

"No."

"Brother, what happened to those hours of conversations we had about being the alpha? We trained, we studied, and we made sacrifices to be the strongest of our species. It's survival of the fittest."

"That's bullshit. Survival of the fittest doesn't negate basic human rights. These people have lives here. They have families." Chris began to slowly sneak deeper into the smoke-filled cabin. Gabby moved with him. Her fist squeezed the handle of her handgun. She shuffled her feet as quietly as possible. The dense fog tickled the back of Gabby's throat and she struggled to subdue her natural urge to cough.

"Spare me your fucking righteous diatribe. You know you don't believe that shit. Would a hungry wolf walk away from its prey because it felt bad?"

"You're right. This is about survival. It's about survival of our species for more than the next fifty years, and it's about my freedom to choose a side."

"When did you become such a righteous asshole? We fought arm to arm, we did some fucked up shit—you know this, and I know this. Now you think you can grow a conscience. Brother, I see right through you."

"You're right. I'm not a good person. This isn't about morals. Soprador pronto."

"You know me. You know that I will have no problem putting a bullet in your head."

"I know. Estroboscópio pronto."

"Your jungle monkeys are no match for us. Just know that you'll be the reason for their slaughter."

"Ahora."

Suddenly, loud blowers came on from both sides of the plane, then strobe lights began flashing. Chris moved swiftly—he exterminated three extraction agents in a matter of seconds. Gabby stayed with him. Shots rang out all around her. They moved into the main hold of the aircraft.

Inside she saw the terrified villagers locked in individual plexiglass chambers. They were huddled in the back corners of their cells, hugging their legs.

Gabby saw an agent step out from between two blockades of cells. She shot first, and the bullet lodged in his shoulder. He lifted his gun. Every part of her being did not want to take another shot, but she forced the trigger down anyway. This time the bullet grazed his neck. He was still up, but Gabby saw the distinct crimson shine in the flashing strobe light covering his black armor. He lifted his arm to fire, but collapsed.

"Enough," boomed Rob's voice as the aircraft's interior lights flickered on.

The man was standing near a control panel. He had pulled one of the villagers out of their cell and held a gun to her head, using her as a shield. She couldn't have been older than twelve. She cried as her body trembled in fear.

"I cut the oxygen to the cells. These specimens will die in five minutes if you don't turn around and walk away."

"Don't do this," Chris said.

Gabby could see the dead bodies of some of Rodrigo's team through the open door at the front of the main cabin. There was no movement. They all must've been killed.

"I'm a survivor, brother. You know this."

"Then survive. Save them. You can stay here."

"And live in a hut in the fucking jungle? I worked too hard for that shit. I'm going to enjoy the fruits of my labor."

"How long do you think you can survive in an AmCorps safe house?"

"Do you know what the safe houses are? I will be living the comfortable life of a millionaire."

"If they let you in, you'll be working for them. Don't let them fool you."

The villagers began to struggle for air.

"Stop," Gabby cried, "they're dying."

"You're a smart one," Rob scoffed. "And you call yourself a doctor."

"Turn their oxygen on," Chris ordered.

"I have absolutely no problem watching them die. The only way they will survive is if you walk off this plane now."

"No."

"Then I'll fucking kill you." Rob aimed his gun at Chris.

Chris pushed Gabby behind him and aimed his gun back, but the young girl completely blocked his shot.

Rob pulled the trigger. Gabby felt the impact of a

bullet push Chris back as it entered his chest. The force was so strong it knocked them back. Chris's head slammed into the plexi cell behind then and they collapsed to the floor. Chris's large body collapsed on top of hers. She immediately heard another shot ring out. Then two more.

The lights in the cabin went out.

"Chris!" Gabby cried as she struggled to get out from underneath his motionless body. There was no response. The cabin was pitch black and silent.

She heard a loud hiss, and then the doors to the plexiglass cells opened. The villagers gasped for air. The lights to the cabin flickered back on, and Rodrigo was standing at the control panel, his gun still in his hand. Rob was lying lifeless, in a heap, at Rodrigo's feet.

"Chris. Chris." Gabby cried. Blood had soaked through his shirt. The bullet hole had gone in right where his heart was. Tears covered her face. She began ripping away his clothes and felt something hard. He had a bulletproof vest on.

"Chris," Gabby yelled, and shook him. "Chris!"

His eyes slowly flickered open. He immediately grabbed his chest and winced in pain as he pulled himself up, taking an inventory of the scene.

"Rodrigo . . . Obrigado Deus pelo Rodrigo!—Thank God for Rodrigo!" Chris bowed his head to Rodrigo.

"Você fez isso, meu amigo." Rodrigo bowed back.

"Our plan worked my friend. Gabs." Chris said, suddenly looking up at her. He pulled her in and hugged her, immediately crying out in pain.

"You probably have a broken rib. How's your breathing? I should check you for a punctured lung."

"It's not broken. I'm fine, just sore." Chris pulled off the old bulletproof vest he had on. The bullet had pierced his skin, but the main force had been stopped. While he was badly bruised, he would survive.

Gabby stood and helped him up. He leaned on her and hugged her again.

"When I thought you were dead, I—I." She looked at Chris.

Gabby was trapped in a tornado of emotion, but in this moment a flood of relief washed over her. Unable to speak, she hugged him.

Tamping down her emotions, she asked "Do you think you'll be able to climb out of here?"

"Yeah, I just need a minute." Chris smiled.

Gabby smiled. "Ok."

As if on cue, Rodrigo guided the surviving villagers out of their holding cells and to the aircraft doors. Gabby and Chris followed, waiting as the villagers took their turn climbing down the broken ladder. The sun was just starting to lighten the night sky. As the survivors emerged from the plane, cheers rose from the surrounding jungle.

Gabby and Chris cleared the plane. There were no survivors. They counted twenty casualties on their side and seventeen on the extraction team. The ladder team waited for them to get off the plane, then joined their unit in the celebration of this victory.

The two of them found a fallen tree trunk to sit on as they watched the sun rise up over the tall trees. From the clearing, they were able to see the mountain peaks that climbed high above the tree line.

"Now what?" Gabby looked at Chris.

"I'm not sure, our work is just starting." He put his arm around her shoulders. "But, we are going to have to leave this area along with the entire village."

That much she knew to be true.

THE END

Acknowledgements

To my dad, Dennis, who turned me into a writer with his incredible stories. While you won't read this book, I know with all of my heart, that these are your ideas. To my mom, Barbara, who is the strongest person I know. You make everything look so easy and you're incredibly graceful as you do it all. Thank you for all that you do for us! To my husband, Ben, who has faith in my ability, even when I sometimes doubt it myself. Thank you! To my boys, Jake and Zac, whose sense of adventure inspires me. To my entire family (Mary, Jonathan, Lauren, Lexi, Aaron, Lisa, Ellie, Evie, Gabrielle, Andy, Drew, Dotsie, Mark, Dave, Maddie, Maya, and all of my family and friends) – thank you for making life so fun! I love you all so much.

To Jay Bonansinga, thank you for allowing me to even attempt to be a writer. Without Hit Me! I would've never thought this was even possible. Your guidance has been truly life-changing. I didn't become a writer because I love writing. I had a story to tell and you showed me how to tell it. It was in this process that I finally discovered what I want to be when I grow up. Thank you! P.S. I'm still in the process of growing up.

To H.D. Gordon, thank you for giving me the practical tips I needed to finally get my first fiction penned. Without that coffee at Starbucks, this book would still be a mess of ideas floating around in my mind. You inspire me as an author, a mother, and a human being.

To Heather O'Connell, publishing extraordinaire, thank you for taking a heap of ideas and turning it into a real book. Your professionalism, thoroughness, and kindness have made my dreams come true in the most beautiful way. I'm so grateful that you agreed to help me and would be totally lost without you!

To my editor, Sandra Haven, you are incredibly talented. Your ability to see where a story needed to go is simply magic. It's a gift.

ACKNOWLEDGEMENTS

To my readers, thank you for reading this book. I hope you enjoyed it!

Much Love, Danielle Gomes

Danielle Gomes is an author, freelance journalist, and brand development specialist. She co-authored Hit Me! Fighting the Las Vegas Mob by the Numbers. When Danielle is not writing she is searching out adventures with her husband and two sons. EVE-0 is her debut fiction novel.

EVE-0 Lucien Series

Lucien, Book 2 – Coming 2022

Dr. Gabrielle Gale and Lt. Christopher Silver may have won a small victory in EVE-0, but their fight is just beginning. Dr. Lucien Sabara wants his active EVE-0 gene and will stop at nothing to get it. With AmCorps on the hunt; Gabby, Chris, and the surviving Matsés attempt to evade capture. Guided by what's left of Trent's work, they head deeper into the jungle and into a world that's controlled by unearthly forces. In a battle between technology and survivalism, can the human race endure?

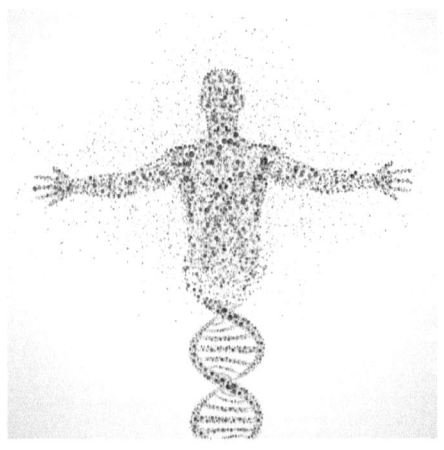